Path To Finding Happiness

By Diane E. Izzard

Scripture quotations are from the HOLY BIBLE, KINGS JAMES VERSION. Copyright 1988 by Devore & Sons, Inc. Wichita, Kansas

Cover image used under license from shutterstock.com

ISBN: 978-0-9970065-1-3

Dedication

For my sister whose strong faith in God and family
is a tremendous influence in my life.

Acknowledgements

Many thanks to my family and friends for their help in making this book possible.

Special thanks to Debby Eye for performing the final edit. Her attention to detail made publishing this book possible.

To my sister, Susan, who gave me the inspiration to write this story.

Chapter One

"Blessed are they that mourn: for they shall be comforted." *(St. Matthew 5:4)*

Jennifer lived a charmed life, at least the first sixteen years. She grew up in St. Paul, Minnesota, as an only child. She was popular in school with many friends, and very athletic. Being five foot nine inches tall helped her excel on the girls basketball team, which won the state championship the previous year. She also displayed her athletic ability on the football cheerleading squad. Jennifer's life couldn't have been more perfect. Her Dad spoiled her by giving her a new red Ford Mustang on her sixteenth birthday. Being an only child Jennifer was very close to her Mom, who was always sharing words of wisdom. The latest advise she received from her Mom when talking about boys was, *"Always stay true to yourself and never let the love of a boy influence you into doing something you are not ready for."* These words meant more than Jennifer realized at the time.

Jennifer's heavenly life all changed in a split second, though. One late spring Saturday evening Jennifer spent the night with her best friend, Elaine, while her parents celebrated their twentieth wedding anniversary. They stayed up late watching scary movies and eating popcorn. Early the next morning Jennifer awoke to the sound of the doorbell ringing. She rolled over and saw it was only 6AM and wondered who would be visiting at this hour. She heard Elaine's parents walk to the front door, and then a male voice. Jennifer crept out of bed and cracked the bedroom door so she could hear what was going on at such an early hour.

"I am sorry to disturb you, but we are looking for Jennifer Ferguson. Is she staying with you?"

Why would someone be looking for me at this hour? Jennifer wondered.

Jennifer quietly slipped on her robe and slippers then walked downstairs. There were two police officers standing at the door talking to Elaine's parents.

"Jennifer's parents were in a car accident and unfortunately didn't survive." Those were the next words Jennifer heard.

Jennifer yelled, "No! That is not possible. My Mom is going to pick me up this morning."

Elaine's Mom rushed over to Jennifer to console her. "It will be all right honey."

Jennifer tried to tell the police they were wrong.

Jennifer's sobs and cries woke up Elaine, who appeared at the top of the stairs. "What is going on?"

"Jennifer's parents have been in a tragic accident," Elaine's Mom spoke up.

Jennifer was in denial and told Elaine's parents, "The police must be mistaken; it can't be my parents they just went out for dinner."

The realization that Jennifer would never talk to her parents again started to sink in when her Mom didn't arrive to pick her up. Elaine and her parents did everything they could to help Jennifer that day trying to explain that her parents were with God in heaven. But that didn't help ease the excruciating pain she felt inside.

Jennifer's grandparents showed up the next day from Florida to plan the funeral and to take care of her. The next few days were a blur and in her grief she just went through the motions of life, trying to make it through each day. Numerous people stopped by the house dropping off food and giving their condolences.

It was raining the day of the funeral, which seemed suitable. It was as if God was crying along with everyone else at the death of Jennifer's parents. She sat in shock looking at the two coffins where her parents laid. She still couldn't believe they were truly gone.

After the service and burial, there was a final gathering at Jennifer's parents house. Jennifer just wanted to be left alone and went to her bedroom to hide. There was a gentle knock on her bedroom door and she opened it to find her youth minister.

Michael was in his thirties, slender, with dark curly hair and a kind face. He was a high school math teacher when he was not facilitating youth activities at the church. He asked Jennifer, "Can I come in?"

"Yes," Jennifer reluctantly replied.

"I can't imagine the pain you are feeling right now. I know that it would be easy to blame God for what has happened, but you should not turn your back on Him. God is grieving with you and will give you the strength to be happy again, if you ask for His help. Our path in life is never clear. It's difficult to understand now, but God has a path for you. The decisions and actions we make each day take us on our path. Grieve for your parents. But do not forget, God will always be with you and help you to find a purpose in the challenges in your life, so you may learn and grow from them. You may stray from your path, but never forget that God is always with you to help you through the difficult times."

Tears streamed down Jennifer's face. She asked Michael, "What have I done to deserve such punishment from God?"

"Your actions didn't cause this. Unfortunately, pain is just a part of life. Put your faith in God and He will help you to find the purpose in your pain," Michael replied.

Jennifer was troubled by the thought of never talking to her parents again and not being able to let them know how much she loved them. "I didn't even have a chance to say good-bye," Jennifer told Michael through her tears.

"Even though they are in Heaven, I believe they can still hear you. Talk to them as if they are right here with you," Michael said

Michael left and Jennifer wiped the tears from her eyes. She looked up toward the heavens and told her parents, "I love you very much and miss you. I wish God would have let you stay with me a little longer. What am I going to do without you?"

Jennifer's Grandma gently knocked on her door and entered the bedroom. "Can I hide up here with you for a little while?" She asked.

Jennifer nodded as tears ran down her face. Grandma lay in bed and wrapped her soft arms around Jennifer like her Mom used to do. Exhaustion had set in and Jennifer could no longer stay awake. Jennifer cried herself to sleep as Grandma held her securely.

When she awoke, the house was quiet and Grandma was asleep next to her. Realization that she hadn't dreamed the last couple of days came flooding back. She was living her worst nightmare. What was she going to do without her parents?

Jennifer later discovered her parents were driving home from dinner when a drunk driver in a large pickup truck crossed the center line and hit them head on, killing them instantly. She only hoped they didn't suffer.

All the Sunday school classes and sermons on the consequences of sinning had Jennifer wondering if God was punishing her for the many sins she had committed in her young life. She felt as if life was going too well and her happiness was bound to end sometime. She wished she could have held onto her happiness just a little while longer.

This would be the first of many challenges Jennifer would face in life as she grew to understand God's love and His plan for her.

Chapter Two

"The Lord preserveth the simple: I was brought low, and he helped me." *(Psalm 116:6)*

Jennifer only had two weeks left before the end of the school year. She was in a daze finding it very hard to concentrate on school work. She somehow managed to finish the eleventh grade in St. Paul, Minnesota before moving to Florida with her grandparents. She had looked forward to her senior year cheerleading for one last season, the senior dance, and hanging out with her friends. Now that dream was over. She hated leaving all her friends, but she tried to look on the positive side. Coming home each day from school with the constant reminder that her parents wouldn't be there waiting for her just reignited the pain. This way she could start a new life, one that didn't constantly remind her of the loss she had suffered.

Jennifer packed her things while Grandma packed a few mementos for her, so she would have something to remember her parents by. Her grandparents arranged to have the house and its contents sold after they left. She stuffed her small Ford Mustang with all her precious possessions, leaving hardly enough room for her and her grandparents to sit. The sense of loss never felt as great as when she walked out of the house for the last time. Grandpa locked the front door and she looked back, remembering all the happy times she had spent as a child there. She was starting a new life and wondered what God had planned for her now.

It took them two long days in the car, but they finally arrived in Cocoa Beach, Florida where her grandparents lived in a three bedroom condo. One bedroom had been converted into Grandma's hobby room, so that left the guest room for Jennifer. Her grandparents had always visited her in Minnesota so there was no need to travel to Florida. This was the first time Jennifer saw her new home. Bone-tired, Jennifer carried her suitcases to the elevator that transported her to the fourth floor. Grandpa opened the door to the condo and Grandma showed Jennifer to her bedroom. At first glance Jennifer thought the room looked about as gloomy as she felt. The walls were painted a cream color. There were light blue curtains hanging over the one window, the bedspread was pale blue and there was one lone painting of an ocean scene on the wall above the bed. The room was furnished with a queen size bed, night stand, and dresser. It basically was as personable as a hotel room.

Grandma must have sensed her disappointment. "Honey, you can decorate the room any way you like. Why don't we go to the hardware store tomorrow? You can choose some paint and new curtains for the windows."

"That would be nice, Grandma." Jennifer plopped her bags down on the floor. It had been an exhausting trip. She had felt claustrophobic with her grandparents in her small car. She just needed some peace and quiet, and time alone to adjust to her new home. "I am kind of tired Grandma. I'm going to unpack and get ready for bed," Jennifer said.

"Well, all right honey, let me know if you need anything." Grandma wished there was some way to take away the pain her granddaughter felt, knowing how difficult it must be for her.

Jennifer found her pajamas buried in her suitcase, put them on and crawled into bed feeling sad and alone. She started to cry and remembered what Michael had said, *"Never forget, God is always with you to help you through the difficult times."*

Jennifer whispered out loud, "God where are you? I need you. Give me the strength to find happiness again." She pictured her Mom's face as she cried herself to sleep.

Jennifer awoke to the warmth of the sun streaming through her bedroom window. She slowly crawled out of bed, squinting at the bright light shining into the room. She looked out the window and smiled. There was a beautiful white, sandy beach below and water as far as she could see. The gently rolling swells made their way to the beach, crashing along the shore. There was a family walking in the sand at the edge of the surf with two young children. The children kept stopping every few feet to pick up shells. To them it must be like finding a treasure as they reached down, picked up the shell and ran over to show their parents. Jennifer suddenly felt sad thinking back to a time when she was so happy and innocent, where the harsh realities of life were not so evident. She dug out some shorts and a t-shirt from her suitcase, dressed, and walked to the kitchen to find her grandparents having breakfast.

"How did you sleep dear? Can I fix you something for breakfast?" Grandma asked.

She didn't want her to fuss. "I will just have some cereal, if that is all right?"

"Are you sure? I can make you some pancakes or eggs."

"I'm not very hungry."

Grandma showed her the selection of cereal stored in the pantry. She looked at the boring selection of heathy bran cereals and settled on frosted mini wheats. As Jennifer poured herself some cereal, Grandma talked with way more energy than she felt this morning. "Why don't we head to town after breakfast and buy some things for your bedroom?" She asked

Jennifer never knew this about Grandma, but she loved to shop. They drove to a hardware store just across the causeway which had many decorating ideas to choose from. She went with a tropical theme since she was now living at the beach. She chose a pastel pink colored paint, her favorite color, for her bedroom. Then she selected seashell wallpaper trim to accent the top of the wall around the ceiling. They also bought some brightly colored tropical flowered material to make curtains and a bedspread. She picked out a small desk so she would have a place to study, and a bookshelf for her many books. Grandma's SUV was packed full by the time they headed home.

The next several days Jennifer spent painting and decorating her room with the help of her Grandma. Jennifer learned a lot about her Grandma in those few days. She loved Grandma's hobby room. One side of the room had a sewing machine with drawers full of sewing supplies. The other side of the room had art supplies complete with an easel and sketch pads. She never knew her Grandma was so artistic. Grandma very patiently showed Jennifer how to sew and make the curtains and bedspread for her room.

They hung the curtains and placed the new bedspread on the bed. They both stood in the doorway and admired their work. The room looked much brighter and cheerier now. Jennifer smiled with satisfaction at the results of their hard work.

Grandma was proud of her. "You did an outstanding job!" She squeezed Jennifer by the shoulders.

Jennifer's mood improved greatly. She was now eager to unpack her bags and store her belongings. She placed some of her school memorabilia around the room. On her dresser she placed a picture of her and Elaine. On her nightstand she placed an old wedding picture of her parents. On top of the book shelf she displayed her cheerleading trophy she had won. It was starting to feel more like home.

Since it was summer, she had two months before school started. Jennifer's grandparents were great, always trying to make her feel at home and cheer her up by including her in activities. She helped Grandma bake cookies. Grandpa even showed her how to play golf. Her grandparents did everything they could to make her feel welcome, but they were not her parents.

Cocoa Beach was nothing like Minnesota. It was hot, sandy, and had no real trees, just palm trees. Jennifer felt like she was in a totally different world. At night she would leave her window open so she could listen to the sound of the waves gently crashing against the shore. Each morning she woke to the sun shining brightly through her window. The ocean was so beautiful and peaceful. She spent many days on the beach her first summer. She missed her friends and was very lonely with no one her own age to spend time with. She just wanted to be a teenager without a care in the world again. She took long walks on the beach just to think, and for some time to herself. In the evenings, she would sit on the patio and listen to the music coming from the Cocoa Beach pier, and wondered how people could be laughing and having such a good time when she was so miserable. It just didn't seem fair.

This particular morning Jennifer went for her normal daily walk on the beach, but noticed the waves were higher than usual. There were several surfers taking advantage of the high waves, enjoying themselves near the pier. She sat on the sand and shielded her eyes from the sun and squinted while she watched the surfers. They floated on their boards just beyond where the waves broke, waiting to catch the next perfect wave. She watched as one surfer started paddling furiously as a wave approached. He lifted himself to a standing position on his surfboard, balancing with his arms as the wave crested. She smiled as she watched him ride the wave to shore. It looked like fun. She enjoyed watching the surfers and lost herself in the water ballet being performed in front of her. It was a spectacular performance between surfer and waves as they danced down the board, maneuvering just to the right point to balance perfectly and receive the ride of a lifetime. Lost in the serene scene, she didn't notice as one of the surfers approached. The sun suddenly disappeared from her face and she looked up to find the source of the shade.

"Hi, I'm Josh," he announced. "Are you visiting from out of town?"

Jennifer looked up at Josh's lean, tan body blocking the sun from her face. Josh had sun streaked blond hair and very blue eyes. He appeared to be around Jennifer's age. Her pale skin from lack of warmth and sun in Minnesota must have given her away as someone not from Florida. "My name is Jennifer. I just moved here from Minnesota. I enjoyed watching you surf this morning. Is it hard to learn?"

"Not at all, if you ever tried it you would be hooked. I could show you the basics if you want to learn."

"I would love to." Jennifer glanced at her watch and was shocked to see it was already past noon. "I didn't realize how late it was. Will you be surfing again tomorrow?" Jennifer asked.

"I like surfing early in the morning when there are no crowds. If you want to learn, be on the beach by eight."

"Do I need to bring anything or wear anything special?"

"Make sure you wear a t-shirt or your stomach will be raw from rubbing against the surfboard." Josh glanced at her pale pink skin. "Make sure you wear some waterproof sunscreen."

"I'll see you in the morning," Jennifer cheerfully replied, trying not to sound too eager. She turned and raced to her grandparent's condo feeling happy, something she hadn't felt in a long time. She decided it would be best not to tell her grandparents about meeting Josh and her upcoming surfing lessons. It would just make them worry.

The next morning Jennifer woke early and put her swimsuit on under her shorts and t-shirt. After a quick breakfast, she just told her grandparents, "I'm going for a walk down to the pier and hang out on the beach. I'll be home by lunch." She grabbed her beach bag and raced out the door before they could ask any questions.

Jennifer smiled when she saw Josh sitting on the beach waxing his board. Josh looked up as she approached.

"I thought you might have changed your mind," Josh said sarcastically.

"No, I'm ready for my first lesson," Jennifer announced enthusiastically.

Jennifer spent the next several hours attempting to surf. Josh used his board to show Jennifer how to stand on the board, first on the shore, then leading her out past the waves. At first, she spent most of her time wiping out, with her head underwater, waves crashing over her. Then it just seemed to click and she actually was standing on the board, water splashing over her feet as she glided toward the shore line. "Yeah, I did it!" Jennifer yelled with delight.

Josh laughed and celebrated along with her. He made her feel at ease. She felt so comfortable around him. She laughed more that morning then she had in months. Before she knew it, it was one o'clock. She was late for lunch. Regrettably she told Josh, "I have to go. Will you be surfing again tomorrow?"

Josh laughed. "You didn't have enough punishment today that you actually want to try again tomorrow? If you can move in the morning, I will be here again at eight. I have an extra board you can use."

"I will see you then," Jennifer happily replied. She turned to run to the condo.

She felt as light as air. She was so happy she floated all the way back to her grandparents. She opened the door to two concerned faces.

"Where have you been? We were worried about you when you didn't show up for lunch."

Jennifer decided she better come clean and let them know what she was doing. "I met a surfer named Josh and he was showing me how to surf."

"I am happy you are having fun, but you need to be careful. What kind of boy is Josh? I want to meet him," Grandpa insisted.

"I plan to meet him again tomorrow at eight for some more surfing lessons. I can introduce you to him then." Jennifer quickly changed the subject before they could ask her any more questions. "I am starved. What is there to eat?"

Jennifer could hardly sleep all night at the thought of spending time with Josh, surfing again in the morning. As soon as the sun came up Jennifer hopped out of bed, cringing from pain. Every muscle in her body ached. A little pain was not going to stop her from surfing again and spending time with Josh. She started to bang around the kitchen so Grandpa would get up. After what seemed like an eternity for him to eat breakfast, they headed to the beach to meet Josh.

Josh was already surfing when she arrived with Grandpa. She waved to get Josh's attention. He caught the next wave and rode it to shore. He lifted his surfboard under his arm and ran up to her.

"Josh, this is my grandfather. Grandpa, I would like you to meet Josh," Jennifer nervously said.

Josh put down his board and shook Grandpa's hand. He smiled and told him, "I am really impressed with how quickly Jennifer learned to surf. She is a natural."

"How long have you been surfing?" Grandpa asked.

"I've lived in Florida all my life and started surfing by the time I was six years old. I am currently working as a lifeguard when I'm not surfing. I will take good care of Jennifer, sir you don't have to worry," Josh responded.

Grandpa seemed satisfied that Jennifer was in good hands and told her, "Make sure you are home on time for lunch today young lady." Grandpa turned to walk back to his condo.

Josh looked at Jennifer with his deep blue eyes and said, "Your grandfather seems nice. How sore are you from yesterday?"

Jennifer didn't want Josh to think she was weak or a wimp and told him, "I feel great! I am ready to dazzle you with more of my superb surfing moves." Jennifer pretended she was surfing, holding her arms out from her sides, laughing.

Josh showed Jennifer to his truck where he had an extra board. "It's a little bit longer than the one you surfed on yesterday, which should make it easier for you to balance and stand up. Is it too heavy for you to carry?" He cautiously handed her the board.

"No, I can handle it." She lied, the board was heavier than she thought it would be. But she was not going to give Josh the satisfaction of thinking she couldn't take care of herself. She struggled but managed to carry the board to the beach.

The first couple of hours Jennifer managed to catch a few waves and not fall off the board. By eleven the wave height started to diminish, so they spent more time floating out past the waves than surfing. They sat on their boards enjoying the rolling movement of the ocean with their feet dangling over the sides, talking.

"Do you stay with your grandparents?" Josh asked.

Jennifer hesitated. "My parents died in a car accident a few months ago, so I live with them now." It was the first time she talked about her parents to anyone since their death. She didn't want to upset her grandparents, so she never mentioned them.

"I'm sorry. It must be hard for you. My Dad left when I was young and my parents are divorced. So, it's just me and my Mom. I live with her in Melbourne."

Suddenly a fin appeared in the water. Jennifer freaked and yelled, "Shark!"

Josh laughed, "Relax, it's just a dolphin. The dolphins enjoy playing in the surf as much as we do. They are natural surfers."

Jennifer laughed at herself for being scared of such a beautiful creature. Now that she knew her life was not in danger, she watched as the dolphin played in the waves and swam around them for several minutes. She had never been so close to such a large wild animal. It was amazing. Jennifer thought it was as if her Mom's spirit was in the dolphin and she was letting her know she was not alone. It was her way of letting Jennifer know she was still watching over her.

Noon quickly approached. Jennifer told Josh, "I have to get home so I don't get in trouble."

As they walked back to Josh's truck with the surfboards, he told her, "I have to work the next several days at the lifeguard stand near the pier. Stop by if you get a chance."

Jennifer's heart fluttered with excitement. "I will. Thanks for the lesson." She ran all the way back to the condo, bubbling with joy.

She couldn't get Josh off her mind and told her grandparents how much fun she had surfing. She couldn't wait to see Josh again. She suddenly had a thought she shared with her grandparents. "My birthday is in three days. Can I invite Josh to supper to celebrate with me?"

Her grandparents looked at each other strangely. "That would be lovely dear. Since it's your special day, you get to choose what you want for supper and what flavor birthday cake you would like," her Grandma said.

"I love anything chocolate, so I would like a chocolate cake with chocolate icing. Can we have french fries and grill some hamburgers and corn on the cob?"

"I think Grandpa and I can manage that," Grandma responded.

The next day Jennifer found the lifeguard stand where Josh was working. He waved and smiled when he saw Jennifer approach with her long brown hair swaying in the ocean breeze. He motioned to the other lifeguard on duty that he was taking a break and climbed down from the stand.

"Hi, how are you feeling today?" Josh asked as they walked to a picnic table to sit in the shade.

"I'm not too sore," Jennifer nervously told him. She tried to get the courage up to ask him to supper. "I really enjoyed surfing and hope we can do it again some time soon."

"I've two more days of work before my next day off. Do you want to surf then, if the waves are good?"

"That would be great." Jennifer hesitated, trying to get the nerve to ask Josh to dinner to celebrate her birthday.

Josh seemed to notice her uneasiness and spoke up. "I get off work at seven tonight. Would you like to go to a movie with me?"

"Yes, that sounds like fun," Jennifer responded, trying to sound calm when her insides were turning upside down. She told him where her grandparents lived so he could pick her up.

"I have to get back to work. I will see you tonight."

Jennifer watched as Josh walked back to the lifeguard stand. She was so excited she ran back to the condo to share the news with Grandma. She burst through the door. "Josh asked me out on a date!" she blurted. "What should I wear?" Jennifer asked as she walked into her room and looked through the clothes in her closet, disappointed at her choices.

Grandma spoke up. "Wearing something new always makes me feel more beautiful and self confident. Why don't we run to the mall and find you something to wear tonight? You can consider it an early birthday present."

"Thanks, Grandma."

They visited one of the larger department stores and Jennifer found the perfect pink short sleeved top and capris to wear with her sandals.

Jennifer applied a fresh coat of pink polish to her fingernails and toe nails when she arrived back at the condo. She dressed in her new clothes and admired herself in the mirror. Her face glowed from all the sun she had gotten surfing.

When the doorbell finally rang, Jennifer about jumped out of her skin. "I'll get it!" she yelled to her grandparents.

She opened the door. Josh was wearing jeans and a t-shirt and smiled when he saw her. "Are you ready to go?"

"Yes, I'm leaving!" Jennifer announced to her grandparents.

"Be home by eleven," Grandpa replied as she walked out the door.

The night was perfect. Josh took her out to eat and then to the movies. They talked so easily with each other, laughing as Josh told her some of his adventures as a lifeguard. During the movie, Josh reached for her hand. The warmth of his hand in hers felt so good. The night was over too soon.

When Josh walked her to the door, she finally got the courage to ask, "My birthday is in two days, would you like to come to supper and celebrate with me?"

"That sounds like fun. What time do I need to be here?"

"Do you have to work?"

"I get off at five, so I can clean up and be here by six."

"That sounds perfect. Goodnight." Jennifer reluctantly closed the door and tried to be quiet so as not wake her grandparents.

Her grandparents, who were never awake past ten, just happened to still be up watching TV when she walked into the family room.

"How was your date, dear?" Grandma casually asked.

The big smile on her face told all. "Josh accepted my invitation to come to supper for my birthday."

"That's nice. Did you have a good time?"

"Yes, Josh and I get along well." She was so elated she didn't know how she was ever going to sleep.

Jennifer drove her Grandma crazy the next two days wanting everything to be just perfect when Josh came to supper. She hadn't seen Josh since their date. She nervously waited for him to arrive. As soon as the doorbell rang, she rushed to open the door. She was surprised to see Josh holding a present in his hand.

"Happy birthday!" Josh yelled as he handed her the present.

Jennifer motioned for him to come in, "You didn't have to bring me a present."

"It's just a little something," Josh replied.

She put the present on the kitchen table and they walked out to the patio where the table was set for supper.

Josh and Grandpa joked with each other on how to cook the perfect burger while Jennifer helped Grandma bring out the rest of the food.

"Everything looks delicious," Josh commented.

"I hope you are hungry because I think Grandma made enough for ten people," Jennifer joked. Jennifer took a big bite of hamburger and commended Grandpa and Josh. "The hamburgers are perfect."

Grandma made sure Josh felt welcome, including him in the conversation. They finished supper and Jennifer helped Grandma clear the table. Grandma lit the seventeen candle on the birthday cake and slowly walked out to the patio to keep them from blowing out. Everyone sang happy birthday and Jennifer closed her eyes to make a wish, then blew out the candles. Jennifer cut the cake and gave Josh a large piece of double chocolate cake along with a big scoop of vanilla ice cream.

After finishing dessert, Josh rubbed his tummy and said, "The food was fantastic. I can't remember the last time I was this full."

"It's time to open presents," Grandma eagerly said as she handed Jennifer the present from her and Grandpa.

"I thought you already gave me my present," Jennifer said as she took the gift from Grandma.

"This is something Grandpa picked up for you."

Jennifer eagerly ripped off the wrapping paper. She was pleasantly surprised when she opened the lid to find a bright pink wetsuit.

"If you are serious about surfing, you will need this as winter approaches so you do not get too cold," Grandpa said, smiling.

Jennifer reached over and hugged Grandpa and kissed him on the cheek. "That is perfect. I can't wait to try it out this winter."

Jennifer then nervously opened the gift from Josh. She was shocked to find a silver chain with a surfboard pendant.

"Thank you so much! Can you help me put it on?" She handed the necklace to Josh and lifted her long silky hair out of the way.

"This pendant is supposed to bring you good luck and many happy days of surfing," Josh said. He reached around her neck and clasped it in place.

Sensing Jennifer wanting to spend some time alone with Josh, Grandma yelled for Grandpa, "Come help me with something in the kitchen."

"I better see what she needs." Grandpa got up from the table and disappeared inside.

"Your grandparents are very nice."

"They can be a little overprotective at times, but they are not too bad," Jennifer laughed. "Thanks so much for coming tonight, and for the necklace. Will you be working again tomorrow?"

"I work the late shift from three till seven. Do you want to surf in the morning? The waves are supposed to be good."

"Yes, that sounds great! I need to practice what you taught me." They stood on the patio staring out at the ocean, listening to the waves, enjoying each other's company until the sun set.

Josh finally spoke up. "The view is magnificent from up here. It's as if you can see to the edge of the earth."

"I am glad you had a good time tonight."

"It's getting late and I better get home so my Mom doesn't start to worry."

"I will see you in the morning." Jennifer said as she walked with Josh to the door.

After Josh left, Jennifer's grandparents couldn't peel her off the ceiling the rest of the night, she was so happy.

The rest of the summer flew by as Josh and Jennifer became closer. They saw each other almost every day. For the first time, Jennifer was dreading the start of school. Josh was also a senior this year but he would be attending high school in Melbourne instead of Cocoa Beach. Josh was the only one she knew in the area. She was afraid she might not fit in and didn't know how she would be treated by the other students.

Josh tried to reassure her. "Living near the beach, everyone is friendly and laid back. You don't have to worry about anything. You will make plenty of new girl friends."

"I hope you are right." Jennifer thought about her best friend Elaine, back in Minnesota, and wished she could be here with her now.

Chapter Three

"Thy shoes shall be iron and brass; and as thy days, so shall thy strength be." *(Deuteronomy 33:25)*

Jennifer insisted on driving herself to school and refused to let her grandparents take her. When she pulled into the school parking lot, she noticed everyone happily greeting each other after being apart for the summer. She gathered up her backpack and told herself, "You can do this." She stepped out of the car and walked toward the school entrance with her head held high. She managed to find her first period English class without getting too lost. She felt so out of place. Everyone wore shorts and sandals while she wore jeans and tennis shoes like she did in Minnesota. She found an empty desk and took a seat. The room was filled with the roar of chatter as everyone greeted their friends after the summer break. Jennifer suddenly felt so alone and wished she could talk to Josh.

The girl behind her tapped her on the shoulder. Jennifer turned around and was greeted. "Hi! My name is Trish."

Trish had a full head of red, frizzy hair, fair complexion with a freckled face and wore braces. "Hi, I'm Jennifer."

"Are you new this year?"

"Yes, I moved here over the summer."

Trish made Jennifer feel welcome. "What classes are you taking?"

They discovered they both had Art History and Chemistry together for the next two periods. Trish showed Jennifer where to go and volunteered to be her chemistry lab partner. After third period, they ate lunch together, and Trish introduced Jennifer to some of her friends. It was not long before they became best friends.

It was as if God put Trish behind Jennifer that first day of school. Of all the desks where Jennifer chose to sit, she picked the one in front of Trish. She made her first day at school enjoyable and helped her survive her senior year.

Trish was very artistic. She loved to draw and act. Jennifer, on the other hand, was more athletic and loved math. Even though they were total opposites, they attended each other's events and encouraged one another.

Jennifer joined the swim team and loved competing. She didn't win many events at first, but later became a strong swimmer and started to place in a couple of races.

Josh and Jennifer continued seeing each other on the weekends and talked almost every night on the phone until it was time for bed. He invited her to homecoming at his school.

She wanted to look glamorous for the dance. Of course it didn't take a lot of persuading to get Grandma to take her shopping to buy a dress. They found a pretty pearl blue sleeveless long dress. As soon as Jennifer tried it on she knew this was the one she wanted. She looked at the price tag and cringed. It was much more than she had wanted to spend.

Grandma seemed to sense Jennifer's uneasiness. "Don't worry about the cost dear. I will buy it for you. It looks just perfect on you."

"Are you sure? I can use my savings to buy the dress, Grandma."

She smiled and explained, "Dear, that is not necessary. Grandpa and I can afford to buy you this dress." She took Jennifer's hand and turned her around so they were facing each other in the small dressing room. "Your parents made sure if anything ever happened to them that you would be well taken care of. You do not need to worry about money."

Jennifer looked into her Grandma's eyes and could see the sadness she felt.

Grandma quickly changed the subject before they both started to cry. "You will be the prettiest girl at the dance." She spun Jennifer around and turned her back toward the mirror.

The night of the dance Grandma helped curl and style Jennifer's hair. She slid on her dress careful not to mess up her hair. She wore new silver sandals, the surfing pendant Josh gave her on her birthday, and pearl earrings that Grandma let her borrow. When finished, she felt like a princess. She looked in the mirror and smiled. Soft curls framed her face with her long brown hair gently flowing down her back.

"You look like an angel." Grandma said, as tears came to her eyes.

Jennifer knew Grandma was probably also thinking of Mom. "I wish Mom could have been here to see me tonight." She hugged Grandma. "Thanks for helping me get dressed."

The doorbell suddenly rang. "He's here!" Jennifer excitedly announced. They both wiped tears from their eyes.

Jennifer rushed to open the door with a big smile on her face. "Wow! You clean up nice," she told Josh. Josh walked in wearing a black tux. She hardly recognized him. She had never seen him in anything more than shorts or jeans and a t-shirt.

Josh was speechless when he saw Jennifer.

"Well, what do you think?" Jennifer asked as she swirled around to show off her new dress.

Josh finally spoke. "You look gorgeous! Here, I got this for you to wear." Josh handed her a wrist corsage with white carnations.

Before they could leave, Grandma took several pictures of them. "You have fun tonight."

Grandpa added, "Be home by midnight."

The evening was magical. Josh took her to a fancy restaurant. They arrived at the prom where they danced and laughed, holding hands the whole time. It was almost midnight before she knew it. Josh drove her home, and they sat in his truck talking for as long as they could without breaking curfew. He walked her to the door. He leaned down and kissed her gently on the lips.

He stared into her eyes, "I had fun tonight."

"I did too, and hate for the night to end."

He kissed her again. "I better let you go before you break curfew and get in trouble. I will call you tomorrow."

Josh released her hand and she reluctantly opened the door and went inside. She loved Josh, but hesitated to tell him for fear it would scare him away.

The condo was quiet, but she saw a light shining from underneath her grandparent's bedroom door. She knew they were still awake, waiting for her to arrive home safely and on time.

Her grandparents bedroom door slowly opened. Grandma appeared and nonchalantly asked, "Did you have a good time at the dance, dear?"

"Yes!" She knew Grandma was dying to hear all the details. "We went to a fancy restaurant and had a scrumptious rich chocolate mousse for dessert. The dance was magical. Josh and I slow danced together for the first time. The ballroom had a large sparkling chandelier hanging from the ceiling and was decorated in the school colors with banners and balloons floating everywhere. The evening was just perfect."

"It sounds wonderful. You can tell me more about it in the morning. You better try to get some sleep before it gets any later."

Jennifer went to bed but couldn't sleep. She prayed to God, "Thank you for bringing Josh into my life. Please do not take him away from me, like my parents." She was so happy but had a sick feeling in the pit of her stomach. It was the same feeling she had when she tried to get away with something she knew was wrong. She feared something tragic would take Josh away from her.

Trish and Jennifer continued to hang out after school working on their homework together and talking about boys. Trish had a crush on a boy at school, and he asked her out on a date that weekend. They were going to the movies together. She was a nervous wreck. Jennifer tried to calm her down.

"What should I wear? What will I talk about?" Trish worried.

"Let's go through your closet and find something you can wear. What about these jeans and this top?" Jennifer held the outfit up for her approval.

"That top makes me look too fat!"

"You have got to be kidding. You are skinnier than me and about three inches taller. Nothing makes you look fat."

"What do I do if he wants to kiss me?"

"Well, do you want him to kiss you?"

"No, not on the first date; I hardly know him."

"I've an idea. What if Josh and I just happen to go to the same movie and sit behind you? If you need me you can just excuse yourself and say you have to go to the restroom. I will meet you there."

"I like that idea. I would be more relaxed knowing you were with me."

So that evening, Jennifer shared her plan with Josh.

Josh was more than happy to accommodate and said, "If everything goes well with Trish and her date, we can double date with them next weekend."

The evening went as planned, and Jennifer sat so she could keep an eye on Trish and her date. After the movie started, Jennifer noticed Trish's date putting his arm around Trish's shoulders. Then he started kissing Trish on the neck and lips. She could tell Trish was not comfortable and kept trying to push her date away.

Jennifer decided it was time to intervene. She walked over and said, "Hi." She pretended to just happen to notice Trish in front of her and to coincidentally be at the same movie.

"I need to go to the restroom," Trish whispered to her date and excused herself. Her date was noticeably upset with Jennifer for interrupting. When they got to the restroom, Trish started to cry. "The night is not going anything like I imagined. I am scared to ride home with him. What should I do?"

"I'll return to the theatre and get Josh. Then I'll explain to your date that you are not feeling well and that I am taking you home."

"He is going to be so mad. Do you think that is a good idea?"

"We can do that or you can go back in and continue to let him grope you."

"You are right; I don't feel safe with him. I am so glad you came tonight."

"Stay here, and I will be right back."

Jennifer told Trish's date, "Trish is not feeling well and I'm going to take her home."

He became visibly upset and yelled, "Bitch! Why don't you mind your own business?"

Josh stepped in front of Jennifer. "You need to watch your mouth."

Jennifer grabbed Josh's hand and pulled him away before a fight broke out in the movie theatre. "Don't let him get to you. Trish is waiting for us."

Everyone was quiet in the car on the way to Trish's house. Jennifer was not sure what to say to make Trish feel better.

"I am sorry for ruining your evening. Thanks for giving me a ride home," Trish said holding back tears.

"You didn't ruin our evening. I am just glad we were there for you. I'll call you tomorrow." Jennifer yelled to Trish as she left.

Josh drove to the beach and parked. It was dark on the beach with only a few lights from the condos reflecting off the water. They took a walk holding hands. The air smelled of salt being carried in by a cool breeze. Jennifer could tell Josh was still fuming over Trish's date's behavior. This was the first time she had ever witnessed Josh lose his temper and come to her defense. "Thanks for helping Trish tonight. No telling what would have happened if you hadn't been there. I love you," she blurted out before she could stop herself. She anxiously waited for Josh's response.

Josh stopped walking and turned toward her, "I love you too." He reached down and softly caressed her lips with his, kissing her gently. They sat on the beach and Josh embraced her with his masculine arms to help keep her warm while they listened to the waves and talked.

"Where are you planning to go to college?" She asked Josh.

"I need to work to save enough money first. Then, I will probably go to the local community college."

It never dawned on Jennifer that Josh's Mom wouldn't pay for his college. Her parents set up a college fund for her the day she was born. She always understood that after high school she was to attend college. It was never a question of whether she would go, but where she would go.

"Do you know where you want to attend and what you want to study?" Josh asked.

"I want to be an engineer like my Dad. I need to start applying at the universities in Florida."

With sadness in his voice he told her, "You will make a good engineer with your analytical mind." He pulled Jennifer to him, leaned down, and kissed her on the temple.

Jennifer suddenly felt very sad at the realization Josh wouldn't be attending college with her.

"It's getting late. I better take you home." Josh helped Jennifer up and brushed the sand off her before walking back down the beach toward the condo. Josh was quiet all the way back.

As they approached her door she asked, "Is everything all right?"

He hesitated. "I'm just tired. I'll call you tomorrow."

Jennifer opened the door and watched as Josh walked away. She had this feeling of impeding doom. The feeling you get when things are going too good. Was her happiness about to end? They finally admitted to each other that they were in love. Was God going to take away her happiness again? She told herself she was just being paranoid.

That night she thanked God for watching over Trish, placing Josh and her at the theatre so they could help Trish; and for Josh's patience and understanding.

It had been six months since her parents died and so much had happened. She almost felt guilty for being so happy, like she was not honoring her parent's memory. She lay in bed talking to them about Josh and how much she wished they could meet him. Then it dawned on her. If they hadn't died, she never would have met Josh.

Chapter Four

"For wisdom is better than rubies; and all the things that may be desired are not to be compared to it." *(Proverbs 8:11)*

Jennifer's senior year quickly came to an end. She had made several friends during the year. There were tears and hugs after the graduation ceremony. They promised to stay in touch. Trish had been accepted at a literal arts college in south Florida. Jennifer planned to attend the University of Florida in North Florida to study electrical engineering.

After the graduation ceremony Jennifer celebrated with Josh. They went out for dinner and then a walk on the beach. They held hands as they slowly walked down the beach enjoying the warm evening and the smell of the salt air as the cool sand caressed their feet. They talked about their plans for the summer. Jennifer had lined up some babysitting jobs, so she could earn some extra cash for college. Josh planned to work as a lifeguard again this summer. After that he thought he might take some classes to get certified as an automobile mechanic.

The summer flew by; the reality of Jennifer moving away to college and Josh staying in Melbourne started to sink in. She dreaded the thought of leaving for college without Josh.

As the day approached, she tried to convince herself that leaving for college was no big deal. She told Josh, "We can talk on the phone every day. I will drive home on the weekends so we can spend time together."

Josh knew how unrealistic that sounded. He understood Jennifer was going to have to study if she wanted to make good grades. "I doubt you will have time to come home every weekend. Let's just see how it goes."

She couldn't imagine going longer than a week without seeing Josh. Somehow she was going to make this long distance relationship work.

The day for Jennifer to leave for college arrived. She gathered up the last few things she planned to take, and Josh helped her load the car until nothing else could fit. She hugged her grandparents good-bye. She turned to Josh and saw the sadness in his eyes. She had told herself she was not going to cry, but she struggled to hold back the tears. She reached up to hug Josh and whispered in his ear, "I love you and will miss you so much."

Josh reached down and lifted her face to his and gently kissed her on the lips.

She couldn't hold back the tears any longer. She ached at the thought of being separated from him.

Josh wiped the tears from her face and gave her one final kiss. He held the door open for Jennifer and closed it once she had gotten in the car. "Drive safely."

"I will call you as soon as I arrive." She started the car and turned on the AC before waving good bye to Josh. She drove away and knew in that instant things between them would never be the same.

Her dorm room was small, with just enough room for two beds, and a small kitchen that was shared with two other dorm rooms. Her roommate, Ashley was petite, only about five feet tall, with brown eyes and dirty blond hair. Jennifer soon discovered Ashley didn't let her size hinder her in any way. Ashley was very smart and ambitious. She was also majoring in electrical engineering. They hit it off right away.

The first couple of weeks at college were crazy. She was taking eighteen hours of classes and couldn't believe all the homework she was given each day. It was nothing like high school. She was quickly overwhelmed.

Sorority rush week began just as classes started. Ashley and Jennifer had received invitations to attend two parties.

"Why don't we go?" Ashley begged Jennifer to attend with her. "We could use a little fun."

Even though she had tons of homework, having a little fun did sound enticing. She convinced herself it would lift her spirits and get her mind off Josh. "Okay, I will attend, but just for a little while. Then I've to get back to my studies."

They attended two parties together where the benefits of belonging to a sorority were presented to them. The sorority sisters explained, along with the scholastically advantage, it was a great way to meet boys. The sororities were often invited to attend the fraternity parties.

After Jennifer informed them that she was already dating someone, the response was, "That won't last long." What did they mean by that? Jennifer wondered. She had no intentions of dating anyone else other than Josh. She met a couple of girls who were juniors also majoring in electrical engineering. They shared with her what professors to stay away from. They were very helpful and offered their assistance if she needed help with any of her classes.

Within a week, Ashley and Jennifer received an invitation to become a pledge for Gamma Phi Beta. The cost was not cheap, but she rationalized being a member could help her with her grades.

Her grandparents were not so easily swayed, though. "All I hear about sororities is the wild parties they have. I am not comfortable with you being thrown into that environment. Would you be living at the sorority house?" Grandma probed.

"It's nothing like that Grandma. The girls are very nice. It will give me a chance to meet more girls on campus and make new friends to study with. The sorority house has limited space, so I will continue to live in the dorm until there is an opening."

After much debate and some hesitation, her grandparents agreed to let her join.

Jennifer was concerned about the cost though. "Do I need to find a job to help cover the expenses?"

"You need to concentrate on your studies," Grandma stressed. "You can use the money your parents set aside for your education."

Ashley was from a wealthy family whose mother had belonged to a sorority in college, so her parents were thrilled that she had received an invitation. She definitely grew up under different circumstances.

Ashley and Jennifer went through the sorority initiation process together. For the next two weeks, they attended classes about the sorority explaining what it represents and means to be a sister. They also were tasked with doing chores for their soon-to-be sorority sisters.

Jennifer just thought she was overwhelmed before. She suddenly realized she needed to stay at school and study all weekend or she would never catch up. She just didn't have the time to drive home and see Josh.

She called Josh when she got out of her last class on Friday afternoon, "I can't come home this weekend. I need to stay and study to prepare for my first test next week." This was the first time their trust for each other was really tested.

"I understand. I know you will come home when you have the time. I have to go." Then he hung up.

His words said he understood, but she could tell in the tone of his voice he was hurt. She was losing him. She felt guilty, like she was betraying Josh even though she was not dating anyone else. Josh suspected otherwise.

She soon took advantage of the benefits of being in a sorority. She struggled to keep up with her studies and didn't do great on the first test. The sorority had created a history file of sample tests for almost every subject being taught. She discovered using the previous test to prepare for her exams helped her tremendously. She was able to get her grades back up to A's and B's instead of C's. She quickly got into a routine at school, getting up early to attend class in the morning, a lab in the afternoon, and studying in the library until late in the evening.

By the weekends, she looked forward to driving home to see Josh; well at least at first. After a few weeks of trying to juggle her time at school and rushing home after her last class on Friday to see Josh, it soon became apparent she needed to spend more time at school if she wanted to keep her grades up. Also, she rationalized the sorority had most of its events on the weekend, so she needed to start helping with them.

She rushed home Friday after class and planned to meet Josh for dinner, so she could explain her situation and return to school on Saturday.

Josh didn't talk much at dinner. She chatted away about school and how much studying she had to do. She finally got the nerve and told him, "I don't have time to drive home every weekend. I miss you, but I need to go back tomorrow to finish a paper due on Monday."

She could tell Josh was hurt. "I'm busy too, so it's probably best if you don't come home for a few weekends." Josh was working full time as an automobile mechanic and was going to school at night to get his mechanic's license. This was not his dream job but it would make him enough money to get by.

Was Josh breaking up with her? "I will definitely be home for Thanksgiving. We can spend some time together then."

Before she had a chance to ask if they were okay he said, "I better get you home I have to get up early for work tomorrow."

When they reached her grandparent's condo, Josh walked her to the door. He grew very quiet, and with a solemn look on his face, kissed her and said, "Good-bye." He turned to leave before she had a chance to say anything.

She returned to college the next day with Josh's behavior in the back of her mind. She was having so much fun with her new friends and discovering new things about herself, she felt guilty for being so happy while Josh was back home working. She was having all these new experiences and freedoms she never had before. Other boys were showing interest in her, but she refused their invitation for a date because of Josh. Between the sorority events and school, she didn't have much time to talk to Josh. She missed several of Josh's attempts to reach her.

When she went home for Thanksgiving, she eagerly called Josh. "What are your plans for Thanksgiving?" She tried to pretend nothing had changed between them.

He sounded strange on the phone. "My Mom's family is in town. I have to spend time with them. Can we get together on Saturday?"

She tried to hide her disappointment and told him, "Sure, I'll see you on Saturday."

Josh arrived at the condo after lunch on Saturday. When she greeted him at the door he asked, "Do you want to take a walk on the beach?" His deep blue eyes stared back at her, but instead of seeing joy that they were together, she saw sadness.

They walked in quiet for a while, holding hands enjoying the warm breeze coming off the ocean. She started to fill the silence with senseless chatter because she was afraid of what he was going to say to her.

Josh stopped, and they sat on the beach at the same spot where they had first met. They watched the surfers by the pier in silence.

She finally got the nerve and asked, "What's wrong?"

"I don't think we should see each other anymore."

"Have you fallen in love with someone else?"

"It's just too painful being separated from you. I know it's best for us to end the relationship while we are still friends. I know you are busy and don't have time for me in your life now. I understand you need to concentrate on school."

She started to cry and through her tears she told him, "I will always love you." She knew in her heart he was right, though. She would only continue to hurt him if they stayed together, but it didn't hurt any less knowing this was probably for the best.

They walked back to the condo hardly saying a word. When they arrived she turned and kissed Josh good-bye. She ran inside and to the solace of her bedroom. She closed the door and cried her heart out. She hadn't hurt this bad since her parents had died. What was she going to do without Josh? She was heartbroken. She loved Josh very much. He had brought her so much happiness when she was at the lowest point in her life. She knew, though, it was not fair to him. School was taking up more and more of her time. She was also changing, becoming more outspoken, confident, and independent; but it saddened her greatly. Josh was a part of who she was. How could she live without him?

After Thanksgiving, she tried to put Josh out of her mind for she had to get ready for finals. She spent every waking hour studying. When she came home for Christmas, the first thing she wanted to do was call Josh and share with him how she had done her first quarter, but realized she couldn't. It just didn't seem fair. They had shared everything for over a year, and Josh was part of her. She was grieving as if a part of her had died. She walked on the beach each morning hoping to see Josh surfing, but they never crossed paths.

Chapter Five

"Let not your heart be troubled: ye believe in God, believe also in me." *(St. John 14:1)*

When college started back in January, Jennifer was glad to get away from Cocoa Beach where there was nothing but sad memories.

She busied herself with her studies and the sorority. She started going to more parties now that she didn't have to be faithful to Josh. It was not long before she was asked out on a date. She had gotten so comfortable being around Josh and talking with him so easily she found it very unnerving not knowing what to expect. She drove Ashley crazy as she got ready for the date. Memories of Trish's date in high school came back to her, and she feared being put in an awkward situation.

Tom picked her up, and they ate at a Caribbean restaurant playing reggae music in the background. They talked over dinner. He was a junior studying civil engineering. He seemed very serious and knew what he wanted to do in life. He was not very athletic or outdoorsy, so they didn't have a lot in common. He was well, boring compared to Josh. Afterwards, he took her to a movie. The evening went well with no major crisis. Tom was a perfect gentleman, but they didn't click like her and Josh did. She didn't know what she was expecting. Tom must have sensed her uneasiness though, because he never called again.

Ashley and Jennifer had studied hard all week. They just completed their midterm exams and had crashed for the evening, putting on comfortable sweats and finding a good chick flick on TV.

Ashley looked over at her, "We should be out celebrating, not hiding in our dorm room. I heard one of the fraternities just down the street is having a party tonight. Why don't we go?"

"I am exhausted from all the late hours. Do you really feel like going to a party tonight?"

"Come on, it will be fun! We can dress up, do our hair and make-up. We don't have to stay late."

"All right, you convinced me. I guess it would be nice to go out and have some fun for a change."

They changed clothes, styled their hair, and put on some make-up. They admired each other's work. "We clean up pretty good. The boys won't be able to resist us tonight," Ashley laughed as they headed out the door.

They walked the few blocks to where the party was being held, but heard it long before they arrived. The music was blaring. People spilled out of the frat house onto the front lawn.

"Let's get something to drink and try to blend in," Ashley suggested as they made their way through the crowd.

There were several kegs of beer at the party. Jennifer had never drunk alcohol before. She knew she was underage, and it was not legal to drink alcohol yet, but thought to herself, "How could drinking one beer hurt?" She felt extremely out of place and wanted to fit in.

Ashley and Jennifer picked up a cup of beer and looked around to see if they knew anyone. Jennifer took a sip of beer and told Ashley, "How does anyone drink this stuff? It tastes like something that was left out on the kitchen counter and spoiled overnight."

"Let's go back outside."

"What?" Jennifer screamed, trying to be heard over the loud music.

Ashley started making her way through the crowd, bumping into people trying to get to the front door. Jennifer tried to follow but was stepped on by a guy who spilled his beer all over her.

"I am so sorry," the guy yelled as he tried to dry the spilt beer with his hand from the front of her shirt.

Jennifer pushed his hand away. "That's all right, this top was old anyway," she joked.

"Do you want to dance?" he asked.

Jennifer thought, What do I have to lose? "Sure." She gulped down the rest of her beer and set the cup on the end table.

She started dancing and having a good time. A beer seemed to magically appear in her hand every time she found her cup empty. Before she knew it, she was lightheaded and could hardly stand. She tried to find Ashley, so they could go back to the dorm when one of the guys she had been dancing with came over and put his arm around her neck. He appeared to be even drunker than Jennifer and was using her as a support to stand.

"Where are you going? The party is just getting started," the guy slurred in Jennifer's ear.

"It's getting late. I'm tired, and need to find my friend Ashley," she yelled back.

"Why don't we go to my room? You can rest there." He started to pull her in that direction.

A voice in her head was telling her, This is not a good idea. You need to get away. But her legs were not following her brain.

He started leading her to his room when Ashley spotted Jennifer. Ashley was with her Big Sister in the sorority. "Do you need some help?" Ashley asked.

Jennifer tried to pull away from the guy who had his arm tightly wrapped around her shoulders.

"Where are you going? We're having fun. You do not need to leave yet." He continued to hold onto her.

Jennifer pushed him away and she stumbled to the ground when he let go. "I have had enough fun for one night."

Ashley helped Jennifer back on her feet. Ashley's Big Sister stepped between the guy and Jennifer. Ashley put Jennifer's arm around her neck and supported her around the waist. "I think it's time we got you back to our room."

Ashley helped Jennifer walk back to the dorm where she collapsed in bed.

"Make the bed stop spinning." Jennifer slurred while putting one foot on the ground.

"Here you may need this," Ashley said as she placed the garbage can beside Jennifer's bed.

"What is that for?" she started to ask, as she leaned over and threw up. She felt like she could just die. "Don't ever let me drink again."

The next morning she woke with the worst headache she had ever had in her life. She slowly lifted herself out of bed holding her head. Ashley handed her three aspirin. "Why did you let me drink so much?"

"I had nothing to do with how much you consumed. I turned around and you were gone. It took me an hour to track you back down."

Jennifer thought back to last night and knew how close things were to getting out of hand. She thanked God for watching over her and wondered if he had a hand in sending Ashley to her rescue. "Thanks for saving me. I don't know what would have happened if you hadn't come along."

"The next time we go to a party let's agree we will stick together."

The rest of her freshman year flew by. Ashley and her managed to pass all of their classes and were looking forward to summer break away from school. Since Josh and her were no longer dating, she dreaded the thought of spending the summer with her grandparents in Cocoa Beach.

Ashley had a boyfriend that was staying in the area for the summer, and she didn't want to leave him to go home to Alabama.

As they packed their belongings to move out of the dorm for the summer, Ashley blurted out, "You know we could find a job and stay here for the summer. We could get an apartment together and save a little extra money for school. What do you think?"

"Where could we find a job?"

"I saw the steakhouse down the road is hiring waitresses. I bet they would hire us."

That sounded so much better than going to her grandparents and moping around all summer. They stopped packing and immediately went to the restaurant and completed job applications. Amazingly enough they were both hired the next day. Now all Jennifer needed to do was convince her grandparents what a great idea this was.

It took some coercion on Jennifer's part explaining, "I already found a job, so you won't have to pay for anything. Ashley will be here with me, so you don't have to worry about me." She held her breath while she waited for their response.

"You have to stay in touch and let us know if you need anything," they begrudgingly agreed.

Ashley and Jennifer couldn't believe their luck. A small two bedroom apartment just became available within their price range located not far from school or work. They signed the lease before someone else took it. They paid the deposit and were handed the keys.

They opened the door to their new home and squealed with delight. It was not much, but it was theirs. They spent that afternoon moving their meager belongings from the dorm to the apartment. They didn't have much in the way of furniture so they sat on the floor until they were able to scrounge some used furniture. They had just the basics: sofa, chair, and beds.

Living in an apartment was a new found freedom she never had before. It felt great. They personalized the apartment by adding some posters to the walls, along with accessorizing the kitchen and bathroom.

They both worked long hours and frequently on different shifts, so they didn't see much of each other over the summer. She now understood what working for a living truly meant. Their new found freedom came with a price, not having time or money to do anything fun. Her life seemed to revolve around work and sleep.

To make rent each month, they lived off grocery store bargains and coupons. A few nights though after a long week, they treated themselves by collapsing in front of the TV, watching a good movie, and eating a quart of ice cream together. Even though life seemed grueling at times, it was great being on their own.

When college started in the fall, Jennifer cut her work hours to thirty hours a week. She registered for fewer classes in hopes of keeping her grades up, still have enough time to support the sorority, and have some fun in the process. Getting little sleep became the norm. She dated but never the same guy for very long. Her heart was just not in it. After a few dates with the same guy when things started to get serious, she would panic and end the relationship. "I really don't have time to date with work and school," she would explain to her date. "It would be better if we didn't see each other anymore." This approach seemed to work until she met John her junior year.

John reminded her of Josh. He was good looking, had curly brown hair, brown eyes, and was well built with muscular arms, stomach, and legs. He was an outdoorsman, enjoyed boating, hiking, scuba diving, camping, and fishing.

When Jennifer was not working on the weekends, John and her would go on a little adventure. They would pull out the Florida trails map and pick a place they hadn't been before and go exploring. During the winter months, they hiked all the trails within a fifty mile radius of the college. They enjoyed watching the wildlife. They saw deer drinking from the springs, wild turkey, bob cat, fox, and every kind of bird you could imagine. Jennifer was fascinated by the wild animals and watched them quietly until they ran away. Occasionally, they ran across a snake which never thrilled her. Most of the time they were as scared of her as she was of them, and they hurriedly slithered away from her.

On a few weekends, they would go on a camping excursion. John had a little pup tent. They set up camp, started a fire, and roasted hotdogs over the flames. Then for dessert, they roasted marshmallows. Everything always tasted better when cooked outdoors after a long hike. They spent the nights cuddled together after a day of new adventures.

She never had anything to fear until one day when they hiked in the Ocala National Forest. It was late spring and the humidity was increasing along with the temperature. They had hiked about eight miles when they heard snorting in the brush. "What is that noise?" Jennifer asked. She stopped dead in her tracks.

"I don't know, but we better turn around." John replied.

Before she could turn she saw a little baby piglet come out from underneath the brush. "How cute," she said as she stopped to watch it.

"We need to leave. The mother is probably not far away. Remain calm, turn around, and slowly walk away from the baby pig."

Just as she turned the mother pig came charging from the brush. "Run!" John yelled as he grabbed Jennifer's hand and pulled her along. He pushed her up the nearest tree as the loud noise from the pig hooves pounded the ground behind her. John managed to jump up another tree just before the pig reached him. The pig hung around for a little while, but eventually left when it determined they were no longer a threat.

"Do you think the coast is clear?" She asked John.

"I can no longer hear the rustle of leaves as they walk through the brush, so they should be far enough away."

They climbed down from the tree and tried to retreat quietly, but found it impossible as the dried leaves crunched beneath their feet. Unfortunately, the tree John so kindly shoved Jennifer up was covered in poison ivy. By the time they reached the car, the inside of her arms and legs were itching horribly. She was covered in a red rash.

John took one look at her and announced, "I think I better get you to the doctor."

Jennifer was given a shot to help with the itching, along with cream to gently apply over the affected areas. She appeared from the doctors office covered in white cream. She held her arms away from her side so they wouldn't rub, and walked carefully so her legs wouldn't touch.

John started laughing.

"What is wrong with you?" She yelled. "I am miserable!" She slugged John on the arm. She could only imagine what she must look like covered in blotches, cream from head to toe, and her hair a tangled mess. She started to laugh to stop from crying. "Look what you have done to me."

"How is this my fault?"

"If you hadn't shoved me up that tree covered in poison ivy, I wouldn't look like this now."

"I could have let the pig attack you instead." John looked at her trying to maintain his composure.

She started laughing again out of frustration. After she got her hysteria under control she asked John, "Can you take me home? I've had all the fun I can take for one day."

John dropped her off at her apartment. She could hardly sleep for a week or wear any clothes that rubbed against her rash. This was another one of life's lessons learned the hard way. Mental note, look for poison ivy before you climb any trees.

Her time with John was never boring. A few weeks later, as it was getting hotter, John suggested going kayaking down one of the local springs. They both rented a kayak for the day. As they glided quietly through the water, she relaxed and enjoyed the scenery.

They quickly left the tourists behind. It was not long before Jennifer spotted a manatee. The manatee surfaced blowing air out it's spout before slowly sinking below the surface. It was enormous, weighing several hundred pounds. She was spellbound as she waited for it to surface again. After a few minutes, and several yards further down the river, it came up again for air. It was a spectacular creature, gray in color with a big nose and whiskers like a large sea lion, with little fins which maneuvered its massive body.

After losing sight of the manatee, they paddled further down the river, deeper into a very swampy area. It looked creepy with Spanish moss hanging from the trees leaning over the water, like you would imagine seeing in a horror movie about swamp monsters. She feared a snake might fall on her as they paddled under the tree limbs. The passageway became narrow. "I think we should turn around and head back," she suggested.

Before Jennifer could turn her kayak around, there was a loud crash just in front of John. "What was that?"

"Paddle backwards as fast as you can!" John yelled. "A very large gator is swimming toward us."

She looked up to see two black eyes looming just above the water, attached to a massive head. A ten foot body trailed behind the sinister eyes, a massive tail moved from side to side, propelling it quickly through the water toward her.

Pure adrenaline pumped through Jennifer's body which allowed her to paddle harder than she ever had before. Her kayak moved through the water so fast she left behind a wake. Once the river opened up, she maneuvered her kayak to a forward position pushing her paddle with all her might to quickly spin around. They didn't stop paddling until they were back where they started.

Out of breath Jennifer said, "That was the largest gator I've ever seen or want to be that close to again."

John laughed and teased, "I never knew a kayak could go that fast. You must have broken some kind of speed record."

"You didn't seem to have any trouble keeping up with me after almost becoming gator bait."

That was the last adventure John and Jennifer would share. Her junior year was over, and John returned home to North Carolina for the summer. His father owned an outdoors store where he helped out during the summer.

John and Jennifer had grown surprising close but the words, "I love you," never were spoken. She enjoyed their time together, but she really had no idea how he felt about her. John always made her laugh and feel better if she was having a crappy week. She had to admit she was going to miss him while he was away for the summer.

Work consumed her during the summer months and she took two classes during the summer term to lighten her load her senior year. John rarely called, and when he did, it was short and impersonal. She started to wonder if John was dating someone else. In their last conversation John casually informed her, "I may decide to stay in North Carolina instead of going back to school in the fall." Before she had a chance to ask him more about it he spoke up, "Well I better run I have to get back to work, bye." Several weeks passed, and she never heard from John again.

Ashley had an on again off again relationship with a boy she had met during one of the sorority parties in the winter. She thought she would surprise him over the summer. She had a couple of days off of work and thought she would drive up to Birmingham to see him. She called his cell phone and a girl answered his phone. "I'm sorry I must have dialed the wrong number," Ashley said as she started to hang up.

"Were you trying to reach Ashton?" the girl asked.

"Yes, I was. Who is this?" Ashley asked, afraid of the answer.

Smugly the girl replied, "I'm Ashton's girlfriend. He is in the shower. Can I give him a message?"

So, when Ashton said he was going home to spend time with his family, he was really spending time with his other girlfriend. Ashley hesitated wondering if she should tell her she was also Ashton's girlfriend, but decided there was no point in hurting her. "No, I will try him later," and hung up. Ashley was not about to share a boyfriend, and never saw Ashton again.

Ashley and Jennifer went back to their weekly ritual on the weekends of crashing in front of the TV at night, watching a good movie, and drowning their sorrows in ice cream. They both decided to swear off boys for a while. They were better off without them.

Chapter Six

"Fear not, for I am with you. Do not be dismayed. I am your God. I will strengthen you; I will help you; I will uphold you with my victorious right hand." *(Isaiah 41:10)*

Jennifer looked forward to her senior year at college. She had completed her hardest classes and mostly electives remained for her to have enough credits to graduate. She increased her hours at work and was able to keep up with her studies and still have time for some fun. The fall term was over before she knew it and Christmas break was upon her. Jennifer looked forward to spending a quiet week at home with her grandparents.

As Jennifer drove to Cocoa Beach, she enjoyed listening to Christmas carols playing on the radio. When she arrived, she was surprised to see Grandpa had lost a lot of weight and was not doing well. She had been so self-involved with everything she had going on that she hadn't bothered to call her grandparents for several weeks to see how they were doing.

Grandma looked tired and she appeared to have aged ten years since Jennifer last saw her six months ago. Grandma shared with her, "Grandpa is battling prostate cancer and the prognosis is not good. He had surgery over the summer followed by radiation and chemotherapy treatments, but the cancer has spread to his pancreas. The doctors give him about four weeks to live."

"Why didn't you call and tell me?" Jennifer blurted out in anger.

"We knew you were busy with school and work. Grandpa didn't want you to be distracted by his illness."

Jennifer was devastated. "There must be something else the doctors can do?"

"Your Grandpa has had a full life with plenty of happy memories. We have been truly blessed to have had so many good years together. We have prayed about this. It's in God's hands now."

"His hands," Jennifer angrily shouted. "Like Mom and Dad were in His hands. I need some fresh air," and she ran out the door toward the beach.

After walking for a while, Jennifer sat on the beach and stared out at the ocean, listening to the waves as they crashed along the shore. Something about the massiveness of the ocean always brought clarity back to her life as she realized what an insignificant part in this universe she was. She had buried the feelings she had for the death of her parents by staying busy with school and work. Those feelings came crashing back at the thought of losing Grandpa. It dawned on her the reason she chose not to communicate or visit her grandparents was because it just reminded her of what she had lost, first her parents then Josh. Now she was going to lose Grandpa.

When she started college, she stopped attending church. She made excuses that she was too busy with school and work. Sunday was the only day she had to catch up on her studies. The real reason ran much deeper than that, though. She was not sure she ever truly forgave God for taking her parents away from her. The bitterness she felt mellowed over time but the hurt never truly went away.

When she returned to the condo she quietly entered Grandpa's bedroom where he was resting. She sat by Grandpa, reached for his hand, and looked him in the eyes. "I love you very much, and I am very grateful for all you and Grandma did for me after Mom and Dad died. I don't want you to think that because I stopped visiting or calling has anything to do with how much I love you."

"I know dear. Grandma and I knew you needed your space to work through your pain and go on with life."

She leaned over and gave Grandpa a hug and kiss.

Grandma and Jennifer tried to make Christmas as special and cheerful as possible for Grandpa. They made his favorite cookies and took him for a drive to see the Christmas lights in the neighborhood. Christmas Eve they attended church services together. Grandpa was very weak but didn't want to miss it. The glory of the season filled Jennifer's heart as she sang Christmas carols. The children in the church put on a short play of the nativity scene and the birth of Jesus Christ. Tears came to her eyes as she asked God to forgive her for turning her back on Him.

After Christmas, Grandpa took a turn for the worse. It had gotten to the point he could no longer get out of bed. Hospice came to the condo and told them what to expect in his final days. It was time for Jennifer to return to college to start her final term. "I can stay and help you Grandma. It won't hurt if I miss a few more days of work and class."

"College is too important, and I do not want you to get behind on your school work. Grandpa and I will be all right, dear."

Leaving Grandpa to return to school was one of the hardest things Jennifer ever had to do. This strong man had watched over her, kept her safe after her parents had passed away, helped assure her life would go on, and she would eventually be happy again. He gave her a reason to get up each day, keeping her busy and little by little she resumed living again. She sat beside his bed and reached for his hand. "I love you Grandpa and will miss you very much. Say hey to Mom and Dad for me when you get to Heaven." She kissed him good-bye as tears streamed down her face.

He gave her some final words of wisdom, "No matter how much sorrow you experience in life, God is always there with you. He will never desert you no matter how hard you push Him away and turn your back on Him. I am going to a wonderful place without pain, filled with peace. Do not cry for me, but rejoice." He wiped the tears from her face.

Jennifer left his bedside and found Grandma in the kitchen busying herself with baking. She managed to control her crying and hugged Grandma. "I will call you every day." She turned and walked out the door knowing she would never see Grandpa alive again.

Grandma called three days later. "Grandpa has gone to be with God. He died peacefully in his sleep last night."

Jennifer sank down to the floor and sobbed. Once she had cried herself dry, she contacted her teachers and was excused from class for the rest of the week. Ashley helped cover her shifts at the restaurant. She drove home to help Grandma plan Grandpa's funeral.

The service was a joyous celebration of life like Grandpa wanted. There was plenty of music and testimony from Grandpa's friends on how he had impacted their lives.

After the funeral, Jennifer went back to the condo with Grandma. The condo seemed so quiet and lonely. "Are you going to be all right by yourself, Grandma? I can stay a few more nights."

"I will be fine, dear. I have several close friends, and I am sure they will be stopping by frequently to keep me company. I know you need to get back to work and school. I don't want you to miss anymore classes."

"If you need anything at all, call me." She hugged Grandma and left to drive back to school.

There is something about a funeral that makes you reflect on your own life and accomplishments. On the drive back to school, she thought about what she wanted now that her senior year was quickly coming to an end. Of course, she needed to find a job, but did she want to get married and have children? She always assumed she would, but what if she never found the right guy? These were things obviously out of her control. She needed to put her faith in God. She realized that God always seemed to put people in her life when she needed them most.

By the end of winter term, Jennifer started applying for jobs in the area. Ashley and Jennifer attended a women's seminar on interviewing skills. They wanted to make sure they were prepared if anyone called them for an interview. The seminar was very helpful. Since she was completing her degree in Electrical Engineering, a field dominated by men, she needed to look and dress professionally along with making sure she knew how to answer the interview questions correctly.

Following the seminar, Ashley and Jennifer looked in their closet and decided they needed to go shopping. At the mall, they tried on suits and dresses to determine what made them look more business like. Jennifer found a navy blue jacket, skirt, and white blouse on the clearance rack that met her price range. Then, they went to the cosmetic counter in the department store to polish their look even more. They needed to look more mature. There is nothing like looking at make-up to make you feel even more insecure.

"Would you like to buy some concealer to help cover the dark areas under your eyes? How about buying a foundation applicators so your make-up will blend better?" By the time they left the cosmetic counter the sales assistant had them feeling like ugly ducklings. They managed to somehow walk away with only buying some base and blush which made a big dent in their finances. Jennifer was now armed with everything she needed to impress her interviewer.

After attending several job fairs, Jennifer received a phone call to come for a second interview. She nervously prepared for the interview which was scheduled at 8AM the next day. She could hardly sleep and didn't eat breakfast for fear of throwing up.

She arrived at the company early and waited in the lobby while the receptionist contacted the person that would be interviewing her. It was not long before a man appeared and greeted her. "I am Harold Barley, Manager of Engineering."

"Good morning, I am Jennifer Ferguson." She firmly gripped his hand to show him she was confident and strong as demonstrated in the seminar.

They walked to a conference room. Upon entering she was introduced to two men sitting at a large wooden table. As soon as formalities were over she took the seat offered to her and the questions began.

"Why do you want to work for our company? Give an example of how you would handle conflict? Describe to us how you would troubleshoot an electrical circuit failure?"

The questions continued for two hours at which time the final question was asked, "Do you have any questions for us?"

Her only question was, "When will you make your decision on who to hire?"

"We still have several candidates to interview and will get back with you within two weeks."

She left not knowing how she did or even if she was in the running. She was totally drained and starved.

Ashley and Jennifer started a ritual of racing home between classes and work to check for messages from potential employers. Jennifer walked in the door and heard, "Yahoo!"

"Did you get an offer?" Jennifer eagerly asked.

"A company I interviewed with a couple of weeks ago left me a message to call. I just got off the phone with them, and they made me a job offer. The only problem is the job is located in Atlanta. I had hoped to find a job in Florida. If I don't accept this offer though, I may not get another one."

"So accept the offer. At worst, if you don't like the job, you will get a couple of year's experience. Then you can change jobs."

"You are right. I'm going to accept the offer."

Jennifer was thrilled for Ashley but had hoped they would find jobs in the same area, so they could continue to live together. She had to start thinking about where she would move after Ashley left. She couldn't afford the apartment by herself.

Jennifer continued to interview and received a phone call one week before graduation. The offer was for an engineering position for a company located in Orlando. It would allow her to stay near Grandma in case she needed her. Without hesitation, she accepted it.

Graduation day had finally arrived. Grandma proudly watched as Jennifer graciously walked down the aisle to receive her diploma.

After graduation, Jennifer found Grandma in the crowd and introduced her to Ashley. "Grandma, I want you to meet Ashley, the best roommate a person could have."

Ashley replied smugly, "What can I say? Jennifer has not been such a bad roommate either," she joked.

Grandma happily announced, "I am so proud of you. I know your Grandpa, mother, and father are watching from Heaven beaming with joy today. Your father would be so happy to know you are following in his footsteps."

Grandma started to get teary eyed. Jennifer gave her a hug. "Thanks for coming. I want to introduce you to some of my friends." Jennifer weaved through the crowd with Grandma in tow, stopping every so often so she could meet some of her sorority sisters.

After some tearful good-byes with friends, Ashley and Jennifer stopped by the apartment one last time. They had already boxed up the belongings they wanted to keep and gave their used furniture to Goodwill. Jennifer helped Ashley load her car for her trip to Atlanta. It was packed full.

"Well, I guess this is it," Ashley said as the elations of graduation faded away.

"I am going to miss you so much. I will call as soon as I find a place to live in Orlando. I'm going to start crying again, so you better leave." Jennifer leaned over and hugged Ashley as she was about to get in her car. She wiped the tears from her eyes. "Have a safe trip!"

"Stay in touch! Visit me when you can!" Ashley yelled out the car window as she drove off.

Chapter Seven

"The sun shall be no more thy light by day; neither for brightness shall the moon give light unto thee: but the Lord shall be unto thee an everlasting light, and thy God thy glory." *(Isaiah 60:19)*

Jennifer found a small second story, one bedroom apartment just north of Orlando. It came with a balcony overlooking what appeared to be a scenic park. She looked forward to having somewhere safe to run after work each day.

She unpacked the car and filled her small apartment with boxes. She spent the day sorting through her things, trying to make the apartment feel like home. She planned to sleep on the floor until she received her first paycheck and could afford to buy a new bed and sofa. It was quiet and lonely without Ashley. Hopefully, she would make some new friends at work and wouldn't be lonely for long.

The first day of work she set her alarm for 6AM to give herself plenty of time to drive to work, or so she thought. She dressed in her navy blue suit with a white blouse and braided her hair, so it was neat and professional. She applied a little make-up to her silky, pale face. Not too shabby, she said to herself as she looked in the mirror.

She grabbed her purse, and left for work. As she drove to work with the other thousands of commuters she soon realized when she merged onto I-4 she may not have given herself enough time to drive to work. The traffic came to a stop. She tried changing lanes to find one that was moving. She slowly picked up speed to a crawl and started to wonder if she would reach work by lunch. Finally, the traffic started to move faster, and she raced the rest of the way hoping to arrive on time.

She stepped into the conference room where the orientation for the new hires was being held and was met by a room full of stares from everyone that had obviously gotten there on time.

"Have you been hired for a secretary position?" the human resource representative asked.

"No, I will be working in engineering as one of the new design engineers," Jennifer proudly told the representative as she took a seat.

She was handed a stack of papers to review and sign. She glanced through the pile. There were health insurance forms, tax forms, a flexible spending form, a life insurance form, a vision care form, a dental care form, and a long term care form. She never knew starting work would require so many decisions in such a short amount of time. After completing the mounds of paperwork, she was required to take several training classes. She started with security, then ethics, timecard familiarization, and on and on. Her first day was over, and she never even left the Human Resource Department.

Her drive home was not much better than her trip to work. Everyone seemed to be in a panic to get home, driving like maniacs, swerving in and out of traffic even though it was barely moving. She feared for her life as she watched the driver in her rear view mirror just inches from her bumper. "What do you want me to do? It's not like I can drive any faster." She motioned to the car in her rear view mirror pointing at the cars in front of her. She drove in heavy traffic all the way home with her hands clenched tightly around the steering wheel. She had never been so glad to be at her apartment before in her life. She immediately took off her uncomfortable suit and put on some shorts, before collapsing on the sofa. Suddenly, the fact that she was starving sank in. She rummaged through the kitchen to find something she could fix fast to eat. She made a peanut butter and banana sandwich. She felt rejuvenated now that she had something in her stomach. She needed to get out of her gloomy apartment and decided to take a walk around the park to clear her head.

The next day she set her alarm thirty minutes earlier and managed to arrive at work just before eight. She was shown to her desk and was introduced to her mentor, Dillon.

Dillon looked to be about five years older than her. He was not unattractive, just not what she would categorize as handsome. He had brown hair, which he wore short to probably ward off the Florida heat, deep brown eyes, which he covered with black rimmed eye glasses, and was about six foot two inches tall, and skinny.

Dillon spent the day familiarizing her with the company procedures and policies along with the business and engineering systems she would be using. She never imagined there would be so much to learn. She soon realized even though she had spent four years in college she knew very little when it came to applying what she learned to the design and fabrication of a product.

She had another gut wrenching drive home and decided she needed to find another way to and from work. She walked into her apartment with her head spinning from data overload. She needed some fresh air and exercise. She changed clothes and jogged through the park. Arriving back home sweaty and out of breath, she felt much better.

The next day she told Dillon where she lived and asked, "Is there a different route I can take to work that might be easier?"

Dillon laughed. "You don't like the speedsters on I-4?"

"I've been to car races that were less dangerous," she joked.

Dillon showed her an alternate route she could take which would help her avoid some of the rush hour congestion. He was a great mentor, patient with her thousands of questions, showing her how to maneuver through the different computer programs. After about two months, she felt she had made progress and started assisting with some designs. Her designs were actually being used in a production environment. It felt good to know that she was making a contribution to an end product.

One Friday after work, Dillon approached her. "Several people are meeting at a local bar if you would like to join us?"

Jennifer was taken back by his offer at first, but thought it would be a good opportunity to make some new friends. "Sure, that sounds like fun."

When she arrived, everyone was drinking and enjoying some appetizers. Dillon introduced her and asked, "What can I order you to drink?"

Jennifer hesitated. She had stayed away from alcohol after getting drunk at the fraternity party during her freshman year. She didn't want to be different from everyone else by ordering a soda so she said, "A glass of wine would be nice."

Dillon ordered her a glass of Merlot, and she sipped it while she listened to everyone talking around the table. It was nice to relax and laugh with her colleagues. Being a woman working in a man's field, she always felt out of place. Her designs as well as her work ethic seemed to be scrutinized very closely. She always made sure she arrived at work thirty minutes early and left work thirty minutes later than everyone else to prove herself. She believed she needed to work twice as hard to be accepted and considered an equal to the men.

Everyone at the bar included her in the conversation and made her feel welcome. With little to eat, the wine Dillon ordered her went right to her head.

"Do you want to grab a bite to eat? Dillon asked. You're starting to look a little pale."

"I am a lightweight when it comes to alcohol. I could use some food before I try to drive home," she shared with him.

While they waited for their burgers and fries to be delivered they talked easily.

"Now that you have been at the company a couple of months, how do you like your job?"

"I love it. You have helped me learn so much since I started."

"Are you originally from this area?"

"I moved to Cocoa Beach after my parents passed away. How about you? Where are you from?" Jennifer quickly changed the subject to focus on him.

"I grew up in the Atlanta area and graduated from Georgia Tech. I also lost my Mom, from breast cancer, when I was ten. So, I know what you must have gone through losing your parents."

Dillon and her talked until about ten o'clock. She got to know a much softer side of him that she didn't know existed. Dillon was also an only child, so he understood what she had gone through. Dillon walked her to her car.

"Are you sure you are safe to drive home now?"

"After all that food, I am fine."

"I will see you on Monday." Dillon said as he closed her car door.

Driving back to her apartment, she smiled to herself at how much fun she had had with Dillon. The last two months working with Dillon she never thought of him romantically, and she never got the impression he was the least bit interested in her. He was very professional, smart, and serious at work. The Dillon she met tonight was a good listener, compassionate, and loved to eat as much as she did. She had seen him in a different light and thought she wouldn't mind spending more time with him.

All weekend she over analyzed the time she spent Friday evening with Dillon. Was he just being friendly or was he interested in being more than a friend? If he wanted to be more than just a friend, was that what I wanted? Was it professional to date someone you worked with?

Would it hurt my credibility at work? Obviously, she was over-thinking and worrying about something that may just be her imagination.

Monday morning came and Dillon treated her as usual and didn't pay any special attention to her. The next several days were the same, and she laughed at herself for thinking that Dillon may consider her more than just a friend.

She had been working ten hour days trying to finish a project and was glad when Friday afternoon arrived. She was looking forward to finding a good book and just relaxing on her patio. She planned to drive to Cocoa Beach on Sunday to spend the day with Grandma. As she was leaving the office, Dillon walked out at the same time.

"Do you have any plans for the weekend?" he asked.

She lied and said, "I hadn't really thought about it."

"I have a couple of theme park tickets I need to use up. Would you like to go with me tomorrow?"

"That sounds like fun. I would love to."

"I will pick you up around nine."

He arrived promptly at nine o'clock the next morning. They spent the day acting like kids again without a care in the world, riding all the rides from roller coasters to water rides to cool off. They pigged out on junk food and drank plenty of water to keep hydrated from the Florida summer heat.

By the end of the day, they were both sunburnt and exhausted. Dillon drove her home.

"Would you like to come in for something decent to eat and drink?"

"I ate so much junk food today I don't think I could eat another bite." He lifted his shirt and pulled it to his nose. "I think taking a long shower is next on my agenda." He laughed and fanned the air pretending to blow away his stench.

"I know what you mean. I am one big sweat ball myself."

"I will see you on Monday," he said as he turned to leave.

He didn't even try to kiss her goodnight or indicate if he wanted to go out with her again. She was not sure what to think of his behavior. Was she the only one that had had a good time?

Sunday, she drove to Cocoa Beach to have lunch with Grandma. When she arrived, Grandma showed her to the patio where the table had been set.

"I thought it would be nice to eat lunch out here and enjoy the beautiful day."

"That sounds great." She leaned on the patio railing and looked out over the ocean, inhaling the salt air, enjoying the warm ocean breeze. Grandma brought out the food as she gazed out over the water. All her worries seemed to melt away as she watched the pelicans effortlessly gliding over the water and listened to the roar of the waves. She had forgotten how much she loved the beach. She hadn't thought about Josh for a while now. She wondered if he still lived in the area and if he ever saved enough money to go to college. She reminisced of the days they had spent surfing together without a care in the world. She missed those days. No deadlines to meet or bills to pay.

"Sit down and tell me what you have been up to," Grandma said as she walked onto the patio with a tray of food in her hand. "Are you seeing anyone?" she pried.

She was not really sure what her relationship was with Dillon, so she didn't mention him. "I've made a few new friends, but mainly I've been busy learning my new job and working long hours. I haven't had time for much else."

"There is more to life dear than work. Don't forget to find time to live and have some fun every once in a while," Grandma said with concern in her voice. "You should know better than anyone that life can be taken away in an instant and every day should be treated as if it may be your last. Life being such as it is, I've planned a vacation to North Carolina in September to see the fall leaves with a friend," Grandma shared, all excited about her upcoming trip.

"Really, that sounds like fun!" Grandma was doing amazingly well and seemed to be having a good time with her friends. She hadn't stopped living just because Grandpa was gone. It was good to see her so happy.

"Unfortunately, it's getting late, and I need to get home. I have to start work early tomorrow. Thanks so much for lunch it was delicious." Jennifer hugged her good-bye. "Call me if you need anything."

Grandma's words kept playing back through Jennifer's head all the way back to her apartment. Was she just cruising through life without a real plan? She hadn't had a serious relationship since John, her junior year of college. Was there someone out there for her?

Monday came, and she had a new outlook on life. She was going to start planning things she enjoyed doing and not wait for someone to do them with. She had accumulated a couple days of vacation and thought about taking a long weekend to drive up to Atlanta to visit Ashley.

Dillon and her didn't cross paths again until Wednesday. He treated her no different than the previous weeks just saying, "Hi," in passing. She didn't know why it upset her so. It was not like they were dating or he had made a commitment to her.

She packed her bag Wednesday night and Thursday after work she drove to Atlanta. The traffic was light, and she made good time arriving at Ashley's around midnight. They stayed up talking until around two in the morning until they could no longer keep their eyes open.

Ashley loved her job and had been dating a guy for about three months that she met through a mutual friend. They had already talked about getting married. Ashley introduced her to him on Saturday when they went out together to eat. He was good looking and very charming. Jennifer could tell he was as crazy about Ashley as she was about him.

Sunday quickly came, and after breakfast Jennifer said her good-byes to Ashley. She drove back to Orlando thinking about her life and where she wanted it to go. She was happy for Ashley and knew after she got married she would have little time, and things between them wouldn't be the same. She found herself being jealous of Ashley.

She wanted everything in life a good job, kids, a faithful husband, and nice house in the suburbs. That is the American dream, right? Why is it she felt she was not complete unless she got married and had kids?

She arrived back in Orlando around six o'clock to a message on her answering machine from Grandma to call her. She called right away to make sure she was okay.

"Have you been watching the weather?" Grandma asked.

"No, I was in Atlanta all weekend visiting Ashley. Is there something wrong?"

"There is a hurricane coming, and it's due to hit the east coast in forty-eight hours near Cocoa Beach."

She immediately turned on the television. The weather was broadcasting on every local station tracking the storm, giving the projected path and time of landfall. Cocoa Beach was right in the center of the projected path.

"Do you need me to come pick you up tonight? You can stay at my place until the storm passes."

"I hate to put you out, but I know if I wait until tomorrow the causeway will be blocked with everyone evacuating the barrier islands."

"I will leave immediately and should be there by eight."

On the drive to Cocoa Beach, the radio announcer was going over the list of hurricane supplies you should have and location of shelters that were open in case people needed somewhere safe to stay. Just before she arrived at Grandma's, the radio announcer blurted out, "As of eight o'clock tonight there is a mandatory evacuation for everyone on the barrier islands."

Chapter Eight

"God is our refuge and strength, a very present help in trouble." *(Psalm 46:1)*

When Jennifer arrived in Cocoa Beach, A1A had already started to get congested with residents preparing for the impending hurricane. Business owners were busy nailing plywood over their storefront windows and homeowners were protecting their homes from the flying debris that was bound to be blowing around in the strong winds.

Grandma eagerly opened the door for Jennifer when she arrived and motioned for her to come inside. "I am so glad you are here," Grandma said as she gave Jennifer a warm hug. "Everyone has been talking about the storm all weekend. Cocoa Beach has never had a direct hit, and I am afraid this hurricane may spoil the record."

The building was abuzz with activity as many residents were carrying boxes down to their cars getting ready to evacuate. Jennifer glanced over at the pile of boxes Grandma had assembled in her living room. "Are you planning on taking all those boxes with you?"

"I tried to pack just what was irreplaceable with sentimental value. There are photo albums, the quilt we made together, valuable documents, a few presents that Grandpa gave me, some clothes, and my medicine."

With her arms full, Jennifer started the trek back and forth to her car until every nook and cranny in her car was filled.

"Well, I hope that is everything because there is barely room for us left in the car."

"There is just one last thing I need to do. Can you help me close the hurricane shutters over the windows?"

The shutters were cranked closed, engulfing the condo in darkness.

Grandma turned on the light in each room as if trying to memorize how it appeared, knowing there may be nothing left when she returned.

She took one last look around to make sure she hadn't forgotten anything before leaving and locking the door on the way out.

The traffic was heavy driving back to Orlando. Many others had decided to evacuate early to beat the rush. It was nearly midnight when they arrived at the apartment. Jennifer was bone tired after driving from Atlanta and then helping Grandma safeguard her precious belongings. She knew she wouldn't be able to sleep until the boxes were unloaded from the car. She slowly moved each box from the car and stacked them in the living room. Finally complete, she joined Grandma on the sofa to watch the latest information on the storm.

"The hurricane has slowed to a forward speed of 5 miles per hour which may allow the storm to strengthen even further. The winds are currently at 110 miles per hour," the weatherman said as he pointed to charts and forecast models. "There could be a storm surge as high as ten feet which would immerse the barrier islands," he continued.

"Oh my, how is my condo going to withstand that?"

"Grandma you know how weathermen are always blowing things out of proportion. The hurricane is still too far out to know where it will hit for sure. I know you must be exhausted. Why don't you take my bedroom and I will sleep on the sofa?"

"Don't be ridiculous, I can sleep on the sofa. I am not going to kick you out of your bedroom."

"Grandma I am too tired to argue. How about we both sleep in my bed? It's a queen and should be big enough for both of us."

Jennifer finally crawled into bed and drifted off to a restless sleep around 2AM with the hurricane looming in the back of her mind. She woke to the sun streaming through the window and realized that in her exhausted state, she had forgotten to set her alarm. She jumped out of bed and hurried to get dressed for work as quietly as possible, trying not to wake Grandma. Just as she was tiptoeing out of the bedroom Grandma woke up. "I'm sorry I woke you, but I need to get to work. Is there anything I can get you before I leave?"

"You didn't wake me; can I fix you something for breakfast?"

"I'm running late for work and have to leave. Help yourself to whatever food you can find. I will stop by the grocery store on the way home. I will call you from work, so you can let me know if there is anything I can pick up for you. I have to run." Jennifer hurriedly grabbed her purse and headed for the door.

When she arrived at work, everyone was standing around talking about the storm and whether work would be shut down the next day. She looked up and saw Dillon walking toward her.

"How are you doing? Have you purchased your hurricane supplies yet?" he asked.

"This is my first hurricane, so I really don't know what to expect. Do you think it will be bad this far inland?"

"We will probably lose power, so you need to make sure you have some flashlights, extra batteries, some non perishable food, and water. If we lose power, everything in your refrigerator will quickly go bad."

"I hadn't thought of that. I was planning to run by the grocery store on the way home and pick up a few things."

"If you wait until then, everything will be gone. You should go during lunch and try to find as much as you can before the grocery shelves are empty. Also, fill up your car with gas. With everyone from the coast evacuating to Orlando, the gas stations will quickly run out of fuel."

"You make it sound like the end of the world is coming. I didn't know there was so much to do to prepare for the storm."

"Call me if you need anything," Dillon said as he walked away.

Jennifer smiled to herself that Dillon seemed to be concerned about her well-being. Maybe she was more than just a friend to him. She started making a list of everything she needed to buy at lunch. She asked her boss, "Would it be all right if I take a long lunch to pick up a few things to prepare for the storm? I will make up my time by working over."

He was very accommodating. "No problem, not much work is getting done today anyway. Do what you need to do to prepare for the storm."

She called Grandma to check up on her and to let her know her plans for shopping at lunch. "Is there anything you need me to pick up for you?"

"I forgot to refill my blood pressure medicine before I left. I will contact my pharmacy in Cocoa Beach and have them transfer my prescription to the Orlando pharmacy. Can you pick it up for me?"

"That won't be a problem. I have to work late tonight to make up my time, so I will see you around seven."

When she arrived at the grocery store, it was a zoo. She had never seen so many people shopping at one time. There were no grocery carts available, so she could only buy what she could carry. The batteries and water had already sold out. She managed to get a loaf of bread and one of the last remaining jars of peanut butter. She found some powdered milk that they could use to eat cereal along with a box of macaroni and cheese and canned beef stew. Next she stopped by the pharmacy. She had planned to use the drive-thru but there was a line of about ten cars. Looking at her watch realizing this was taking longer than she had planned she decided it might be faster to go inside. The line inside was even longer. People waiting for their turn to pick up prescriptions stood in a line all the way down the aisle.

Finally, she had Grandma's prescription in hand and drove to the gas station to fill her gas tank on the way back to work. She was met by another line of cars waiting for a pump to become free. She joined the line and waited thirty minutes before she finally made it to a pump. Frustrated she quickly discovered the station only had high test gasoline left. Knowing she had no choice she paid the extra amount for gas.

She at least felt a little more prepared for the storm as she made her way back to work just in time to see everyone leaving. She ran into Dillon walking out as she was headed to her desk.

"You were right about the panic before the storm. I couldn't believe the crowds and lines. It was worse than when a blizzard was predicted to hit in Minnesota. It's like we are going to be cut off from the rest of the world with the panic I witnessed."

Dillon laughed, "When people get stressed, they eat, so they buy anything and everything just in case the worst happens. Hopefully, the storm will hit south of us, and at worst we may be without power for a day or two. If you need help after the storm has passed, call me."

She was pleased that Dillon seemed to be genuinely concerned about her. It was nice to know that Dillon was there if she needed help. She stayed at work another two hours to try to make up some of the time she spent away from the office during lunch. After another long day with little sleep over the weekend and the night before, she was totally exhausted. She didn't think she would ever arrive home. The roads were packed with people trying to get home from work, along with people evacuating from the coast. At least work was shut down on Tuesday to help keep the roads clear for the evacuation. She was grateful for that, so she could spend the day with Grandma relaxing. She laughed at the thought of trying to relax as a hurricane approached; what was she thinking?

When Jennifer arrived home, Grandma was sitting in front of the television watching the hurricane updates. Grandma was very concerned about her condo located so close to the beach being able to withstand the storm surge and winds that were predicted.

To get her mind off the storm, Jennifer told her, "We need to cook everything in my freezer, so it won't go bad in case we lose power. So for dinner we have a smorgasbord of hamburgers, hotdogs, frozen vegetables and for dessert, ice cream."

"I am not very hungry, but I can help you cook."

Even though Grandma didn't think she was hungry, she ate a hot dog and hamburger along with a large bowl of ice cream. They were stuffed.

"Why don't we go for a walk through the park to help work off some of this food? Some fresh air will do us both some good."

"You may have to carry me, I ate so much."

They walked slowly around the lake enjoying the warm evening. There were more people out than usual enjoying the evening with their family and dogs before the storm hit. They stopped to rest on one of the park benches and watched the ducks swimming in the water.

"I am not getting any younger you know. I am going to die one day, and I want to make sure you will be all right. Since your parents didn't have any siblings, you do not have any aunts or uncles to call if you need help. I don't want you to grow old and alone. Life is too short to not share it with someone."

"Where is this death talk coming from? You are healthy, and won't leave me anytime soon."

"I know dear, but you never know when God will call you to heaven and you need to be prepared."

"You have nothing to worry about when God decides to take you. I have a good job and make good money. I will be fine."

"I am not worried about you financially. It's emotionally that concerns me. You can't go through life pushing people away every time they start to get close to you. You will end up alone and unhappy."

Jennifer tried to make light of Grandma's serious conversation and teased her. "You are too cantankerous to die and have many years left to live, but when that day does come for you to join Grandpa and my parents in Heaven, I will be fine. I've made several friends at work, and I know God has a plan for me. If that plan includes marriage, then I will meet someone and fall in love."

"You used to be such a happy, carefree girl. Your parent's death forced you to grow up way too fast. I know there is a free spirit still inside you and hope you will experience love again."

Jennifer thought back to her and Josh. She remembered the pain as if it were yesterday when the relationship ended. Her heart broke and never truly recovered. In college she would tell Grandma how much fun she was having but she was only going through the motions. She didn't want her grandparents to worry and would say everything was fine for their benefit but never truly believed it herself. She understood they wanted her to laugh and be happy again, but how could she do that after all that had happened?

Sitting in the park next to Grandma she felt sad for what she had lost but knew in her heart God was by her side no matter what happened. She tried to persuade Grandma not to worry. "You made sure I got a good education so I could always support myself. You have molded me into the strong and responsible woman that I am today. You should be proud of your accomplishment and how I turned out. I know God has a plan for me, and I believe the purpose for all the hurt will be shown to me one day. He will show me my path to finding happiness again. You don't need to worry about me." She reached over and squeezed Grandma's hand. "We better start walking back before I am too tired to move, and it gets too dark."

Grandma seemed satisfied with her answer, and they completed their walk around the lake in silence enjoying the beauty around them knowing it could all be gone tomorrow.

When they arrived back at the apartment, reality set back in as they sat glued to the television. The weatherman showed the estimated rainfall amounts, possible wind impacts, storm surge projections, and the updated hurricane projected path. It was now forecasted to hit just south of Cocoa Beach but track across Orlando before exiting off the west coast of the state in the Gulf of Mexico. The impacts will start being felt as early as tomorrow afternoon. They sat mesmerized by the television, waiting for the hurricane updates every three hours hoping the path would change and wind speed would drop.

After another restless night with the storm looming in the back of her mind, Jennifer awoke at daybreak. The anticipation of what the day would bring gave her a sense of dread. The day looked as any other August day in Florida, hot and humid. She quietly got out of bed so as not to wake Grandma. Grandma had come to bed late after watching the weather updates, worrying about her condo. Jennifer quietly slid on shorts and a t-shirt and left for a morning run through the park to help improve her mood. There was an eerie stillness to the hot air this morning. To the east, she could see dark clouds looming above the horizon indicating what was still to come. Her breathing was labored as the air seemed heavier than usual. By the time she returned home, she was drenched in sweat, but felt rejuvenated and ready to face another day.

She was greeted by a wonderful aroma from the kitchen. Grandma had been busy cooking while she was out. "I was not sure which one you would prefer, so I made both eggs with bacon and pancakes."

"I need to jump in the shower and cool off before I stuff myself for breakfast. I'll hurry."

When she returned, the smell of fresh coffee and bacon filled the air and she realized how hungry she was. "After all the food we ate last night, I can't believe I am saying this, but I am starved. It all smells so enticing."

They ate as if it was their last meal before the storm. She remembered what Dillon had said about stress making people hungry and now understood what he meant.

After breakfast, they once again sat glued to the television as the latest weather updates were being reported. There were weathermen located live all up and down the coast to catch the first glimpse as the winds started to pick up. The outer bands started hitting the coast just as the sun was setting.

Jennifer remembered Dillon telling her to have plenty of drinking water in case the water treatment plant was impacted by the storm; so they filled every empty container she owned with water. When finished, there were pots, bowls, and buckets of water placed all around the apartment. Then, she pulled out every candle and flashlight, placing them on the kitchen table in case they lost power. She lived on the second floor so she was not worried about flooding, but she was concerned about wind. She had windows along the front of the apartment and the glass patio door that could shatter if hit by flying debris.

As night approached, dark clouds started swirling through the sky and a gentle breeze formed. For supper, they ate reheated leftovers and tried to finish the rest of the perishable food.

They both curled up on the sofa and prayed for God to watch over and protect them. They continued watching the television as the rain and wind started to pick up around midnight. As the night went on, the apartment started to moan as each gust of wind grew stronger. By 2AM, there was a constant roar as the rain pounded against the windows and roof. The eye of the storm was now approaching the coast and tracking just south of Orlando.

Just when she thought the apartment couldn't take any more abuse, another heavy band of wind and rain slammed against the building. The noise was deafening. The wind blew relentlessly, sending debris crashing against the side of the building. She thought the roof may blow off at any minute. They were suddenly thrown into darkness as the power went out.

Jennifer nervously groped for the flashlight and lit a candle to give them some light. "Grandma, we better move to the bathroom. It's the strongest room in the apartment, and there are no windows."

She placed a blanket and some pillows in the bathtub. They huddled together listening to the storm which seemed even louder now in the darkness with no noise from the TV to help drown out the sound. The only light came from a candle she left burning on the vanity. She decided to save the flashlight batteries for later. It continued pounding till about 5AM, when it slowly started to subside. Feeling the worst was over, they climbed out of the tub and into bed to try to get a little rest.

After just a couple of hours sleep, Jennifer woke to a dim light coming through the bedroom window as the dark skies started to lighten. She quietly crept to the living room and opened the blinds. There was debris and water everywhere. It looked as if a bomb had exploded. Trees were stripped of their leaves, and there were several trees lying across the road. It was still raining, and the roads had turned into rivers overnight as the rain fell harder than the drainage system could handle. She feared the apartments on the first flood may be flooded. She grabbed her umbrella and walked outside to inspect the roof for damage. Shingles littered the parking lot and were blown on top of cars. Some of the car windows were shattered from flying debris. She reached her car and found the windows intact, with just a few dings on the hood and sides from where debris had impacted. There was water flowing underneath the car but none inside it. She trudged through the waterlogged parking lot to where she could see the roof. The roof above her apartment appeared to be intact, but there were definitely areas where the shingles were missing.

She went back inside and looked around the ceiling for any signs of leaks. There were some water stains on the ceiling and water on the floor by the patio door. She grabbed a towel out of the bathroom to soak up the water. The power had been out for about five hours now and the temperature in the apartment had started to rise with no air conditioning. It was eerily quiet with no appliances or air conditioning running. She didn't want to open the windows until the rain had stopped, to limit the water damage.

Grandma walked out of the bedroom, hair sticking straight up, still in her clothes from yesterday. "It looks like we survived. How bad is the damage?"

Jennifer opened the blinds on the patio door to show her the destruction. "Oh my, it looks like we won't be going anywhere anytime soon."

"I think we were the lucky ones. Other than some roof damage, we came out of it pretty unscathed. Are you hungry this morning?"

"Not particularly, after all we ate last night. I could really use some coffee though."

"Well, without power I am not sure how I would heat the water for coffee. Could you settle for a bowl of cereal and some orange juice this morning?"

The rain turned to a drizzle, and by lunch, people started slowly emerging from their shelter to examine the damage. The neighborhood came alive with the roar of chainsaws as everyone gave a hand to help clear the street and roadways. By supper, the first electric truck was spotted in the neighborhood to repair the downed power lines. Grandma anxiously wanted news on coastal damage to see if her condo survived the storm. They found a neighbor who was listening to a battery operated radio and several neighbors gathered around to hear the damage reports. The causeways were still closed due to the hazards across the roads. A1A had boats and debris lying on the road making driving treacherous. Law enforcement urged residents to stay where they were for the night, and they would be allowed back on the island tomorrow. The residents were assured that the area was being patrolled by police to catch looters from stealing people's possessions from their damaged homes and stores.

"Grandma, it looks like you are stuck staying with me for another night."

"That's all right. At least you don't snore like your Grandpa used to," she laughed.

The sun started to break through the clouds and the humidity soared. Jennifer wiped the sweat from her face. The apartment was getting too hot to stay inside without air conditioning. "Grandma, why don't we sit out on the patio and try to stay cool."

They sat watching the activity going on outside to restore the neighborhood when a car pulled into the parking lot below them. Jennifer was surprised to see Dillon get out. She waved down to him from the patio and yelled, "I'm glad to see you made it through the storm." Jennifer returned inside to open the door for him. "What are you doing here?"

"I had no way of contacting you with the phone lines and cell phone towers down. My apartment is flooded, so once the roads were clear, I decided to check on you and see if you needed anything."

Jennifer smiled to herself at the thought that Dillon was worried about her. "It was so scary listening to the storm pounding the building all night long. Other than a little leak, everything seems fine."

"I didn't make out so well. My apartment is on the ground floor and has about a foot of water inside. Some carpet and furniture will need to be replaced. I'll have to start looking for a new apartment immediately. I'm also without power."

"You are welcome to sleep here tonight on my sofa. You will have to excuse the mess. My Grandmother evacuated with all her valuable possessions."

"I might take you up on that offer."

Grandma walked into the room and held out her hand. "Hi, I am Jennifer's grandmother."

Jennifer was so excited to see Dillon that she had forgotten she had left her Grandma sitting on the patio. "I'm sorry Grandma, this is Dillon, a friend from work."

"It's nice to meet you Dillon." Grandma gave Jennifer that look that said what have you been hiding.

"I don't want to put you out. The thought of staying in my place tonight doesn't sound that inviting and I know all the hotels are full with people that evacuated from the coast."

"I don't know how comfortable it will be here tonight without air conditioning, but it has to be better than your place. I honestly would feel safer with you here just in case more problems arise overnight. You would actually be doing me a favor." Jennifer gave Dillon her pitiful look hoping to guilt him into staying.

"You make it hard to refuse. I appreciate your offer and will stay just until tomorrow when I can start looking for a new apartment."

Suddenly, they heard a cheer come from the neighbors as the power came back on.

The first thing Jennifer did was turn on the air conditioner. Nothing ever felt so good as the cold air blowing out the vents. "I didn't realize how late it was getting. Is anyone hungry for some supper?"

Grandma jumped up from her chair. "Let me help you make something." She followed Jennifer into the kitchen.

While Jennifer rummaged through the kitchen, trying to find something to fix, Grandma asked, "So, why have you not told me about Dillon?"

"I told you we are just friends and nothing more," Jennifer whispered, so Dillon wouldn't hear her.

"He seems to care about you more than just a friend. I can see it in his eyes."

"You are just imagining things Grandma. Now behave yourself, and don't embarrass me in front of him. Here, set the table while I fix supper." She handed Grandma plates and silverware.

Jennifer managed to cook a hot meal of canned beef stew and biscuits for supper.

"This is delicious. I didn't realize how hungry I was," Dillon said as he ate vigorously.

"I am glad you like it." Jennifer laughed. "It's hard to believe that canned beef stew could taste this good." She realized after what they had gone through last night, she was just happy to be alive.

"Dillon, why don't you relax while Grandma and I clean the dishes." Jennifer handed Dillon the remote control so he could watch TV. She didn't want to give Grandma the opportunity to be left alone with Dillon.

Once the kitchen was cleaned, they joined Dillon in the living room watching the damage reports. Grandma kept pointing out areas she recognized where the buildings had partially fallen into the ocean. Her condo was not on the news, which hopefully meant it was not severely damaged.

They were all exhausted after several nights with no sleep, worrying about the storm. Jennifer brought out some clean sheets, blanket, and pillow for Dillon to use on the sofa.

"Do you want me to help make up the sofa for you?"

"No, I'm going to stay up a little while longer before calling it a day. Get some rest, and I will see you in the morning."

By the time Jennifer changed clothes, brushed her teeth, and climbed into bed, Grandma was fast asleep in bed.

Knowing Dillon was here to watch over her she felt at ease. She finally was able to relax and instantly fell asleep. When she woke, she heard the sound of laughter coming from in the living room. She looked at the pillow next to her and saw Grandma was already awake. Fearful of what Grandma might say to Dillon she threw on shorts and a t-shirt. She rushed out the bedroom, her hair a tangled mess, with no make-up. She found Grandma and Dillon sitting on the sofa drinking coffee and watching the news.

"What are you two laughing about?" she cautiously asked.

"Work is still without power this morning, so we don't have to report today," Dillon said.

"Great!"

"Would you like a cup of coffee, dear? Grandma asked. It looks like you could use one."

Jennifer remembered her hair and tried to run her fingers through it to get it to lie down. "That sounds wonderful." She poured herself a cup of coffee and joined them in the living room.

"Is there any news of when the roads will open today?"

Dillon spoke up. "The news reported the causeway will open at 9:00AM and that residents would be allowed to return to their homes, but warned people to stay away from downed power lines. Most of the power is still out."

"That is good news. Grandma, I know you have been anxiously waiting to see if your condo survived the storm. I can take you home after breakfast." She sipped her coffee, watching the news and storm damage reports. An aerial view was being broadcast from a news helicopter. The camera zoomed to show the cars on the Beachline expressway. There was already a line of slow moving cars heading east along the expressway as residents tried to return home. The highway had become a parking lot as everyone waited for the causeway to reopen.

Jennifer groaned at the thought of being stuck in that traffic with nowhere to get more gas. "Grandma we might need to wait until after lunch before we leave to avoid being stuck in traffic all day. I don't want to run out of gas before we arrive."

"I agree. I don't want to be stranded on the highway either. I can wait a few more hours to get home."

"Thanks for supper last night, somewhere dry to sleep, and the coffee this morning. I need to check on my place and contact my apartment manager to determine how long it will take to repair my apartment. I also need to sort through my belongings and see how much can be salvaged. Call me when you get back from your grandmother," Dillon said.

Jennifer was pleased that Dillon wanted her to keep in touch with him. "Don't you want some breakfast before you leave?"

"I'm not much of a breakfast person."

"You are welcome to stay another night here if you need to."

"Thanks for the offer, but hopefully I will be able to find a new place to stay tonight," Dillon said as he walked out the door.

Jennifer watched as Dillon drove away. "Grandma, what did you and Dillon talk about before I got up this morning?"

"Not much dear. I asked him about what he did at work and how long he had been dating you."

"You didn't dare ask him that, did you?"

"Yes, I did."

Jennifer was embarrassed to ask, but she wanted to know how Dillon responded to Grandma's question. She waited for Grandma to say something and when she didn't asked, "So what did he tell you?"

"He said you had only been out on a couple of dates and that he has enjoyed the time you have spent together."

What did he mean by that? Jennifer thought to herself. Does that mean we are dating?

"Why did you not tell me you were dating someone from work?"

"I wasn't really sure we were dating. We spent a day together at a theme park, but he hasn't asked me out since. We work together, so it would be very awkward if we started dating."

"You are just making excuses. Young people date their colleagues all the time. I can tell you like him. Maybe you should ask him out, so he knows you are interested."

"Grandma, I can't believe you suggested that. I wouldn't feel comfortable being that forward. If he wants to see me again, he'll ask. I just need to give him more time."

"Sometimes you just need to drop subtle hints to let him know you are interested in him. Like tell him, *I have a craving for lasagna tonight, but the recipe makes more than I can possibly eat by myself. You would do me a favor if you would come over and help me eat it.* Give Dillon a reason to see you again, and a little push never hurts. What do you have to lose?"

Jennifer thought to herself, maybe Grandma was actually right. Maybe Dillon didn't think she was interested in him and inviting him to dinner would show him differently.

***

After breakfast they continued to watch the news until it reported the causeway was open and traffic was moving freely. Jennifer crammed all Grandma's boxes back in her car and hoped they wouldn't be returning with her. They started their slow trek toward Cocoa Beach.

The traffic was heavy, but at least it was moving. As they approached the coast, the damage became more apparent. Billboards, trees, and debris littered the side of the highway. They could tell where chainsaws had been used to clear trees from the roadway. There was also sand lying on the roads where the waves had crashed over the highway from the Banana and Indian Rivers. As they approached the first condos in Cape Canaveral they noticed some visible roof damage. They also saw that one of the historic restaurants along A1A that had been around since the Apollo days, had been totally destroyed by fire. When they arrived at Cocoa Beach, the police reduced traffic from four lanes down to two because of the damage to the road. The place looked like a war zone. There was debris everywhere. She feared the worst for Grandma's condo.

They finally made it. It took them two hours when normally it would have taken them an hour. The condo parking lot was almost empty. "It doesn't look like too many residents have returned yet," she told Grandma.

"This time of year the snowbirds are still up north, so there are not many people staying here."

She parked the car close to the entrance. Jennifer looked up through the windshield at the tall structure. "Well, the front of the building doesn't appear to be damaged. Hopefully that is a good sign." Jennifer knew the back of the building faced the ocean and may not have survived as well in the storm. "Let's leave all your stuff here until we are sure it's safe to return."

They entered the lobby and were met by damp heat and a musty smell. It was obvious the power was still out and there was no air conditioning to cool the building. It also meant the elevators were not working.

"Let's walk out onto the pool deck to check out the back of the building," Grandma said.

They stopped dead in their tracks. The gorgeous beach that once ran behind the condo was gone, along with the dunes that protected the condo from the surf. The pool area was destroyed. The pool was now teetering on the edge, about to fall into the ocean.

Jennifer grabbed Grandma's trembling hand and told her, "It will be all right. The pool can be fixed and the beach replenished. Let's walk up to your condo."

With no elevators they slowly walked up the dark stairwell to the fourth floor, being careful not to trip. They could hardly breathe the air inside the stairwell was so hot and stale. They were both out of breath by the time they reached the fourth floor landing. They stepped into the hall and Jennifer stopped to let Grandma catch her breath. One of Grandma's neighbors came out of her home to greet her.

"I am so glad you made it through the storm safely," Grandma said as she hugged her neighbor.

"The building manager told us today that there is some roof damage which caused water damage to the condos on the top floor, but other than that the building is sound and can be occupied. Repairs to the roof, pool area, and replacing the dunes will begin as soon as someone can be contracted to do the work. With so much damage to the island, it may take awhile. Oh, and the power may be off for several more days."

"That sounds much better than some of the places we saw on our way here." Grandma's mood improved instantly at the good news. She opened the door to her condo and they looked inside. Everything was as they left it. Jennifer helped Grandma lift the hurricane shutters and open the patio doors to let in some light and fresh air into the room. A gentle breeze blew in off the ocean helping to cool it down inside. It was hard to imagine that not just forty-eight hours ago the winds were gusting to over one hundred miles an hour.

Grandma insisted on staying even though she didn't have power. She wanted to clean out her refrigerator before all the food started rotting. She found her flashlights and candles so she would be able to see after dark. Her next door neighbors assured Jennifer they were also staying and would keep an eye on Grandma.

She was not thrilled with leaving Grandma alone but understood how it must feel to be back home. She carried just a couple of Grandma's boxes up from the car. After walking up four flights of stairs twice, carrying boxes, she told herself, This is crazy. Once the elevator is back in service, I can bring up the rest of the boxes. She set the load down in the kitchen and rested to catch her breath.

"I will come back on Saturday. Hopefully by then you will have power restored and I can deliver the rest of your belongings. Are you sure you will be okay by yourself?"

"I will be fine, dear. I have plenty of non perishable food to eat and the neighbors are here if I need anything."

"Call me when the phone lines have been restored." Jennifer hugged her and walked back downstairs to the car.

The drive back to Orlando had much less traffic, and she made good time getting home. The sun had just started set. She was disappointed when she arrived and there was no sign of Dillon. Her apartment seemed quiet after all the activity the last couple of days. She tried calling Dillon's cell phone and there was no answer. I am sure he must be busy, she told herself. She called to find out the status of work for tomorrow. The power was back on, so she had to report to work in the morning. It would feel good to get back to a normal routine.

She made herself a peanut butter and jelly sandwich for supper. She made a mental note to stop by the grocery store tomorrow on her way home from work to re-stock her refrigerator.

The next morning she arrived at work and listened to everyone's horror stories. Some still had no power or running water. Others had their cars damaged from fallen trees or floodwaters. She felt very lucky.

Dillon stopped by her desk, "Sorry I missed your call last night. I was busy moving into another apartment while mine is being renovated. Thanks again for letting me stay at your place."

"Do you need help moving?" she offered.

"No, I've already moved everything that was not damaged. Did your Grandma make it home to her condo?"

"Yes, her condo was not damaged, thank goodness. The pool is slowly washing into the ocean, and she is without power. Other than that everything seemed to be fine."

"I'm glad to hear that. I have to get some work done today and will talk to you later."

Once again, Dillon ran out of her life before she had a chance to mention coming over for supper. It was probably for the best. She had a project to finish, and she was buried in work herself. Maybe she would try again later in the week. Jennifer worked over each night and on Saturday. She wanted to make her original project completion deadline after missing two days of work.

After work on Saturday, she drove to Cocoa Beach to check on Grandma. The roads had been repaired and were back open. Most of the stores had reopened, but there were still a few closed due to the extent of the damage. Grandma's power had been restored, but she still had no phone. Jennifer unloaded the rest of Grandma's boxes, grateful to have the elevator working again.

After she brought up the last box, she asked Grandma, "How are you doing?"

"I am fine. I went to the grocery store yesterday and replaced all the food in the refrigerator that I had to throw out. Have you asked Dillon out for supper yet?"

Grandma had a way of getting right to the point and didn't beat around the bush. She was determined to find her a boyfriend. "I've been too busy at work making up for the lost days from the storm. I will try to catch Dillon next week and ask him, I promise." She knew she would never hear the end of it from Grandma if she didn't.

"Life is too short, dear, to work all the time and never have any fun," Grandma persisted.

Jennifer stepped out onto the patio and looked out over the ocean. She immediately became calm and relaxed listening to the waves crashing against the shore as the sun reflected off the water. She watched as a couple of dolphins played in the surf. She smiled at the memory of the day she surfed with Josh and thought the dolphin was a shark.

She was awakened from her day dream. "Can I talk you in to staying for supper before you return?" Grandma asked.

"That would be nice."

Grandma fixed a healthy supper of chicken, rice, and a salad. They sat on the patio talking and enjoying the evening breeze as the sun set. Reluctantly she told Grandma, "I need to leave. Let me help clean the dishes before I head home."

"I can get it dear. Go ahead and drive back before it gets any later."

On her way back to Orlando she tried to understand the feelings she experienced every time she went back to the beach. She felt drawn to it like that was where she belonged. She always had a sense of peace and forgot the stresses of everyday life when she was there. She yearned for the days when she could walk on the beach and surf with Josh without a care in the world. Would she ever find someone to love her and make her as happy as Josh had?

She arrived after dark to her lonely apartment and thought of the days with Ashley in college. They would find a good movie and eat a quart of ice cream to make themselves feel better. She scooped a large portion of ice cream into a bowl and enjoyed the cool sweet treat while she watched a teary romance movie on TV. It seemed to fit her mood.

***

Sunday, she awoke to the sound of the phone ringing. It was Dillon. "There is a sci-fi convention going on downtown. Do you want to attend with me today?"

Still half asleep she responded, "That sounds like fun."

"Good, I will pick you up in an hour."

She was suddenly awake. "Wait. What should I wear? I've never been to a sci-fi convention."

"Wear whatever you like. Not everyone dresses up like their favorite science fiction character."

Jennifer jumped out of bed and looked in the mirror. Her hair was a frizzy mess. She felt fat and guilty after eating all that ice cream the night before. She took a quick shower and managed to tame her hair by putting it in a pony tail. She dressed in shorts, a cool short sleeved cotton top, and comfortable sandals in case there was a lot of walking. The doorbell rang just as she finished applying her make-up. She opened the door and smiled. Dillon was dressed in a Star Trek uniform.

"Don't laugh, I know this is a side of me you haven't seen yet."

"I bet you are a blast on Halloween," she giggled.

"Are you ready to go?" he asked, in a hurry to leave.

"Yes, lead the way, protector of the universe," she snickered

"You are confusing me with Superman," he said as they walked to his car.

They arrived, and she soon felt out of place. Everyone was dressed in full costume like Dillon. This was definitely a convention for nerds.

Dillon showed her around, and they stopped by all the booths selling everything from comic books to crafts. Dillon held her hand as they walked down the aisles of exhibits; talking and laughing all afternoon.

By the time they arrived home, it was dark. Dillon walked her to the door. "Would you like to come in for something to drink?" Jennifer asked

"No thanks, maybe another time. I need to get home and get out of this hot costume. This is definitely not the outfit to wear when it's almost 100 degrees outside. Thanks for going with me today."

"I had fun. Thanks for inviting me." Jennifer hesitated then blurted out, "Would you like to come over for supper one night this week? I have a craving for lasagna and could use some help eating it all."

"I love lasagna and could definitely help you eat it."

"How about Wednesday at around 6:30?"

"I can't wait." He leaned down and kissed her on the lips. "I will see you tomorrow at work."

She closed the door and smiled, glad that Dillon finally made his intentions clear. He did think of her as more than just a friend. She was so happy she could hardly sleep.

Chapter Nine

"If ye abide in me, and my words abide in you ye shall ask what ye will and it shall be done unto you." *(St. John 15:7)*

Jennifer started eating lunch with Dillon during the week and spending time with him on the weekends. One weekend he introduced her to astronomy. Multiple falling stars were forecasted in the eastern sky. Dillon drove out past where the glow of the city lights could reach. He parked in a field and announced, "We are here."

"Where exactly is 'here'?" Jennifer asked.

"You don't need to worry. A friend of my father's owns this property and knows we are here tonight. Just watch where you step. He grazes cattle here part of the year."

Flashlight in hand, they tromped through the field to scare away any snakes. Dillon set up his telescope and placed a blanket on the ground, so they could lie on the ground and watch the sky. Dillon pointed out the different constellations and some of the planets. Jupiter was very bright that night. Then, Jennifer saw her first shooting star streak across the sky. She squealed with delight as several more raced overhead. The show continued late into the night. The temperature began to drop and Jennifer started to shiver with chills. Dillon wrapped a blanket around both of them and they snuggled together staring up at the sky. It was fantastic. Jennifer was in awe at the beauty of the night sky and never realized how many stars there were.

She felt so comfortable around Dillon and had grown to enjoy his company immensely. As if he knew what she was feeling, Dillon rolled onto his side and gave her a long passionate kiss. He pushed her long, brown hair away from her face and stared into her big, brown eyes. "I know we have only known each other for a short time, but I've fallen in love with you."

"I love you also." Jennifer leaned over and kissed him again.

They made love for the first time in the field that night as the stars continued to streak through the sky.

Dillon and Jennifer grew even closer over the next couple of months and they spent all their free time together.

At Christmas, Dillon invited Jennifer to spend the holiday with his family. He wanted her to meet his Dad and step-mother who lived in Atlanta. Jennifer was torn between wanting to spend Christmas with Dillon or her Grandma, not wanting to leave Grandma alone over the holidays.

She called Grandma and explained the situation.

Grandma of course encouraged her to go with Dillon and not to worry about her. "Several of the retirees in the condo complex are getting together for Christmas. I am just glad you are happy and have found someone to enjoy the holidays with. I will be fine. Enjoy yourself."

"Merry Christmas, Grandma! Maybe we can celebrate New Year's Eve together."

"That would be nice. Have a safe trip!"

The day before Christmas Eve, Dillon and Jennifer left for Atlanta immediately after work. Dillon's car was packed with suitcases and Christmas presents for his family. They arrived around midnight.

When Jennifer opened the car door she couldn't believe how cold it was. When they left Orlando, it was in the 70's. The shock of the freezing temperatures quickly chilled her to the bone. She had forgotten that the rest of the states were experiencing wintertime temperatures which were much colder than Orlando. It reminded her of Christmas when she lived in Minnesota. Dillon wrapped his arms around her to help keep her warm. They walked together up the brick sidewalk to the front door of his Dad's two story colonial style house.

The house was decorated for Christmas with candles in the windows, icicle lights hanging from the eaves, and lights flashing on every bush and tree in the front yard. It reminded her of Christmas with her parents. Her Mom and Dad always loved decorating the house for Christmas. The day after Thanksgiving they would get out the Christmas lights and spend the day outside putting up decorations. She didn't realize how much she missed that until now.

Dillon opened the door, and Jennifer was immediately embraced by Dillon's Dad and step-mother. "Come in and get out of the cold. Hi, I am Doris and this is Dillon's Dad, Albert."

Jennifer stepped inside and was glad for the warmth. "Your house is beautiful. I love all the Christmas decorations you have on display. Thanks so much for having me."

"I know you must be tired after your long drive. Let me show you to the guest room."

She followed Doris up the stairs and was shown to her room. She placed her suitcase on the floor by the bed. "Thanks, this looks lovely."

Dillon stuck his head in her room. "My room is just next door if you need anything." Dillon gave her his wicked grin.

She peered into Dillon's bedroom, and it was as if she had stepped back in time. His Dad hadn't changed the room since Dillon left for college. "Look at all those science awards. You must have really been a nerd in high school," she teased him.

"I guess Dad likes keeping the room as it's for my sake. Maybe he thinks I will return one day."

"I know how hard it must have been for your Dad to let his only child leave."

Dillon walked Jennifer back to her bedroom. "Get some rest. I will see you in the morning."

It felt lonely sleeping in a strange bed with Dillon just next door. After the long day, she was so tired, she drifted off to sleep in no time. She awoke to the sounds of laughter coming from downstairs. It was already morning. She climbed out of bed, shivering from the cold. She quickly dressed in jeans and one of the few sweaters she owned to ward off the cold. She walked into the kitchen to find Dillon and Doris busy making breakfast.

Dillon smiled at the sight of her. "How did you sleep?"

"Like a rock. I didn't realize how tired I was. What smells so good?"

"Doris always enjoys baking cookies on Christmas Eve. She made my favorite oatmeal- raisin-chocolate chip cookies, which are in the oven cooking now. Would you like some coffee?"

"I would love some."

Dillon handed her a large mug of coffee. "Is there anything I can help with?" Jennifer asked

Doris joyfully responded, "Just relax and enjoy your coffee. I've already put a breakfast casserole in the oven."

Jennifer sat on the bar stool in the kitchen while they talked about Christmas traditions.

"Our family always goes to Christmas Eve church service," Dillon shared.

"I used to do that with my parents in Minnesota."

"Our church has a music program where many of the holiday hymns are sung, along with a sermon. Afterwards, we enjoy driving around the neighborhood looking at Christmas lights."

"That sounds like fun!"

Dillon's Dad walked into the kitchen and teased Dillon, "Have you eaten all the Christmas cookies yet?"

Dillon joked back, "No, I saved one for you."

Jennifer could tell Dillon and his Dad were close by the way they loved harassing each other. Being an only child herself, she knew how much time Dillon must have spent with his Dad growing up. Jennifer sometimes wondered how nice it would have been to have a sister to talk to, someone to laugh with, and share the good times as well as the bad. Then she realized she may not have been as close to her parents if she had a sibling to share their attention. She decided she was glad to have been an only child, to have had her parents all to herself for the few short years they had.

They spent the day cooking and enjoying time together. She hadn't laughed so hard in a very long time. After supper, she dressed in the warmest clothes she owned, and went to church with Dillon and his family. After church, they drove around and looked at the Christmas lights in the neighborhood. Some of the displays were absolutely amazing with lights synchronized to music.

When they arrived back home, Doris asked, "Who wants some hot chocolate?"

Everyone yelled, "I do!"

They sat in the family room drinking hot chocolate and watched a Christmas movie. Jennifer felt like a kid again, all excited about opening presents Christmas morning.

Jennifer had struggled to come up with a Christmas gift for Dillon. After much thought, she decided against buying him boring clothes and purchased a new zoom lens for his telescope. It was a little pricey, but she knew he would love it. She had no idea what he had bought her.

When she went to bed, there were only a few gifts under the Christmas tree, and she thought Dillon's family must not exchange a lot of gifts for Christmas. When she woke and walked downstairs Christmas morning, it was as if Santa Claus had truly come, as presents spilled out onto the floor from underneath the Christmas tree. At first, she thought she didn't buy enough gifts for Dillon's family, but soon found out that most of the gifts were either handmade or didn't cost much. For example, Dillon's Dad was always losing his keys. So, Dillon gave him a device he could attach to his key ring. When he lost his keys, all he had to do was press a remote to set off a sharp, shrill noise so he could find his keys. Doris crocheted scarves for Dillon and Jennifer to keep them warm in the winter.

Jennifer was overwhelmed with the special gift Doris had given her. Dillon had told Doris that Jennifer enjoyed cooking. Doris made a copy of her family's favorite recipes and created a cookbook for Jennifer.

"I am a true believer that the way to a man's heart is through his stomach. I wanted to share some of Dillon's favorite recipes with you."

"Thank you so much! That is so sweet of you to do that for me." A tear came to Jennifer's eye when she realized that this woman, who she had only met yesterday, was welcoming her into her family and into their lives. "I will have so much fun making these recipes for Dillon and keeping his stomach happy."

Next, she opened the gift from Dillon. When she removed the Christmas paper, she could tell the box was from a jewelry store. She nervously opened the box to find a gorgeous necklace with a diamond heart pendant. She leaned over and kissed Dillon. "It's beautiful. Can you help me put it on?" she asked as she handed the necklace to Dillon and lifted her hair out of the way.

After opening gifts, they spent the day cooking, eating, and watching football games on TV. Before she knew it, it was time for Dillon and her to drive back to Orlando. They only had to work four days before they were both off again for New Year's Eve and New Year's Day.

Jennifer asked Dillon on the way back to Orlando, "Can we spend New Year's Eve with Grandma, since I didn't get to spend any time with her for Christmas? There is always a spectacular fireworks display on the beach at midnight, and we could watch from Grandma's balcony or go down to the beach."

"That sounds like fun! Why don't I make reservations at one of the local restaurants so no one has to cook?"

"That would be nice." Dillon was always so considerate. On the ride back to Orlando she called Grandma from her cell phone to go over plans for New Year's Eve.

After discussing the agenda for New Year's Eve, Grandma informed Jennifer, "I've a surprise to share with you. I will tell you all about it when you arrive."

She wondered what Grandma was up to and couldn't wait to hear. Four days of work dragged on before she could find out what Grandma had in store for her.

Finally, New Year's Eve arrived and she begged Dillon, "Let's leave early. I am dying to find out what Grandma has to tell me."

Dillon teased her, "You are like a kid going to Disney World, growing more excited each passing minute."

As they drove through Cocoa Beach, Jennifer noticed most of the hurricane damage had been repaired along A1A and everything looked back to normal. They arrived at Grandma's condo around five. Dillon made reservations at a restaurant on the beach for six.

Once they arrived, Jennifer grabbed Dillon's hand and hurried him up to Grandma's condo and rang the doorbell. Grandma opened the door, and Jennifer blurted out, "What is this surprise you have been keeping from me?"

"Well, I am happy to see you too!" she joked. Grandma showed them into the living room. "I would like you to meet Robert. We met at a Christmas party a few weeks ago. Robert is also widowed and has just recently moved to the area to start a new life and be closer to his two children. He is a retired doctor."

"It's very nice to meet you." Jennifer smiled and looked into Robert's warm, blue eyes and gave him a welcoming hug.

Dillon spoke up and said, "I made reservations for six at the restaurant on the pier. Since it's New Year's Eve, we better leave early so we don't lose our table."

At dinner, Jennifer got the chance to get to know Robert better. He was very polite-making sure Grandma was comfortable. He spoke highly of Grandma during dinner and told Jennifer how much fun he'd had with her the last few weeks. Jennifer could tell Grandma enjoyed his company. She was giggling like a little school girl every time Robert made a joke.

While they waited for dessert, Jennifer excused herself to go to the restroom and Grandma followed her. Once in the seclusion of the bathroom Jennifer said, "Now that I have you alone, Robert seems very nice. I am so glad you have found someone to spend time with again."

"I was not sure how you would react. I was afraid you might think it was too soon after Grandpa had gone to start dating anyone."

She laughed, "I am thrilled you have someone in your life who seems to make you very happy."

They returned to the table to find Dillon and Robert talking about football and the New Year's Day bowl game.

After a lush dessert, they went back to the condo to watch the fireworks at midnight. Instead of going upstairs with Grandma and Robert, Dillon suggested to Jennifer, "Why don't we take a walk on the beach? I could use the fresh air after all the food we devoured."

"That sounds wonderful."

Dillon reached down and grabbed Jennifer's hand. They slowly walked down the beach to where the fireworks were being launched. Even though it was getting dark, the beach was crowded with tourists and snowbirds down for the winter.

As the sun set and darkness engulfed them, Dillon and Jennifer sat on the beach listening to the waves. They talked easily with each other. The night was cool with the wind blowing off the ocean, so Dillon took off his jacket and wrapped it around Jennifer's shoulders. They cuddled together on the beach as the crowd counted down to midnight. Just at the strike of midnight, Dillon turned and gave Jennifer a tender kiss. This was truly one of the best New Year's Eves Jennifer could remember, and it was not over yet.

Dillon turned to Jennifer, "I've one more surprise for you tonight." He handed her a velvet covered jewelry box to open.

Jennifer nervously opened the box, not knowing what to expect. She lifted the lid and was in shock. A gorgeous sparkling engagement ring was staring back at her. She started to shake all over as tears came to her eyes.

Dillon reached for Jennifer's quivering hand and kneeled down on one knee in front of her. "I can't imagine my life without you. Will you marry me?"

She yelled, "Yes!" then threw her arms around Dillon's neck.

Dillon gently pulled Jennifer's lips to his. They kissed passionately as the fireworks boomed above their heads.

Chapter Ten

"Consider what I say; and the Lord give thee understanding in all things." *(II Timothy, 2:7)*

Jennifer wanted a spring wedding when it was not too hot and many flowers were in bloom. They agreed on May tenth as the day they would be married in Atlanta. Dillon wanted to be married in the church he grew up in with his family. They planned a small ceremony with just close friends and relatives. Jennifer asked Grandma if Robert would mind walking her down the aisle since Dad and Grandpa couldn't. Robert was thrilled. Since he had two boys, he never had the opportunity to walk a daughter down the aisle.

Jennifer had just five months to plan the ceremony. With the help of Grandma and Dillon's step-mother, Doris, the event was going to be very special. A country club was reserved for the reception where dinner would be served, following the ceremony. It was a little pricey but Dillon helped cover the cost. Dillon helped choose the invitations and assemble the guest list. They registered at several department and home improvement stores. Jennifer got lucky and found a wedding dress already in stock that fit her perfectly. Everything was ready and she anxiously awaited for the day to arrive.

Dillon and Jennifer drove to Atlanta the day before the wedding. Jennifer stayed in a hotel with Grandma and Robert. She didn't want Dillon to see her on her wedding day for fear of bad luck.

The day was perfect. The sun was shining brightly. The church grounds were ablaze with color from the azaleas and tulips in bloom. Inside, the church was decorated in pink carnations and white roses.

Jennifer arrived at the church two hours before the ceremony. She nervously paced while Doris and Grandma helped with her wedding dress, styled her hair, and applied her make-up.

Finally ready, Grandma held her at arms length, with tears in her eyes. "You are just beautiful. Your parents would have been so happy if they could have been with you today."

"Thank you Grandma." Jennifer gently hugged Grandma making sure not to mess up her hair or smudge her make-up. She was a nervous wreck fanning herself, trying not to sweat. Her anxiety must have been apparent.

Doris shared the story of how she met Dillon's father. "I was thirty years old when I met Albert at a church function. I belonged to a different church, but on this particular Sunday, our two churches came together to share an evening of fellowship. Dillon's father was five years older than me and already had a son. It was not how I pictured falling in love and getting married, but God had other plans for me. It was evident that Albert and Dillon needed me and that God had a hand in bringing us together. Over the last twenty years, Albert and I have changed, but it has only brought us closer together. Marriage is not always easy. You will have years where everything runs smoothly and you are very happy together. Then, God may throw a bump in the road to test your faith and your love for each other. Remember facing the conflicts together will only bring you closer."

Jennifer smiled at Doris, "Thank you for your help and all you have done to make me feel part of your family. I don't think I could have done it without you and Grandma."

Then, there was a knock at the door, and Robert was standing there so handsome in his tux ready to walk Jennifer down the aisle.

Grandma adjusted Jennifer's veil and told her, "Don't worry. You and Dillon will be very happy together." She took Jennifer's hand and placed it in Robert's. "Just relax and enjoy your special day."

Doris and Grandma were escorted to their seats.

Robert placed Jennifer's hand around his arm as the music for the marriage march began. "Are you ready?"

Jennifer nodded her head nervously and took a deep breath, releasing it slowly to calm her nerves. They started their slow march down the aisle toward Dillon, who was smiling brightly, and very handsome in his white tux.

The day was a blur. Jennifer hardly remembered the ceremony and reception. Thank goodness it was videotaped, so she could watch it later.

Dillon and Jennifer spent their first night as husband and wife in a fancy suite in a luxury hotel in Atlanta before leaving for their honeymoon the next day. They joyfully boarded a cruise ship and sailed around the Caribbean for the next five days. They relaxed in the sun and enjoyed being together. Their evenings were spent eating extravagant meals then lounging on their private patio watching the sun set. This was followed by gentle caresses, kissing, and eventually making love.

They returned to work and reality. Jennifer had moved all her belongings into Dillon's apartment the day before they were married. There were boxes stacked everywhere. They soon realized as Jennifer emptied her boxes, that all her belongings were not going to fit.

They looked at the mess stacked in the living room. Jennifer spoke up, "We have to find a bigger apartment."

"You know, with both of our salaries we should be able to qualify for a loan to buy a house," Dillon said.

"I hadn't thought about that. That would be great! Imagine having a garage for our cars and an office where you can keep your telescope and space memorabilia."

"I see your true motive. You are just trying to find a place big enough to hide all my sci-fi stuff."

"That's not true! I would just enjoy decorating a place together and making it our home."

Dillon grabbed Jennifer and kissed her on the head. "I'll contact a real estate agent tomorrow and determine what price range house we can afford with our income."

Within a week the real estate agent found the perfect place. It was a small three bedroom, two bath house on a half acre lot located just ten miles from work. The price was right. They couldn't believe their luck when their offer was accepted.

Forty-five days later they moved into their first home. They spent days unpacking and Jennifer added a female touch decorating the house. She enjoyed picking out window treatments, rugs, new towels, and some new furniture. Once settled in, she invited Grandma and Robert over for dinner to show them the house.

Grandma arrived with a housewarming gift and another surprise. "Robert and I have decided to get married! We are going to have a small ceremony with just family and a few friends in two weeks. I hope you and Dillon will be able to attend."

Jennifer was shocked. She didn't know why she hadn't realized this was possible at Grandma's age. She quickly removed the shocked expression from her face, smiled, and gave Grandma and Robert a big hug. "I am so happy for you! Dillon and I will definitely attend."

They spent the evening talking about the wedding and what they planned afterwards. "We have made arrangement to get married at my church in Cocoa Beach. Robert is renting a house, so he is going to end his lease and move in with me. That means you are still welcome to come and visit and stay in your old room any time you want."

"It sounds like you have carefully thought this through and everything is decided. Is there anything I can help with?"

"We just want to keep the wedding simple. Having you there will mean so much to me."

Before Jennifer could even adjust to the idea of Grandma getting married her wedding day arrived. Grandma wore an elegant, long, cream colored dress and Robert was in a nice suit. Robert's two sons attended the ceremony, and Jennifer finally got to meet them. They were thrilled their Dad was remarrying and had found someone to spend the rest of his life with.

After the ceremony, they all met back at Grandma's for a buffet style supper to celebrate their union. It was a joyous occasion and a good excuse for family to spend some time together.

The weeks following Grandma's wedding, work picked up. Dillon was promoted to a manager and spent extra hours at work making sure his department performed to company performance targets.

Jennifer was also very busy on a new project and spent extra hours making sure it was complete on time. No matter how busy Dillon and her were, they always spent Sundays together.

Jennifer started feeling run-down and tired all the time. She just didn't have the energy she used to and stopped jogging after work to see if that helped. She was getting plenty of rest but was still tired. She finally decided to make an appointment to see a doctor. She didn't want to worry Dillon, so she didn't mention the appointment to him. She left work a little early to make it to the doctor's on time.

The doctor asked her what seemed like a thousand questions. "How long have you been experiencing tiredness? Have you changed your diet? How much caffeine do you drink? Have you been feeling depressed..." He asked her to urinate in a cup, so he could run some tests. She sat in the cold examination room for what seemed like an eternity before the doctor returned with her test results. She was concerned it might be something serious. "What is wrong with me?"

The doctor smiled back at Jennifer, "You are pregnant. I want to start you on pre-natal vitamins and that should help with the tiredness. You need to schedule an appointment with your OBGYN to determine how far along you are."

She sat there stunned. "Are you sure? I've been taking birth control pills, so I didn't even consider the fact that I might be pregnant."

"Yes, I am positive. Birth control pills are not 100% effective as you have learned."

She thanked the doctor and walked back to her car in a daze. She sat behind the wheel trying to rationalize what she was just told. I had gained a little weight but just figured it was from not exercising as much. Dillon and I had talked about having children one day, just not this soon. Will he be happy when I tell him the news? How am I going to keep up with my work schedule and raise a child? She drove home slowly, thinking about the baby growing inside her.

She arrived home to find the house was quiet. Dillon was still at work, so she busied herself making supper while she waited for him to arrive.

Dillon walked in and she could tell he'd a bad day at work. "I am beat and glad to be home."

"I made your favorite for supper. Pot roast with potatoes and carrots along with an apple pie that I picked up from a bakery."

He joked, "You either are buttering me up for something or have some horrible news to share with me."

She hesitated, then blurted out, "I'm pregnant!"

At first, Dillon stood there and didn't say a word. Then, after what she said had a chance to sink in, he asked, "We are going to have a baby?"

She nodded her head up and down. He lifted her into the air and gave her a big kiss.

Then he started firing off questions. "How far along are you? Have you told your grandmother? What color should we paint the nursery...?"

His reaction was better than she could have possibly imagined.

The next seven months she dealt with morning sickness and being very uncomfortable during the heat and humidity of the summer months in Orlando. Dillon was fantastic helping out around the house making sure she didn't overdo it. He went to every doctor's appointment with her to make sure she and the baby were healthy. The day they were told,

"You are having a girl!" Jennifer thought Dillon would be disappointed that it wasn't a boy, but he didn't care as long as the baby was healthy.

*****

Jennifer's water broke around 2AM on a Friday morning. "Dillon wake up. It's time to go to the hospital!"

"Okay, I'm awake." He threw on his clothes and calmly loaded Jennifer and her bag into the car before racing to the hospital.

After a very long, painful labor, she gave birth to a beautiful baby girl weighing six pounds and seven ounces. They named her Hope.

Jennifer had never been so totally in love with anything before in her life, as she was the second Hope was placed in her arms. Her tiny little fingers and toes could all fit inside Dillon's big hands. She had the cutest nose and Dillon's deep brown eyes. She was mesmerized by Hope and never wanted to let her go.

Twenty-four hours later, Jennifer was released from the hospital and they took their precious angel home. Their focus immediately changed from themselves to their gift from God. Their world was suddenly turned upside down and it totally revolved around their fragile little girl.

At first, they put Hope's crib in their bedroom, so they could hear if she needed anything during the night. Hope seemed to wake up hungry every fours hours to be fed. During the week, Jennifer took care of Hope, so Dillon could rest for work. On the weekends, Dillon helped take care of Hope so Jennifer could get some rest. After four weeks, Jennifer started to look for a day care where she could leave Hope, when she returned to work. Trusting someone to watch over Hope was going to be very difficult. After visiting several day cares in the area, whose employees seemed competent and the centers were clean, she just couldn't bear the thought of leaving her little girl in a stranger's hands. She decided to check into having someone come to the house to stay with Hope. She discovered it would only cost about fifty dollars more, and Hope would receive personalized attention that she wouldn't get at the day care. She convinced Dillon that even though it was more expensive, this was what was best for Hope.

Jennifer interviewed ten candidates before deciding on a woman that was a retired nurse and had raised three children of her own. Her name was Rachel. She was willing to come to their home each morning by 7 AM and stay until 5 PM when Jennifer would arrive home from work. She was satisfied that Hope would be in good hands with Rachel. She would be able to return to work and not worry about Hope all day, or so she thought.

The day came for her to return to work, and she was a nervous wreck. She had stocked up bottles of breast milk in the refrigerator, so Hope would have plenty to drink while Jennifer was at work. She gave Rachel all her contact information and told her to call for any reason.

She found it very difficult to concentrate once she arrived at work. Her desk was piled high with assignments from being gone, but all she could think about was Hope. She must have called home five times to make sure Hope was all right that first day. Slowly, she began to trust that Rachel knew what she was doing and that Hope was just fine without her.

Hope was a very happy girl, always smiling, giggling, and rarely crying. After two months, she was sleeping six hours at night allowing Jennifer to get some rest.

Dillon and her photographed Hope endlessly not wanting to miss any new feats she performed. They recorded her from the first time she rolled over, started to crawl, to when her first tooth came in. The day she stood up and took her first step was a monumental moment in their eyes. She was growing up fast, and of course, they thought she was the brightest and prettiest girl there was.

When Hope turned three, Jennifer started to notice she stumbled occasionally and her motor skills seemed to be declining, instead of getting better. She took off work to take her to the doctor. They ran every test from checking her reflexes, CAT scan, and blood work, trying to determine what was wrong.

After two weeks, the doctor called and asked that she and Dillon come to his office. Jennifer knew that if the doctor wanted to talk to them in the office it couldn't be good, and prepared herself for the worst.

Jennifer tightly held onto Dillon's hand as the doctor tried to explain. "Hope has a rare form of muscular dystrophy. She will continue to lose her coordination and movement in her arms and legs as the disease progresses. Eventually her heart muscle will be affected and surgery will need to be performed to install a pacemaker. The disease progresses at different rates, but I do not expect Hope to live more than three years.

There are some drugs that can help slow the paralysis, but currently there is no cure."

Jennifer refused to believe what she was hearing and that the doctor must be mistaken. How could God give her such a precious gift, and then take her away? He couldn't possibly be so cruel.

Jennifer managed to hold herself together until they reached the car, and then broke down and sobbed as Dillon held her.

Dillon's reaction was different. He was angry. He was not the type of person to show his emotions, and he just withdrew, trying to hide his hurt. He started spending more and more time at work. He couldn't stand to spend time with Hope knowing she was going to be taken away from him.

Jennifer wanted to spend every second of the day with her, to enjoy her for as long as she could. She took an extended leave from work. She wanted to make sure Hope was happy and comfortable.

The next two years their lives revolved around doctors and physical therapist appointments trying to keep Hope's muscles strong. Hope was losing her battle, though, and was now confined to a wheelchair.

None of this seemed to faze her little girl, though. She was just as happy and never complained about anything. Hope loved to read, so Jennifer took Hope to the library every week to find books they could read together. She was a very smart girl and knew she was different from the other little girls in her story books. Jennifer told her how special she was. She wanted her to know about God and how she would be with him one day. She read Bible stories to Hope. One day, she shared the story of David and Goliath. "David was a shepherd boy that watched over his father's sheep. One day, he was asked to deliver some corn and loaves of bread to feed the army fighting against the Philistines. When David arrived, he heard the men talking about a great warrior named Goliath. The men of Israel feared Goliath for he was so big and strong. When David heard that the army needed someone to fight Goliath, he said, "The Lord will protect me as he has done in the past against the lions and bears. I will fight Goliath for you." David didn't have any great weapons. He just had his sling and some smooth stones with him to battle Goliath. As Goliath approached, David placed a rock in his sling, whirled it over his head, and released the rock. The rock flew with great speed and hit Goliath right in the head, killing him instantly. David became a hero. He was honored for being so fearless and putting his faith in God."

Hope had been quiet as Jennifer told the story, and she now spoke up. "I am fearless like David. I do not look strong, but I am inside."

"Yes, you are sweetie." Jennifer hugged Hope as a tear came to her eye. "It's time to get some rest." She turned out the light and sat with Hope until she fell asleep. She was definitely her David helping her to stay strong for the battle ahead. God chooses special people to perform his work, and he chose Hope to bring joy and laughter to the lives of people around her. Jennifer's heart was breaking as she couldn't imagine life without Hope.

The day Jennifer dreaded came all too soon. Hope's heart started to fail. Surgery was scheduled to install a pacemaker, but they knew it would only keep her heart pumping for so long.

Dillon and Jennifer didn't want Hope dying in a hospital, in a strange place, with tubes coming out of her. Instead, they chose to let her pass peacefully at home. She slowly became bedridden and didn't have enough energy to go outside. Jennifer would lie in bed with Hope, watching her favorite cartoons and listening to her laugh.

In the wisdom of a five and a half year old, Hope knew she was dying and tried to comfort Jennifer. Her brave little girl didn't fear death and asked, "Will I be able to see you from Heaven?"

"I believe you will, and one day I will join you in Heaven. Until then, your grandparents will be there with you. You will like them very much."

Jennifer stayed with Hope every night, listening to make sure she didn't stop breathing. Exhaustion set in one night and Jennifer dozed off while holding Hope in her arms. When she awoke, Hope was gone. Her scream of agony brought Dillon running into the room. They cried together, holding their precious angel.

After the funeral, Jennifer tried to figure out what to do with her life. The last two and a half years she had done nothing but take care of Hope. She left Hope's room as it was, for she couldn't bear to give anything away. She would sit on Hope's tiny bed, feel her presence, and wonder if she was looking down on her from Heaven.

The sadness drove Dillon and Jennifer apart. He couldn't get over the anger and hurt he felt over losing his little girl. Dillon started working seven days a week just so he wouldn't have to come home and be reminded of Hope.

Jennifer fell into a deep depression and was totally lost. She no longer knew what she was supposed to do with her life now that Hope was gone. She had no energy and all she wanted to do was sleep. She wished to wake up and find that it was all a bad dream and Hope was in her bed. Each day though, she woke to realize she was living a nightmare.

Dillon arrived home from work upset to see her still lying around. "You have to get on with your life and go back to work. You can't just keep lying around feeling sorry for yourself. I need some fresh air." He slammed the door on his way out.

After Dillon stormed out, Jennifer knew in her heart he was right but just didn't know how to go on with her life. She grabbed her purse and keys. She drove to Cocoa Beach to talk with Grandma.

Sitting on Grandma's patio, staring out at the beach always seemed to bring clarity to her life. Grandma and her talked to well past dark.

"I know your heart will never be the same, but you have to find the strength to start living again. God has a purpose for you, and you need to find the good in this tragedy and turn it into something positive and wonderful."

Driving back home Jennifer thought of Grandma's words. *"Make something positive out of the hurt you are feeling."* That is when it dawned on her. I know what God wants me to do. I should start a school for handicapped children. Schools do not offer the resources necessary to educate handicapped children. I will create a school in Orlando that will allow handicapped children to spend time with other children like themselves, where they can learn. For the first time in weeks Jennifer felt that she had a purpose again.

Chapter Eleven

"Forbearing one another, and forgiving one another, if any man have a quarrel against any: even as Christ forgave you, so also do ye." *(Colossians 3:13)*

When Jennifer arrived home, she wanted to share her idea with Dillon. She found him asleep on the sofa and didn't want to disturb him. The next day, after Dillon returned home from work, she enthusiastically shared her idea with him. He thought she was crazy.

"You have an electrical engineering degree. You want to throw away all that education and money to teach? What do you know about teaching handicapped children and running a school?"

All she wanted was a little support, but instead she felt like Dillon slapped her in the face. She thought he would be happy that she had finally figured out what she wanted to do with her life. She had taken their horrible experience and wanted to turn it into something good, but he was not the least bit understanding. She tried to explain, "I can go back to college to earn a teaching certificate. I can also take some nursing and child development courses."

"Where are you going to get the money to do that?" Dillon angrily asked. "We barely have five hundred dollars in our bank account after paying off Hope's medical bills. You haven't contributed to our income in over two and a half years. I've had to pay all the bills, on my salary."

"I can pursue getting a school loan and possibly a grant to cover the cost."

"I can't deal with this right now. I've had a long day at work and all I wanted was a peaceful evening to relax, for a change." He grabbed his keys, slammed the door, and sped away in his car.

Sarcastically, Jennifer asked herself, Was I really asking so much from you that you couldn't give me just a little support? She started to cry. She was so frustrated with Dillon's attitude. Every time she tried to talk to him lately, it ended in an argument. He seemed to twist her words around as if she was threatening him in some way. She knew she just needed to give him time to accept the idea.

Dillon didn't return home that night, and she was concerned that he may have been in an accident. The next morning she called his office and left a message. At lunch, he returned her call and gave no explanation for where he had stayed overnight, just that he was all right. He hung up before Jennifer could say another word.

Jennifer hoped Dillon would eventually understand her need to teach. She busied herself researching colleges in the area. She found a local college with the curriculum she needed to get a teaching certificate. She submitted her transcripts and application to attend. Then, she searched for possible loans and grants she could qualify for.

It didn't take long for her to receive an acceptance letter from the college. She started signing up for classes immediately. School was scheduled to start in just two weeks. She figured she would use her charge card to pay for classes and books. She hoped she would be approved for a loan or grant in time to cover her charge card bill.

It had been over six years since she had attended college, and she prayed she still remembered how to study. All the pre-requisite courses from her engineering degree were accepted by the university, so all she needed was an additional twenty-five credit hours to obtain her teaching certificate. She signed up for five classes her first term which would put her more than halfway to receiving a certificate. If everything went as planned, she should be able to graduate with her new degree by spring.

Dillon continued to work long hours and seemed to spend as little time at home as he could. They rarely spoke anymore.

Jennifer threw herself into school, and for the first time in a very long time, she felt she had a purpose and reason to keep on living. Her first week of school was a bit overwhelming, but in one sense, she was better off now than when she went to school the first time. She didn't have the distraction of work or school social events to deal with this time around.

A month into her term, she was sitting at the kitchen table studying when Dillon came home early. He walked into the kitchen, and she looked up from her book. "What are you doing home so early? Is everything all right?"

Dillon blurted out, "I want a divorce. I just came home to pick up my clothes and move out."

Jennifer was shocked and didn't know what to say. She knew Dillon was not happy, but hadn't realized their relationship had come to this. "I know we can work this out if you would just talk to me."

"I've nothing more to say to you."

"Have you met someone else? Is that why you have made yourself so scarce lately?"

Dillon hesitated and said, "Yes. I met someone at work that shares the same interests as me and enjoys spending time with me, unlike you."

"That is unfair. You are the one who keeps leaving every time I try to have a conversation and never wants to spend any time with me."

He retaliated, "Why do you think that is? Because all you ever want to do is talk about Hope," as he answered his own question.

"You have hardly said a word to me about Hope since her funeral. I thought you just needed some time." She realized this was his way of dealing with losing Hope. He just wanted to forget she ever existed. With sadness in her voice Jennifer said, "You know there is nothing you could have done to save Hope. Neither one of us are at fault."

"I'll come back tomorrow to get my clothes while you are in class." Once again, he stormed out of the house.

He slammed the door on his way out and left her sitting there crying. "How did our relationship come to this? We used to be so happy."

When she came home from school the next day, Dillon had emptied his closet and left a note in the kitchen.

I have contacted a Real Estate firm to sell the house. You'll need to find another place to live.

How could he do that? This was the only place she felt close to Hope. He couldn't take that away from her, too. Not knowing what she should do next, she called Grandma in tears.

After talking with Grandma on the phone for over an hour, Grandma managed to calm her down and gave her the name of a good attorney in the area. "Don,t worry about the cost. I will pay the attorney fees for you. Just call him right away so Dillon does not take advantage of you."

Jennifer met with the attorney the next day. "Dillon can't kick you out of your house, because both of your names are on the loan. Since Dillon is the one filing for divorce, you can ask for alimony to help cover the cost of the mortgage, but you need to show good faith by making an effort to find a job to pay some of the expenses."

Jennifer immediately contacted a temporary job agency in the area. She was told there were several companies in the area interested in hiring engineers part time. She submitted her resume to two of the companies and was hired within a week. She was able to work from noon until six each day, so she could continue going to school in the morning and studying at night after work.

Dillon agreed to the divorce terms to pay for half of the mortgage for no more than five years. After that time, if she couldn't afford to stay in the house on her own, it would be sold and any equity divided equally.

There was no way to prepare herself for divorce. Even though she knew the day was coming when Dillon and her would no longer be married, when it came she was very sad. It just seemed like one more thing in her life she had failed at. After class and work, she drove to Grandma's and took a long walk on the beach. She just needed time to think and clear her head, which the gentle roar of the ocean always seemed to do. She walked south for several miles thinking back on her life and the mistakes she had made. She was deep in thought when she saw some surfers offshore. She suddenly realized that she was exhausted and sat on the soft sand to rest. She watched the surfers for a while remembering how free she felt when she surfed. The surf was rolling in nicely. The surfers waited patiently for just the right wave and their patience paid off as she watched them ride to shore. She smiled, remembering the exhilaration she felt when she caught a wave, water splashing over the board, hitting her in the face then the rush of flying over the water. It seemed like a lifetime ago that she felt that free.

She rested there feeling a sense of peace for the first time since Hope passed away. She reminded herself that God was with her, and he would give her the strength to pick herself back up and keep going to face whatever life had to offer.

The shadow of a surfboard across her face brought her out of her trance. She looked up and was surprised to see Josh standing above her.

He joked, "Would you like to learn how to surf?" just like the first time they met.

"I had a very good instructor a few years ago. I think I still remember how." She laughed.

He sat down beside her. They talked as easily as if it was just yesterday when they last spoke and not ten years ago.

"I own the surf shop behind you."

She turned around and saw a rustic wooden structure partially built on stilts to protect it from the high tides. "Wow, that is great! When did you open it?"

"Just over two years ago when I saw a for sale sign on this empty building. It looked like a perfect place to open a surf shop. I never finished college. You were always the studious one," he rationalized. "I did take some business classes and was able to save enough money as a mechanic to open the store. It will never make me wealthy, but I feel like the richest man around getting to do what I love for a living."

She finally got up the nerve and asked him, "Did you ever marry?"

"I never found anyone that made me as happy as you," he sadly responded. "How about you, did you marry?"

Her insides jumped for joy to know he still cared about her. "I frequently thought about you the last ten years and wondered what had happened to you," she confessed. "I even walked on the beach hoping to get a glimpse of you, but never did until today. If you only knew how many times I wanted to pick up the phone and call you. Ironically, I,m back in school." Jennifer told him about getting married to Dillon, and about Hope; how painful it was to lose her, and that Dillon never got over the loss which is why their marriage ended.

"I am so sorry you have had so much sadness in your life. I admire your courage for going back to school and pursuing something which could make a difference in a lot of people's lives. It will help bring happiness to others as well as yourself again."

Before she knew it, the sun was setting. "Grandma must be worried by now. I need to get back."

"Can I give you a ride?"

Jennifer looked down the beach in the direction in which she had come. "I didn't realize how far I walked. I would appreciate it."

On the way to the condo, Josh casually mentioned. "I've enjoyed talking with you today. Do you have time in your busy schedule to spend some time with me on Sunday? My store will be closed so I can pick you up at ten, and then we can have brunch in Orlando and spend the day together."

Jennifer felt like a nervous teenager, like the day when Josh and her first met. She was still just as attracted to him as she was then. His blond hair and lean body hadn't changed much. She gave him directions to her house in Orlando and told him, "I am so glad we found each other again. I've really missed having you in my life." She leaned over and kissed Josh on the cheek.

Chapter Twelve

"I will say of the Lord, He is my refuge and my fortress: my God; in him will I trust." *(Psalm, 91:2)*

Josh and Jennifer spent the next several weeks getting to know each other again. Jennifer looked forward to time she spent with Josh, and he slowly helped her heart heal from losing Hope. He was by her side the day she decided to finally box up Hope's clothes and toys and donate them to a local charity.

She painstakingly sat on the floor of Hope's bedroom and went through every item in the room remembering the good times she spent with her. Josh walked in to find her crying as she placed each item in a box.

"Hope will always be in your heart, and packing up her belongings doesn't mean you will forget her," Josh reminded her.

"You are right. I've been holding onto her things for fear of losing my memories of her. This room is a part of her and letting it go is one of the hardest things I've ever had to do." Josh hugged her as tears ran down her face.

Once everything was packed up and loaded in her car, Josh rode with her to the donation center and helped her unload the car. She felt a sense of peace come over her as if Hope was watching and gave her approval to go on with her life.

After the winter term, Jennifer graduated with her teaching certificate. She had taken several classes on child development to help prepare for what lay ahead. She was still working part time as an engineer to pay the bills and now needed to decide how to proceed. She could continue taking more classes or she could start looking for a location to open her school and determine if she could obtain funding to proceed.

Josh once again was the answer to her prayers. He called her and asked, "Can you help me teach a surfing class on Saturday?"

"Sure, if you really think I can help. It has been a while since I last surfed. I might be a little rusty."

At first, she couldn't imagine why Josh wanted her at his class and how she could possibly help. When she arrived at the surf shop on Saturday, the parking lot was full. She walked down to the beach and stopped suddenly at what she saw. She smiled, realizing why Josh asked her to help. There were several handicapped children eagerly waiting to learn how to surf, who were accompanied by their parents.

Jennifer caught up with Josh who had a big grin on his face. "I thought I could put some of your education to work." He immediately introduced her to his class. "I would like you to say hi to Jennifer. She will be helping me today."

"Hi!" the kids yelled in unison.

She looked around and noticed each child had a different handicap. She met each one and even though some were battling cancer, partial paralysis, or had Down syndrome they didn't perceive their condition as a handicap. She looked into their eyes and saw the same determined look that Hope always had. Their eyes sparkled with excitement, ready to face whatever challenge arose, never doubting for a second they couldn't overcome their handicap. That day was filled with many triumphs, not to say the children didn't struggle. They overcame each obstacle until they finally rode their first wave into shore at the cheers of their parents. Jennifer had never been so tired but happy in her life, by the end of the day. The children were amazing. Once again, Josh came to her rescue and proved to her that she was ready to start her school.

She talked to several of the parents during the surf lessons and most of them were home schooling their children. They loved the idea of their child being able to attend a school that would focus on their special needs, along with giving them the opportunity to learn with other children like themselves. Most indicated they would consider sending their child to a school like that if one existed.

On Sunday Josh helped her search the web for different organizations that might help provide funding to start the school. She already had researched what it would take to apply for a charter school in Florida. Even though the state would provide some funding, it wouldn't be near enough to make the school a reality.

Now the real work began. Her goal was to have the school up and running by the start of the upcoming school year, which gave her less than four months. She made a list of everything she needed to accomplish. First she needed to obtain the school board's approval to proceed with the charter school and to find a location for the school. Once she did that, she needed to find skilled teachers and order all the books and supplies. To say the least, she was overwhelmed.

She quickly came to the realization that she couldn't continue to work for the temporary agency and have the school opened by fall.

Once again, Josh came to her rescue. She discussed her dilemma with him. "To be able to have enough time to start the school by the fall, I need to sell the house, so I can live off the equity. I can live with Grandma to keep my expenses down and find a place of my own once I start work again."

Josh interrupted her. "You know I've never stopped loving you. Even though we have only been back together for a few weeks now, I have waited ten years to ask you this question. Will you marry me?"

"Yes!" she yelled. She threw her arms around his neck and kissed him passionately.

She immediately picked up the phone and called Grandma. When Grandma answered, she announced, "Josh and I are finally getting married!"

"Congratulations! I couldn't be happier for you both. What can I do to help you prepare for the wedding?"

"We haven't had a chance to decide on a date yet. I will call you back as soon as we come up with a plan."

Then she then called Dillon and explained. "I no longer need the house. Thank you for helping with the mortgage payments. I want to put the house up for sale immediately." She felt like she was somehow betraying Dillon when she shared with him, "I am getting married to my high school sweetheart."

"I'm happy for you Jennifer. If you like, I can meet with a real estate agent and put the house on the market?"

"That would be very helpful. Let me know if you need me to sign anything." She hung up the phone happy to hear that Dillon had moved on with his life also. It was the first conversation they'd had in months that didn't end in a fight.

She couldn't wait to marry Josh. "How about we get married next weekend?"

"You do realize that's only four days away?"

"I know, but if you don't mind, we could have a simple ceremony at church with just a few people."

Four days later, they were married with Josh's Mom Harriet, Grandma and Robert present.

After the ceremony, they all went out to eat to celebrate. During dinner, Josh shared with his mom Jennifer's plans for starting a school for handicapped children in the area. Josh squeezed Jennifer's hand, "I am so proud of her for taking on such a big project."

Jennifer blushed, "I still have a long way to go. I haven't even found a location for the school yet."

"I might be able to help with that," Harriet replied.

Jennifer had forgotten that Harriet worked in the Melbourne high school administrative office. "Really, do you know of a place I could use for a school?"

"I just heard of a charter school that will no longer be operating after the end of this school year in the Eau Gallie area. I was notified the students would be attending Melbourne High School next year. I can obtain the owner's name for you, so you can determine if the building would be suitable for your needs."

"That would be wonderful!" She jumped at the offer.

Josh's house was located close to his surf shop and across the street from the beach. Since property in this area was prime, it had a very small back yard with another house just a few feet away. Josh and Jennifer spent the rest of the weekend moving some of her furniture and belongings to Josh's house. Since Josh's house was much smaller then Jennifer's, it was quickly evident that all her belongings were not going to fit. They agreed on what to keep and donated the rest. Josh happily let Jennifer convert his bachelor pad into a home.

Josh and Jennifer celebrated their honeymoon on the beach, which seemed fitting since that was where they met. Josh surprised her by buying a bottle of champagne and packing a picnic. She browsed through the contents of the picnic basket and realized Josh had remembered all her favorites. It was filled with chocolate, strawberries, a baguette and brie cheese. She placed a blanket on the beach to spread their smorgasbord on. They relaxed on the beach and munched on the treats and sipped champagne, enjoying their first evening as husband and wife. They snuggled together watching the waves gently rolling to shore. The effects of the champagne made Jennifer giggle. Josh stopped her laughter by covering her mouth with his. After the sun set they made love on the dark, secluded beach while being serenaded by the sound of the crashing waves.

Chapter Thirteen

"Lay not up for yourselves treasures upon earth, where moth
and rust doth corrupt, and where thieves break through and steal:
But lay up for yourselves treasures in heaven, where neither
moth nor rust doth corrupt, and where thieves do not break through
nor steal:
For where your treasure is, there will your heart be also." *(St.
Matthew 6:19-21)*

Jennifer felt amazing, knowing her life was back on the right path.
She focused all her time and energy on starting her school. Harriet called
early Monday morning to give her the address and contact information
for the charter school that had recently closed. Jennifer immediately
called the owner of the building. He was happy to hear she might be
interested in renting the building and agreed to meet her at noon, to tour
the school.

Jennifer made a list of questions to ask the owner and then dressed
for her noon appointment, excited at the prospect of finding a place to
start her school. She prayed the rent would be cheap enough for her to
afford and the space would provide the needed resources for the special
children that would attend. She drove to the school, arriving early. She
anxiously waited for the owner on this warm, sunny summer day. From
the outside, the school didn't look like much. It resembled an office
building with few windows, cream colored metal siding, and padlocked
doors at either end. Just as Jennifer's clothes were starting to stick to her
from sweat, the owner drove up.

She politely extended her hand and introduced herself. "Hi, I am
Jennifer. As I mentioned to you on the phone, I am looking for a space
where I can start a school for handicapped children."

"Nice to meet you, I am Fred Martin. Let's get out of this heat and go
inside."

Fred removed the padlock and opened the double doors to a dark and dreary looking hallway. To Jennifer's surprise it was cool inside. He must be running the AC even though no one is using the building, she thought to herself.

"To our left and right are ten rooms that were used as classrooms."

The classrooms were the same dull, cream color as the interior walls of the building and the floors were tiled in vinyl that had faded from age.

"At the end of the hall, there are separate girl and boy bathrooms and some office space."

She made note that there was a handicap stall in each bathroom, but additional handicap facilities would need to be added.

"Past the offices is a small cafeteria and kitchen. The appliances are fairly new in the kitchen."

"I had hoped the building would come furnished, but I don't see any desks in the classrooms or offices."

"All the furniture was removed at the end of the school year and sold."

"Is there a playground on the premises?"

Mr. Martin showed her to the back of the school where there was a dilapidated playground. The basketball rim had rusted and was falling down, along with a rusted swing set. The wood that made up the jungle gym had rotted and weeds were taking over the whole area. The entire play area would need to be rebuilt and made wheelchair accessible.

It was not in as good condition as she had hoped. On the positive side, the kitchen was not in bad shape. There was a large refrigerator and stove that still worked. Metal tables were available at which the children could sit and eat their meals. The place would need a lot of work to get it ready by fall, but with some volunteers it was possible.

"How much do you want, to lease the property?" she asked as she held her breath waiting for the answer.

"I have a son with Down syndrome, and I have a vested interest in having a school he can attend. I realize it's going to need some work. I will let you rent it for the next two months for free to give you an opportunity to prepare the school to open. After that, the monthly rent will be three thousand dollars a month."

"That is very generous of you, Mr. Martin. I want to make this school somewhere special for the children who will be attending." She held out her hand and vigorously shook his hand. "You have a deal. I look forward to meeting your son."

Once again, God led her to the perfect place. The school location was thirty minutes from her home, but in a central location in the county to hopefully benefit as many children as possible. She could picture classrooms painted in bright colors with wooden tables where the students could work, along with computers for each teacher to aid them in teaching. She wanted to line the walls of the classrooms with bulletin boards, so the children could display their work.

The next day she signed the lease, still not sure how she would come up with three thousand dollars a month for rent. She hoped God would show her the way.

She spent the rest of the afternoon and into the evening creating a web page to spotlight the school and inform the community of the planned opening in August. She provided an email address where parents could contact her with questions, along with a request form for parents to let her know if they were interested in sending their child to the school. This would give her an avenue to respond to questions and concerns from parents. It would also help her plan for how many teachers she would need to hire.

When Josh came home, she gave him a big hug. "I am now the proud lessee of a school. I have your Mom to thank for finding it. It does need some work though." She explained the condition of the building and playground to Josh. "Let me show you the web page I created." She dragged Josh to her computer.

"That looks great! Can I suggest also including a link for accepting donations to raise funds to help offset start up costs?"

"I never thought about that. Do you really think it would be appropriate to ask people for money?"

"From how you just described the condition of the school, I don't see how you will be able to make the needed improvements unless you take out a loan or ask for donations. I know there are many people in this community that would be eager to help."

She kissed Josh. "I hope you are right."

With the web page created, she waited for social media to go to work for her.

After supper, Jennifer organized a plan of where to begin. Before she quit for the night she opened her web page and was amazed at what she saw. She already had received some comments from her post. All were positive. The parents where thrilled to finally have another option for educating their child, other than the normal school system, which didn't provide the attention their child needed. Bullying by other children was another issue mentioned by one parent for why their child had to be removed from the public school. She sat there smiling as she read the comments, realizing how badly this community needed a school like hers.

Now that she had a location, she needed to obtain approval from the local school board to proceed. The monthly school board meeting was scheduled on Wednesday night. She contacted the school superintendent and asked to be added to their agenda. She also submitted her application to start a charter school to the school board to review.

Tuesday she worked all day on her presentation, outlining her vision and business plan along with how her school would greatly benefit the community. She changed her presentation many times before she was satisfied with the wording. She was not comfortable speaking in front of a large group of people she didn't know. Her stomach was already in a knot thinking about it.

The next day she kept herself busy so she wouldn't think about the school board meeting that night. She was a wreck by the time she was ready to leave for the meeting.

Josh tried to reassure her, "Just speak from the heart. Show the passion and determination you have for making the school a success. There is no way they could turn you down."

"My always positive husband, I wish you could go with me, but I know you have a surfing lesson tonight." She leaned over and gave him a loving kiss. "How did I survive without you all these years?" She looked into Josh's eyes and could see the love he had for her. With Josh by her side, she felt like she could do anything.

"I guess you were just lucky to find me again." Josh modestly laughed.

"How do I look? Do I look like I could run a school?"

"You look fine. Quit stalling and go before you are late for the meeting."

She kissed Josh one last time for good luck and rushed out the door for the school board meeting.

She entered a large room packed with people, and found a seat near the front while she waited for her turn to speak. School uniforms were also on the agenda that night. This was a highly emotional topic of whether to allow children the freedom to dress as they liked versus standardizing what they wore by requiring a uniform. The reasons for it were that it would reduce the distractions in the classroom, along with eliminating the gang attire. She hadn't realized gangs in the area had become an increasing problem. After a lengthy discussion, the school board finally voted. The vote was three to wear school uniforms and four against, so the measure didn't pass, due to the concern of the additional cost to parents.

Suddenly, she heard her name being called, and she nervously made her way to the front of the room. She nervously started her presentation. Josh's words kept playing in her head. *Show your passion for the school.* She went through her scripted presentation discussing the financial data, along with the benefits to the community. Looking at the bored faces of the board members she could tell they didn't understand how important this was to her. She had to get their attention. Unplanned, she closed her presentation and told the audience and board members about her daughter, Hope, as her eyes started to fill with tears. She explained, "Hope was a brave girl, and even with her disability, she never lost her desire to learn. She was such a special girl who taught me about living. I wish she could have attended such a school if she had lived." Suddenly she knew the name for her charter school. "I want to name the school Hope Academy to symbolize the hope we all have for our children."

The audience stood up and started to clap. She noticed she was not the only one shedding a few tears. Now tears of joy started flowing at the overwhelming support from the community. After establishing order, the board unanimously voted to approve the school.

With the board's approval, she was ready to start fixing up the school. When she arrived home, she told Josh about how his suggestion of speaking from her heart won the approval she needed. She discussed with Josh everything she needed to be able to open the school.

Josh asked. "How is the fundraising going?"

She hesitated and admitted, "It has started out slower than I had hoped, but after tonight's school board meeting, I am hoping donations will start pouring in."

She looked at the clock, and it was almost midnight. Her adrenaline had worn off from all the excitement. She was exhausted. She noticed the light blinking on the answering machine. "I wonder who called while we were out?" She played the message and immediately recognized the voice. It was from Dillon. "The real estate agent called today with an offer on our home. Call me so we can discuss whether to accept the offer or not."

She decided it was too late to return Dillon's call. She would have to wait until morning to hear how good the offer was. It was difficult to sleep even though she was so tired. She worried about her financial situation and prayed God would help her find the needed resources. She desperately needed the money to be able to open the school on time. She could hardly wait until morning to call Dillon.

She knew Dillon would wake early for work, so she called him at 6AM. The phone rang several times before he picked up.

"Hi, it's Jennifer. Sorry to call you so early, but I was dying to hear the offer you received."

"It's a full offer from a client that wants to close immediately and pay cash. They are moving from California and need a place to live next week when they and their belongings arrive in Orlando. The only contention is they want us to pay half of the closing cost."

She couldn't believe her ears. This was the answer to her prayers. "Of course, accept the offer. This is more than I had dreamed we would get." Dillon and her would split about forty-thousand dollars from the sale. That would give her twenty-thousand to use to fix up the school. "How are you doing?" Jennifer asked.

"My job is keeping me busy, and I am engaged to be married in a month," Dillon nonchalantly threw in.

She didn't know why she was surprised to hear he was getting married again, but it made her hesitate as she remembered their wedding and how much fun they used to have together. "I am so happy for you."

"I have to run. I will let you know as soon as the closing is scheduled."

She hung up the phone, now wide awake and excited, knowing that she would have enough money to finish the school. She woke Josh with kisses and hugs telling him the good news.

After Josh left to open the surf shop, she started a shopping list for the school. She could charge everything, and then once the house closed, use that money to pay off her charge card.

Her first stop was the home improvement store to buy paint and paint supplies. She delivered everything she bought to the school and then realized what a monumental task she had undertaken. She sat there trying to figure out where to start when her cell phone rang. It was Grandma.

"How are you doing, dear?"

Jennifer caught her up on the last couple of days of finding a school and obtaining the approval of the school board. Then she told her, "I have no idea how I am going to get the school ready in time for classes to begin in August. There is just too much work to be done."

"Don't worry. Robert and all of his golf buddies will be more than happy to help you."

Within two hours, Robert was at the school with ten other guys he recruited. They were all retired, but in great physical shape, and tan from enjoying the outdoors in Florida.

They tore out the old vinyl flooring, then washed and patched the holes in the walls to ready them for painting. By the end of the day, everyone was dirty, sweaty, and smelling pretty bad; but the place was ready to be painted in the morning. She thanked everyone for coming.

The next day, amazingly enough, Robert and his team of workers all showed back up to help paint. Everyone was dressed in torn t-shirts, old jeans, and baseball caps to protect them from the paint.

She passed out paint rollers and brushes. They each took a room. Typical of guys, they made it into a competition to see who could paint the fastest and complete their room first. She laughed at the way the men poked fun at each other. She shook her head at them and walked toward the kitchen. She needed to pick up all the tables and scrub the walls before she could start painting. She stacked all the metal tables out in the hall. She put on rubber gloves and got to work finding the wall behind the grime.

By lunch, she had scrubbed her fingers to the bone. She walked out of the kitchen area to find the guys admiring each others work. She looked in the classrooms and was astonished how just a little brightly colored paint could cheer up the rooms, making them look new again. She told the guys, "The rooms look great. Take a break while I pick up some BBQ I ordered us for lunch."

When she returned, the men had set up a couple of metal tables in the hallway, and she passed out plates and food to eleven hungry men. She sat with the men, eating, and listening to the guys talk about sports and playing golf. These men truly enjoyed living. She was very blessed to have their help. God once again was watching over her.

After lunch, they painted the kitchen and cafeteria area. As the sun sunk low in the horizon they finished painting the last wall. They all stood back and admired what they had accomplished with pride.

"I could never have done this by myself and appreciate your help more than you can possibly imagine. Before I let you get away though, do you have any ideas for how I can improve the playground?"

Several men voiced their thoughts on what they wanted to build. They had great ideas from a treehouse with a wheelchair ramp to an obstacle course that the children could use to improve their motor skills.

Robert spoke up, "Don't worry about the playground. We will be back in a couple of days to build a playground the children will love."

She gave them all a hug as they left.

When she arrived home, there was a message on the machine from Dillon. "The house is scheduled to close tomorrow at 10AM at the Estate Title Company in Orlando. Give me a call to confirm you will be there."

She hadn't seen Dillon since he stormed out of the house that night after work. The divorce was handled through their attorneys, so they never had to see or talk to each other. She knew it was going to be awkward facing him tomorrow.

She picked up the phone and returned his call. He answered the phone right away.

"Hi Dillon, this is Jennifer. I got your message, and yes I am available for the closing tomorrow. I will see you there."

After she hung up the phone, she thought about what they had shared together. The memories she had with Dillon were some of the happiest and saddest in her life. Unfortunately, their love couldn't endure the saddest times, which drove them apart. But without it, she would have never made her way back to Josh.

Josh interrupted her thoughts and asked, "Is everything all right?"

"I'm just tired." She gave him a kiss. She shared with him the closing details and then laughed as she described the painting competition between the guys. "The school looks great now that it has been freshly painted. Robert and his friends are eager to help and have also agreed to refurbish the playground for me."

He smiled, "Those guys sound like nothing more than big kids and constructing the playground will be prefect for them."

She lay in bed pleased with the progress that had been made on the school. She knew the most expensive items were still to come, though; new flooring, furniture, and computers. She hadn't received the donations she had hoped from the web site. How was she going to afford everything she needed? As more ideas came into her head, she drifted off to sleep.

Chapter Fourteen

"Trust in the Lord, and do good; so shalt thou dwell in the land, and verily thou shalt be fed." *(Psalm, 37:3)*

Jennifer arrived at the office where the closing was being held a few minutes early. The real estate agent was already present and escorted her to a large conference room with plush seats. She was introduced to the people buying the house, Angelia and Chuck.

She welcomed them to the area and told them, "I hope you will enjoy your new home."

Dillon walked in and their eyes met. She smiled at him as he was being introduced to the buyers.

They sat together at the table and pretended it was not the first time seeing each other since their divorce. The closing started, and just as when they bought the house, they signed their life away once again. There were a couple of pages reflecting the amount which would go to their mortgage company to pay off the existing mortgage and the equity that would be distributed to them. She felt a twinge of sadness once the closing was complete. This was the last thread of her life connecting her to Hope. She reluctantly handed the keys to the new owners and congratulated them. She stood up to leave before she started to cry, and walked to the parking lot.

Dillon sensed how hard this was for her and called out to her before she reached her car. He pulled Jennifer into his arms and gave her a hug.

She hugged him back and told him, "I know how difficult this must also be for you to relive the pain we shared." She wiped the tears from her face and took a deep breath. "Thanks for helping with the mortgage payments, so I could complete college. I'm starting a school for handicapped children like I dreamed. I've named the school Hope Academy, since she was the one that inspired me to start it."

He smiled, and with no anger in his voice said, "I am pleased you didn't listen to me about how crazy I thought your idea was, going back to school. I wish you nothing but happiness, and I am glad you found a way to pick up the pieces and go on with your life."

"I am also happy for you and wish you and your new bride the best."

They said their final good-byes. Jennifer drove away knowing she would never see Dillon again and that another chapter in her life had closed.

Jennifer met Josh for lunch. They celebrated the closing and the fact that she was mortgage free. "What do you think would be the best use of the twenty-thousand dollars I received from the closing?" she asked Josh.

"One of the guys I taught to surf owns a furniture store in Melbourne. He might be willing to give you a discount on office furniture for the school."

"That would be great! How soon could you talk to him?"

"My last lesson is at three o'clock today. I'll call Frank to make sure he is available, and we can go together to the store after work. Once Frank hears your idea for the school, I am sure he will be more than glad to help."

She felt as giddy as a little girl on her birthday, waiting for Josh to arrive home from work so they could go shopping for school furniture together. Josh arrived home just after three, hurriedly changed from his surfing gear to street clothes, and drove them to the furniture store.

They walked in and Jennifer was amazed at the size of the store. It had everything you could imagine to furnish a house or business. She looked around the floor samples for office furniture.

Frank approached them, "I hear you could use some furniture for your new school. Let's go to my office, and I can show you what we have in stock through our catalog."

After Frank asked them to have a seat by his desk, Jennifer explained, "I need to buy multiple pieces of furniture to prepare my school for opening. The school is going to cater to handicapped children in the area. I want to offer an environment where parents will feel comfortable leaving their child, knowing they are in good hands. The school is as much for the parents as for the children. It will give the parents a network of other parents experiencing the same challenges as them. The children will be able to interact with other kids in their age group going through the same difficulties. They will be able to learn from each other."

"It's great what you are doing for the community. Josh explained to me how your funds are limited. I am more than eager to help in any way I can."

Frank showed Jennifer their catalog of office furniture. "I will sell anything you want in the catalog at cost. I would also like to donate one thousand dollars to help the school get started."

"That is so generous of you, and I am so grateful for your help." Jennifer looked through the catalog of office furniture and found wooden tables she thought would work best for the students. She could put two students per table. They were open, which would accommodate wheelchair access. She ordered fifty tables and ten faculty desks. The total came to twenty-one thousand dollars, even with the discount. She made final arrangements to have the furniture delivered to the school in two weeks. She thanked Frank again for his help before leaving, in shock that she had just spent that much.

As Josh drove home, Jennifer started to stress over the lack of funds.

"Have faith that God will show you the way," Josh once again reassured her.

She knew he was right. That night she prayed for God to help her find the funds to complete the school and find the resources needed to install the flooring and computers for the school.

Friday morning she woke well rested, for a change and with a new drive to finish the school. She drove to the school with a cooler full of drinks and sandwiches for the guys who were busy building the playground. She arrived to find Robert and his golf buddies almost finished. She was awestruck at what she saw. It was better than she could have ever imagined. There were monkey bars, some low to the ground so children in wheelchairs could reach them, a slide with a handicap ramp, a fort with wheelchair access, and a new basketball rim that was lowered so the children in wheelchairs could play. They even included park benches so the teachers or parents could watch the children enjoying themselves. It was magnificent. The sidewalk was made from pressure treated wood so the wheelchairs could easily be maneuvered. The landscaping was fantastic. They had created flower beds with brightly color flowers around the perimeter of the playground along with some small trees which made the playground look more like a park.

"You guys did a fabulous job. I can't thank you enough for all you have done. The children will love their new play area."

"We have one more surprise for you," Robert said. "Ralph has a nephew that owns a flooring store in the area. Ralph contacted his nephew last night, and his company is willing to donate all the flooring for the school."

Ralph handed Jennifer the contact information for his nephew. "Order whatever you need, and the store will cover the expense."

Jennifer was speechless as tears came to her eyes. God had answered her prayer. She ran over to Ralph and gave him a big hug as tears ran down her cheeks.

Ralph, fighting back tears himself, told her, "What are you waiting for, go to the store and order the flooring before my nephew changes his mind!"

She wiped the tears from her face and laughed. The store was only about thirty minutes away. When she arrived, a sales associate showed her to the owner's office. His office had just a basic desk and filing cabinet. It was not elaborate like you would imagine a store owner having.

She introduced herself and told him about the school and how much she appreciated his generous donation.

He offered her a chair and explained the different flooring materials available. "I suggest going with a bamboo material. It will hold up against wear, the wheelchairs will be able to maneuver easily, and it's softer than tile. The look will make the classrooms appear as they did fifty years ago with hardwood floors."

"That sounds perfect!" She hesitated before telling him how many square feet of flooring she needed, afraid he might change his mind. When she shared the amount he didn't flinch.

"I will order the bamboo planks today. It should arrive in a week. I have several floor installers that work with me. I already talked to two of them this morning. They are willing to donate their time and services to install the floors."

God really does work in mysterious ways, Jennifer thought to herself as she stood up. "Thank you so much. You have no idea how much this means to me." She shook his hand. "Please come to the grand opening ceremony in August."

"I look forward to visiting the school."

On her drive home, she couldn't wait to tell Josh her prayers had been answered once again. Josh was giving surf lessons until eight o'clock, so she planned a late supper with him.

As soon as she arrived home, she called Grandma to tell her the wonderful news about the school furniture and flooring. "You will have to stop by the school and check out the playground that Robert helped build."

"I am so excited to hear things are going so well."

"I have two last big expenses, refurbishing the bathrooms to make them more handicap accessible and buying the computers."

"Don't worry; I know God will help you find a way."

Jennifer seemed to be hearing that a lot lately. "It seems like forever since I last saw you. Why don't you and Robert come over for supper on Sunday, so we can visit and catch up?"

"That sounds good, but let me check with Robert to make sure he doesn't have plans to play golf."

Jennifer hung up the phone and started looking for plumbers in the area that might help with the bathroom refurbishment. She needed hand rails installed in each stall along with lowering the sinks and drinking fountains, so they could be reached by children in wheelchairs. She found a plumber who would donate his time and make the changes at cost. It still was not going to be cheap, though.

Next, she opened the school web site to start reviewing resumes for teachers. She was surprised to see that there were over fifty resumes posted. There must be a lot of teachers needing work in the area, she thought.

She read through the resumes, focusing on ones that had experience in working with handicapped or slow learner programs. She found ten candidates with experience that really impressed her. While most had worked in a school environment there was one candidate that actually taught a computerized homeschool program for handicapped children.

She started contacting the ten potential candidates to set up times for interviews the following week. Just as she hung up the phone from scheduling the last interview, Josh walked in the door, still damp and smelling of salt from the ocean.

He kissed her then announced, "I'm starved and in desperate need of a shower."

While he showered, she threw together spaghetti and a salad for supper. She enjoyed the time they spent together in the evening. Whatever stresses or concerns that had built up during the day seemed to melt away after she talked to Josh about them. He was always so positive and provided words of encouragement and ideas to help boost her self-confidence.

This evening was like many others. After supper, Josh and her cuddled together on the sofa watching television. She rested her head against Josh's chest, and he wrapped his arms around her neck. Before long, he started caressing her body and kissing her all over. Josh carried her into the bedroom where they made passionate love, then they fell asleep in each others arms.

Chapter Fifteen

"I will lift up the cup of salvation and call on the name of the
Lord." *(Psalm 116:13)*

Jennifer interviewed the ten teachers. They were all quite impressive. She never knew there were so many talented teachers in the area to choose from. She now had the hard part of deciding which five teachers to offer the positions. She might be able to hire more teachers once she determined how many children actually registered for school.

She sat at home reviewing her notes, trying to determine whom to hire. The reason given by most of the candidates for wanting to teach was because they felt they could impact someone's life. Money was never a factor when becoming a teacher, and they knew the rewards came from watching the children learn. Based on the funds she had available, she couldn't offer much in the way of salary and still be able to meet her infrastructure cost. She just hoped the teachers would accept the job offer.

She decided that the school would be treated like a corporation in which the teachers would be part owner. For an incentive, she told the potential teachers they would be included in the daily decision making process. She wanted their feedback on how to improve the school's operation and ideas to improve the children's learning environment.

After much debate, she managed to narrow down the ten candidates to the five most appealing applicants. She called each one and to her surprise, they all accepted the position even with the low salary. She told the new teachers to stop by the school during the next two weeks and personalize their classroom any way they liked.

Pleased with herself at finally having a staff, she drove to a local discount store for school supplies. When she arrived, she asked one of the cashiers, "Could I please speak to the store manager?"

She waited for several minutes before a nice looking lady in a suit appeared. With a pleasant smile she asked, "What can I help you with?"

She explained about the school she was starting and her limited funds dilemma. "Could you possibly offer me any discounts in support of the school?"

"I am sympathetic to your situation and know the school will be an asset to our community. I've a niece who is battling leukemia who could benefit from such a school. I can sell you the school supplies at cost, which includes any computers we sell. I can have a sales associate help you find everything you need."

"Thank you so much. I hope to meet your niece soon. She would be more than welcome at the school whenever she is well enough to attend."

God once again sent her to someone who could help. She practically emptied the shelves of their school supplies. Then, she was shown to the electronics area, where the sales associate demonstrated the many different computers available.

She had wanted to buy a computer for each student to use, but since she was out of money and using her credit card, she found something that might work as well. She was shown a video projection system which could display the computer image onto a pull down screen. That would be perfect for providing more learning material for the students and limit having to use black boards. She ordered six computers and five video projection systems, which the store agreed to deliver to the school in a week.

She waited as the cashier rang up her purchases, trying to figure out how she was going to pay for all of this. The total came to just under twelve thousand dollars. She pulled out three charge cards and charged the maximum amount on each one. That left her about a thousand dollars short and she wrote a check that drained her bank account.

Driving home, she prayed to God to help her find the funds once again to cover the expenses and to help her find the words to explain to Josh what she had just done. She should have asked him before she spent that much money on the school. She didn't want to put his business in jeopardy by using all their funds. How was she ever going to be able to pay off the charge cards?

When she arrived home, she went to the office, turned on the computer, and brought up her latest bank statement to make sure she had enough in the balance to cover the check she just wrote. There was just enough, but she couldn't afford to buy food this week.

As she stressed over what she had just done, she brought up the school donation web sight. When she saw the donation total, she was shocked. Someone had donated fifty-thousand dollars to the school! She couldn't believe what she was seeing. It must be some kind of computer error. She reviewed the school bank account associated with the donation site and the balance reflected just over fifty-thousand dollars. She wiped tears from her eyes, "Thank you God," she said out loud. The donation was made anonymously. Who would have donated that much money to the school? she thought to herself. What had she done to deserve so much from this community?

The door opened, and Josh walked in. She ran to him, wrapped her arms around his neck, and kissed him. "You are not going to believe it, but someone donated fifty-thousand dollars to the school!" She dragged Josh into the office and pointed to the computer screen.

With a bewildered look on his face, he stared at the screen. "Who donated it?"

"A name was not provided. My money woes are over!" she yelled. "I now have enough money to open the school on time. The only thing left to do is finish the bathrooms." She told him about her shopping expedition. "I worried all the way home how I was going to pay for everything I just bought. God came to my rescue once again and answered my prayers."

Chapter Sixteen

"The Lord is my light and my salvation; whom shall I fear? The Lord is the strength of my life; of whom shall I be afraid?" *(Psalm 27:1)*

The school grand opening day finally arrived. The new teachers had decorated their rooms in preparation for the first day of school. The community was invited to the open house to tour the school and see how their donations were used. Jennifer made dozens of cupcakes and chocolate chip cookies to welcome the guests.

As the mayor and school commissioner cut the ribbon across the front door, she said a few words. "I want to thank everyone for coming today and helping to make this day possible. Children are the most important people in our lives. Our goal is to give them the attention and education they deserve. The teachers and I are available if you have any questions. There are refreshments in the cafeteria at the end of the hall."

She opened the double doors to welcome everyone inside. Mr. Martin, the owner of the building, approached her.

"I would like you to meet my son Tristan."

It was obvious to Jennifer that Tristan had Down syndrome. She kneeled down to Tristan's level and held out her hand. "Nice to meet you, Tristan. I think you will really like this school. I hope to see you next week."

Tristan was very shy and hid behind his Dad's leg. "The place looks amazing. I plan to bring Tristan next week and see how he adapts to the new school."

"Great! Let me show you around inside." She walked with Tristan and his Dad into one of classrooms. Tristan eyes lit up when he saw the cardboard figures of the Disney characters hanging from the wall.

"He really likes Winnie the Pooh. He watches the movies and shows over and over again," Mr. Martin shared.

"That is good to know. We will make sure to use the characters in our learning tools."

Jennifer mingled with the visitors, answering many questions. Several parents voiced their pleasure of the effort made to make the classrooms, bathrooms, cafeteria and play area handicap accessible. The staff received nothing but warm welcomes and congratulatory comments from everyone that visited that day. By the end of the day, thirty children had registered to start school in a week.

Upon arriving home, she told Josh, "The day was a huge success. We had over fifty people visit the school today and an additional ten children signed up for classes. All of my hard work is finally paying off."

Josh leaned over and gave her a kiss, "I never doubted it for a minute."

"I am glad you were so confident because I've been having this recurring nightmare that after all this hard work, I arrive the first day of school to find no one but me there."

The next day she met with the teachers to make final preparations for classes to begin in just six days. They strategized on how to divide up the students by their handicap. During registration, she had the parents indicate their child's mental or physical handicap, along with any special needs they required while at school.

Obviously, some students would need more attention than others. They divided up the mentally challenged children into two classrooms with five students each. The teachers felt the students with learning disabilities would have more behavioral issues and need more attention. The students with physical handicaps were divided up by age. There would be seven in two classrooms and six in the remaining classroom. They discussed lesson plans and techniques. Jennifer learned some helpful hints from some of the more seasoned teachers.

Grace, one of the teachers, was also a registered nurse. She agreed to be responsible for making sure medications were administered as directed by the student's doctors. She made a list of each child requiring medicine while at school, the drug name, dosage, and frequency the medicine was to be administered. She created a program on her computer to alert her when shots or pills were required.

The day before the students arrived, the kitchen was stocked with food and drinks. Jennifer's heart was racing as she took one final look in each room to make sure she hadn't missed any details. The next day would be the day she worked so hard for. Jennifer inhaled deeply and slowly released her breath, to calm down after running around all day. She prayed for God to give her the strength and knowledge she needed to handle whatever may arise.

She went home and tried to relax with Josh but lists of things kept going through her head. Did she remember to adjust the thermostat on the air conditioner so it wouldn't be too hot? Did she put wipes in each classroom for the children to use? Did she pack enough water? That night she could hardly sleep a wink. She was so excited and nervous at the same time.

She awoke before daybreak and quietly dressed so as not to wake Josh. She drove to school and unlocked the doors and switched on the lights to all the rooms. She sat in the quiet, admiring everything that had been done to prepare for this day. The classroom walls were lined with bulletin boards waiting to be filled with the student's work. The new desks and computers sat in each room waiting to be turned on. The smell of fresh paint still hung in the air. It would soon be replaced by the scent of children hard at work, with sounds of laughter and chatter.

She greeted the teachers as they arrived. They were just as excited and eager for what the day would bring. The teachers booted up their computers and opened their lesson plans.

Jennifer's class was made up of handicapped students ages five to eight. She planned to start the day off measuring each student's scholastic ability to determine their grade level. She smiled as the first student arrived with her mother.

"Good morning, this is Sarah," her mother said. "Sarah has difficulty walking and speaking, but is very bright."

"Sarah, you are going to be in my classroom. Let me show you to our room." Sarah reminded her a lot of Hope with big brown eyes, brown hair, and a look of determination on her face.

"You are my first student to arrive today. You must be excited to start your first day. Let's find you a table." She made Sarah comfortable and gave her some school supplies to place in the drawer of her table.

Sarah's mother squatted down beside her daughter and looked her in the eyes. "I can stay with you a while if you like."

Sarah shook her head back and forth and pointed toward the door indicating she wanted her mother to leave. Sarah was much braver then her mother, and Jennifer knew how difficult it must be for her mother to leave her little girl.

She took Sarah's mother by the arm and asked, "Would you like a cup of coffee? I made a fresh pot this morning in the cafeteria. We will take good care of Sarah, you don't have to worry."

Sarah's Mom was noticeably emotional, "This is the first day I won't be with Sarah since she was diagnosed with her illness."

"I understand, and if it will make you feel more comfortable, stay in the cafeteria for a little while to make sure Sarah won't need you." She pointed the way down the hall. She knew if it had been Hope's first day of school she would have wanted to stay close also.

As the other students arrived, the classrooms slowly filled up, along with the cafeteria as anxious parents waited to see if their child would be okay without them. As the hours passed, the cafeteria slowly emptied out as the nervous parents listened to laughter coming from the classrooms.

The first day was a major success in Jennifer's mind, with only a few students getting frustrated when they couldn't understand something right away. This was the first time many of the students had been with other children with similar challenges as themselves. She could see the bond the students immediately formed, trying to help each other. When one student would get upset, another student would be there to comfort and encourage them. When she looked in their eyes, she saw the same courage and eagerness to learn that Hope had had.

She drove home that night totally exhausted, but so happy. Josh laughed as she told him, "The parents were more emotional at leaving their child at school than the children were at being left." It sunk in that her dream had become a reality.

Chapter Seventeen

"Then spake Jesus again unto them, saying, I am the light of the world: he that followeth me shall not walk in darkness, but shall have the light of life." *(St. John 8:12)*

Josh and Jennifer settled into a routine. He worked at his surf shop from nine in the morning until around six at night, unless he had a late lesson. She woke early and was at school by seven to start greeting the children by eight. The children were released from school at three in the afternoon, and she stayed until four to help pick up around the classrooms and talk with the other teachers. She listened to how the students were progressing and if they were experiencing any issues.

Watching the children laugh and play made Jennifer yearn to have a child of her own. She was scared of the possibility of having another child born with the same illness as Hope; yet she still wanted to have a large family. She missed having brothers and sisters, being an only child. She wanted to make sure her child had siblings.

She decided on her way home from work to discuss the topic with Josh that night at supper. She arrived home and started cooking. She worried whether Josh was ready to start a family. They hadn't talked about having children since they were married. She didn't know if Josh was just waiting for her to bring up the subject or if he was not ready yet. She worked her stomach into a knot by the time Josh arrived home.

They sat down at the table to eat, and Jennifer tried to find a way to bring up the topic of children without being too blunt.

"You are awful quiet tonight. Did you have a rough day at school today?"

"The kids are wonderful. They are so eager to learn and help each other when one of them is struggling with their lesson." Then Jennifer blurted out, "Have you thought about starting a family of our own? I know we discussed having children when we were both very young. I just wondered if you still wanted to have a large family one day."

Josh had just stuffed a large spoonful of beef casserole in his mouth. She waited for what seemed like forever for Josh to chew his food and speak. He looked her in the eyes and said, "Yes, I still want to have children."

She breathed a sigh of relief.

"I just didn't want you to feel pressured into having children until you were ready. That's why I never broached the subject."

"I am ready." She smiled at her caring considerate husband. She walked over and playfully sat in his lap and asked, "Do you want to start trying to have a family right away?"

Josh gave her his wicked bad boy grin, picked her up and took her to the bedroom. They made love and cuddled in bed until they both fell asleep.

The school year was flying by. She started to worry that her hopes of getting pregnant were not in God's plan. Months had passed since Josh and her started trying to have a baby. Then she realized her period was late. Her period had always been irregular but it had been eight weeks since her last one, and she started to hope that she might be pregnant. She didn't mention the fact to Josh that she was late just in case it was a false alarm. She decided to stop by the pharmacy on the way home from school to buy a pregnancy test. When she arrived home, she nervously opened the box and took out the test strip. She urinated on the strip and waited for the color to change as she paced back in forth in the bathroom.

She stared at the stick and then read the directions again to make sure she had performed the test correctly. The stick indicated "+" which meant she was pregnant. She squealed with delight. Josh would be home in an hour. She busied herself with making supper while she anxiously awaited his arrival.

As soon as Josh walked in the door, he knew something was up.

"Why do you have that funny look on your face?"

"We are going to have a baby!" she yelled.

He ran over and threw his arms around her waist, lifting her in the air. He suddenly realized there was a baby inside her and gently put her down, patting her tummy.

"How do you feel? Do you have any morning sickness? How far along are you?"

"Slow down. I just took the home pregnancy test after work. I will make a doctor's appointment tomorrow to make sure the test was accurate and that the baby is well. I don't want to tell anyone until I am sure the baby is well."

"I understand. I won't say a word, but you know your Grandma. She will know something is up as soon as she lays eyes on you."

"You are right. I will have to avoid Grandma until I know everything is all right."

First thing the next morning, she called her doctor to schedule an appointment. It was her lucky day. There had just been a cancellation, and he could see her right after school.

She arrived a little early and sat in the waiting room with the other expectant mothers. One woman, sitting across from her, appeared as if she might be having twins she was so huge. "When is your due date?" she politely asked.

"I'm still four weeks away, but I can't imagine he will stay inside me that long. I haven't been able to see my feet in two months and can barely stand without help."

Jennifer thought to herself, That is going to be me in seven months. What was I thinking?

Jennifer's name was called, and she was escorted to the examination room. She nervously waited for the doctor, sitting on the cold metal table to be examined.

The doctor ran a quick test and informed her, "You are definitely pregnant. Based on when you had your last period, I would guess the baby is about seven weeks along. I will know better once we do a sonogram during your next visit in thirty days."

She asked, "What are the chances the baby could have muscular dystrophy like Hope?"

"It's a genetic trait, so it's hard to say. The father may have been the genetic carrier for Hope and you may have nothing to worry about. Once the baby is older, I can run a test that will show if the baby carries the gene. For now, you need to concentrate on getting plenty of rest and eating right. I will give you a prescription for pre-natal vitamins. Make another appointment to see me again in thirty days."

She left the office fairly elated, knowing she was definitely pregnant. She talked to Josh during supper. They both were dying to tell their family that she was expecting and decided to share the news cautiously.

Josh called his Mom as soon as they finished eating. "You are going to be a grandmother!"

Jennifer heard a cheer of delight come over the phone as Josh answered her questions. Josh hung up the phone. "She is just a little overjoyed, to say the least, that she is going to be a grandmother. She is already talking about having a baby shower for us."

"Give me the phone. It's my turn." She dialed Grandma's phone number and waited for her to answer. "Hi Grandma, I called to share some good news with you. I am going to have a baby!"

"Robert come here. Jennifer is pregnant," she could hear her say. "We are both thrilled. How are you doing? Is there anything you need?"

She could hear the concern in her voice and knew she feared the same thing she did. What if the baby is born sick like Hope? To calm Grandma's fears, she told her, "I prayed about having another child. The children at school have shown me, whether my baby is healthy or not, having children in my life makes me whole. I know God will be by my side and give me the strength I need."

"I know God will be with you, dear. I just don't want to see you suffer any more than you already have. It seems like ages since I last saw you. Why don't you and Josh come to supper on Saturday?"

"Josh and I would love to. How about we come over around seven?"

"Sounds good, can't wait to see you."

She hung up the phone and suddenly realized she was exhausted. "Now that we've shared our good news, I am beat and need some rest." She got up to walk to the bedroom, then stopped and turned back toward Josh, "Would you prefer a boy or a girl?"

Josh reached for her hand, looking in her eyes. "It doesn't matter to me as long as the baby is healthy, and I can teach him or her how to surf." Then he playfully lifted her off the ground, carried her into the bedroom, and threw her into bed.

"What if they don't want to learn to surf?"

"Of course they will want to surf," Josh replied. In Josh's mind, there was no chance their children wouldn't surf.

On Saturday they arrived at Grandma's for supper. The conversation revolved around the baby. "How are you feeling? Is there anything we can do to help? Have you discussed names yet? Do you want a boy or a girl?" This went on and on. "I want to buy a crib for the baby."

"I'm planning to go shopping next weekend to start looking for baby items for the nursery and to register in some of the department stores for gifts. Would you like to come with me?" she asked Grandma.

"Yes, I would love to! It has been so long since I shopped for baby items. You can show me the crib you want."

Josh and Jennifer laughed all the way home at how excited Grandma was about the baby.

The next few weeks were a blur between school and starting to prepare for the baby. Her sixteen week appointment with the doctor had arrived. Josh didn't want to miss seeing the sonogram and left work early so he could go with her.

The doctor lifted her shirt and squeezed cold jelly on her stomach. He rubbed the sonogram paddle around her abdomen. She could faintly hear the baby's heartbeat.

"Everything looks to be progressing normally. The baby is about eighteen weeks along. How are you feeling? Are you experiencing any morning sickness or bleeding?"

"I feel great. I tire more easily and have been sleeping a little more, which I know is to be expected."

"Would you like to know the sex of the baby?"

Josh and her both eagerly said, "Yes!" in unison.

"Congratulations, you are going to have a boy."

Josh yelled, "YES!" It was obvious that was what he wanted. She just wanted the baby to be healthy.

"Your due date should be around June sixth."

"Great, that will be during summer break from school, so I won't miss teaching any classes."

"Make an appointment to come back in four weeks."

Josh and her talked about decorating the nursery all the way home now that they knew the sex. Josh wanted a surfing theme, painting the walls blue and placing a mural of the ocean on one wall.

So, over the next several weeks they worked on the nursery and bought everything they would need for the baby.

The next four months passed quickly as her stomach expanded. The last week of school had quickly arrived and the children were so excited. She planned a special graduation for each child to show their parents what they had accomplished during the year. Each child had a bulletin board displaying their successes. The children wanted to impress their parents and posted everything from artwork to math tests on their bulletin boards. The parents were invited to attend the last day of school.

She never saw thirty children more proud of themselves. They joyfully took their parents to the bulletin board, eagerly showing them everything they had accomplished.

She called each student's name and handed them a piece of paper showing what grade they had completed.

The students had brought gifts for their teacher. Some with tears streaming down their face, hugged their teacher and said good-bye for the summer. The parents had nothing but praise for the faculty for all they had done for their child.

The teachers were as ready for a break as the children. She met with the teachers before everyone left for the summer to discuss improvements that could be made to prepare for next year.

Along with some software upgrades, it was suggested to obtain cameras for the computers. This way class could be taught virtually to any student unable to physically be present in class due to their illness. She agreed that that was an excellent idea and planned to buy what was needed over the summer and have it installed.

All of the teachers had become very close and planned to keep in touch with each other over the summer. Everyone told her to call as soon as she gave birth.

She went around to all the classrooms to make sure the computers and lights were turned off. She stopped and looked down the hall before closing and locking the doors for the summer. She thought to herself, "I managed to survive my first year of teaching." What a magnificent feeling!

She was as excited as the students that school was out for the summer. When she arrived home, she announced to Josh, "I am free!" The baby started kicking inside her. "I think our son is also happy." She took Josh's hand and placed it on her tummy, so he could feel the baby kick. Josh leaned down and kissed her belly. She had just four more weeks until her due date.

Chapter Eighteen

"In him was life; and the life was the light of men." *(St. John 1:4)*

As her due date approached, she grew more and more uncomfortable in the Florida heat. She sat under the air conditioner vent trying to stay cool. Josh teased her for keeping the house so cold. "It feels like the arctic in here," he complained. "I am going to have to take out a loan to pay our electric bill this month."

"If you could just convince our son that it's time to come out, I wouldn't be so hot." That night she was so uncomfortable she couldn't sleep. She got out of bed at 2AM for the fifth time to go to the bathroom, when her water broke.

"Josh wake up, the baby is coming!" he yelled. She changed her clothes and gathered her bag she had prepared for the hospital.

Josh jumped out of bed, fully awake now, and threw on his clothes. He was so excited he ran out the house barefoot.

"Don't you think you should put on some shoes?" She pointed at his feet. "It took me nearly twenty-four hours to deliver Hope, so I am sure we have plenty of time. You don't need to hurry."

Josh managed to find his shoes and loaded her and her suitcase into his truck. They arrived at the hospital at 3AM.

Once admitted, the doctor examined her. "The baby is currently breeched. Sometimes the baby will turn themselves around without any help. I will continue to monitor you, but if the baby does not turn on its own, it will be safer and easier on you to have a c-section."

The doctor left the room and Josh grabbed her hand. "I feel so helpless. Tell me what I can do to make you more comfortable."

"Just stay with me and pray that the baby will be healthy."

After six hours, the contractions had gotten much worse. The doctor examined her, "You are now dilated 6 cm. The baby still has not turned. I am going to have the nurses start prepping you for a c-section."

Grandma, Robert, and Harriet anxiously waited for news outside the maternity ward, so Josh left Jennifer's side just long enough to give them a status report.

The nurse administered an epidural, and she was now numb from the chest down. She was awake but could no longer feel the severe contractions. The doctor placed a curtain below her neck, so she couldn't see him make the incision to remove the baby. She held onto Josh's hand for dear life as the doctor started the procedure.

Within no time, the baby was removed from her womb. "Josh would you like to cut the umbilical cord?" the doctor asked.

Josh looked around the curtain and saw their son for the first time. He took the scissors from the doctor's hand and cut the cord. Then Jennifer heard their son cry for the first time, as tears streamed down her face.

The doctor handed the baby off to a nurse where he was placed on a table to be examined and cleaned. The crying baby was gently wrapped in a small blanket then handed to Josh.

Josh tried to comfort their son by talking to him. "It's all right my handsome boy. I will protect you." As soon as the baby heard Josh's voice, he stopped crying. Josh leaned down to show Jennifer the baby while the doctor finished taking care of her.

"He is perfect."

Josh handed the baby to her, and she held their son in awe, looking at the true miracle in her arms. Tears of joy ran down her face.

"What is his name?" the doctor asked.

"Jonathan Anthony, named after my father and grandfather," Jennifer said.

Jonathan weighed eight pounds and two ounces, over a pound more than Hope. She had faith that God was watching over her and that Jonathan was healthy and disease free.

She had to stay an extra day in the hospital due to having a c-section. The nurses let her hold Jonathan often to breast feed him. Josh went home to get some rest and to make sure the Surf Shop was running smoothly without him.

As she breast fed Jonathan, she looked into his big blue eyes. They were the same sky blue eyes that Josh had. He didn't have much hair but what little he had appeared to be blond. He had the cutest fat cheeks with dimples. His little fingers strongly gripped her thumb while he ate.

Grandma stayed with her until Josh returned just in case she needed anything. "Can I hold my great-grandson for a little while?"

"He just had a big meal, so he will probably sleep for a while." She handed Jonathan to her.

"It has been such a long time since I held your Mom when she was a baby. I forgot how small babies are." Jonathan made a gurgling noise in response to Grandma's voice. "What are you trying to say there big boy? Are you ready to go back to your Mama?"

Grandma handed Jonathan back to Jennifer. He slept in her arms until the nurse returned to take him back to the nursery.

"Get some rest. I will quietly read until Josh returns."

The next day she was released from the hospital with her little bundle of joy. She was still very sore, and the doctor told her no heavy lifting for a while. Once home, Josh waited on her hand and foot to give her a chance to heal and rest.

Within two weeks, she was much stronger and had much less pain. She watched over Jonathan, taking every precaution to make sure he was safe. She moved Jonathan's crib into the master bedroom, so she could listen for him at night. She wanted to make sure nothing happened to him.

Jonathan quickly developed a routine of crying every four hours to be fed. After the first month, Jonathan let her sleep almost six hours straight before he woke to be fed. He was a happy boy and rarely cried other than to eat.

Time was quickly approaching for her to return to school. Jonathan now weighed fifteen pounds and was becoming a chubby baby with cute rolls of baby fat. It just made him cuddlier. He was also becoming much more active, moving his arms and legs and smiling all the time.

There was much she needed to do to prepare for the new school year. She had to find a day care to take care of Jonathan during the day while she worked, which she was dreading. She also needed to buy the cameras for the teacher's computers and install them so class could be taught virtually when needed.

When Josh arrived home from work she asked, "Can you watch Jonathan while I shop for school supplies?"

Josh leaned over Jonathan's crib and lifted him into his arms. "It will be nice to have some male bonding time with my son. Take your time. We will be fine."

When she left, Josh was blowing on Jonathan's stomach making him laugh.

She returned to the department store that was so helpful last year, and once again, they offered her a discount. She was able to purchase everything she needed to start the school year.

When she arrived home, she found Jonathan bathed and sound asleep in Josh's arms in the recliner. She smiled to herself and realized how blessed she was to be married to such a wonderful man; he was such a good father.

She leaned over and kissed Josh. "Was Jonathan any trouble?"

"Jonathan fell fast asleep after our play time. Did you find everything you needed for school?"

She showed Josh the cameras she had purchased for the computers. "It will be great having the capability to teach the children who are not physically able to attend class in person this year. Now all I need to find is a day care facility to take care of Jonathan while I am at work. I am a little concerned at the thought of leaving Jonathan with total strangers, though."

"You know there are several very good day care facilities in the area. Why don't you visit some tomorrow to determine which one you like the most?"

"I guess you are right. I will try to keep an open mind and check on several tomorrow."

The next morning she made a list of day care centers to visit. She opened the door to leave and ran into Grandma, who had stopped by to see her great-grandson.

"How are you two doing?" she asked as she held out her arms to hold Jonathan. "He has gotten so heavy."

"Jonathan never misses a meal," she joked with Grandma. "Are you familiar with any day care centers in the area?" she probed.

"Are you sure you want to leave Jonathan with a total stranger? Something could happen to him."

"I share your concern, but what other choice do I have?"

"Well, you could let me take care of him."

"You would be willing to do that for me?"

"Of course, I would love spending time with Jonathan. At his age, all he does is eat and sleep. I am sure he would be no trouble at all."

"I would only need you for about seven hours a day. Josh's surf shop doesn't open until ten, so he can watch Jonathan until 9:30. School gets out at 3:00, so I can hurry and be home no later than 4:00. It would be wonderful if you could watch him. It would save me from having to worry about him all day long."

"Like I said, I would love getting to spoil my great-grandson."

"Thank you so much! This weekend I will go over his schedule with you and let you know where to find everything you will need."

When Josh got home, she shared the good news with him. He agreed he had no problem taking care of Jonathan between seven, when she left for school, and nine thirty when Grandma would arrive.

With that taken care of, she just had a few more days to finish planning the school year. There were an additional ten students registered to start this year. She met with the teachers, and they discussed which class the new students should be placed. Everyone agreed they could absorb the increase in students without having to hire another teacher.

On the first day of class, Jennifer had a difficult time saying good-bye to Jonathan. She went back over everything Jonathan would need and had prepared for Grandma. "Bottles, diapers, wipes, formula..."

"You are going to be late for work. I am sure your Grandma can handle whatever may arise," Josh said as he pushed her out the door.

She quickly forgot about Jonathan when all the children started to arrive. There were a few tears, but most were excited to return and get the year started. The original thirty knew what to expect and helped the new students adjust. She was amazed at the love the kids had for each other. There was no bullying or intimidation like in the county schools. Everyone was accepted with whatever handicap or mental capacity they had.

At the end of each school day, she rushed home to find Jonathan either sleeping or playing with Grandma. She worried about Grandma overdoing it, but Grandma assured her she was fine.

The days finally started to cool off as Thanksgiving and Christmas arrived. Since this was Jonathan's first Christmas, he was showered with toys from all of his family. Josh and her invited Grandma, Robert, and Harriet over to watch Jonathan open his presents. Jonathan was more interested in the wrapping paper than the presents, since he was only seven months old.

After the presents were opened, Jennifer laughed as she watched Josh and Robert sitting on the floor playing with Jonathan's train set he had received for Christmas.

Jonathan was now crawling and getting into as much trouble as possible. She had to keep a watchful eye on him. Josh and her had child proofed the house, making sure all the cabinets had child proof locks on them; but that didn't stop Jonathan from trying to get into trouble.

The Christmas break was over too soon, and it was time for her to return to work. The school year was going well. She was contacted by two parents after Christmas break. Their child's condition had worsened and they couldn't return to school.

She instructed the parents on how to log onto the classes virtually, so if their child felt well enough, they could watch the lessons for the day. The students could hear their teacher and view the material being covered from the comfort of their own home. This way if the students' condition improved, they could return to class and not be too far behind the others in their grade.

Unfortunately, one student was terminally ill, and she was not going to be able to return to class. She knew how hard it must be for her parents to watch as their child's condition worsened.

Jennifer received the phone call she dreaded from Sarah's father. "Sarah went to be with God last night."

This was particularly hard on her. Sarah was the bright-eyed, cheerful, determined girl that was the first student to arrive the day school opened. She was so smart, such a fighter, strong, and confident. Even though she had difficulty talking and struggled in class, she was eager to participate and play with the other students. She never complained and never missed a day of school until a few weeks ago.

"Sarah was a very special girl and will be greatly missed," she expressed to Sarah's father. "I was so blessed to have her in my life for the last year and a half. I know how difficult this time is for you and the pain you must be going through. She will always be in your heart, and I know in time God will lead you to find happiness again in your life as he did mine."

This was the most difficult day she had since starting the school. She told the other teachers after school. Tears and hugs were shared along with their happy memories of Sarah.

This was the hardest part of being a teacher for special needs children. Letting these precious gifts from God touch their lives and hearts knowing one day they may not return to school. It's gratifying though, to think they made a small difference in their lives for however long they lived.

All the teachers attended Sarah's funeral on Saturday. They watched as the small, white casket was placed in the ground. Memories of Hope entered her mind, but instead of being sad, she was happy knowing that Sarah was with Hope in heaven.

Spring quickly arrived in Florida, and they were all ready for spring break. She was looking forward to spending the week with Josh and Jonathan, relaxing on the beach and playing in the sand.

When she arrived home, she heard Jonathan crying, which was unusual. She quickly opened the front door and raced into the house. Jonathan was standing in his playpen crying. She reached down and picked him up to comfort him and found his diaper was wet. She looked around and noticed Grandma sitting in the recliner. She appeared to be sleeping. Jennifer leaned down to touch her. Grandma was cold to the touch. She checked for a pulse and couldn't find one. Jennifer collapsed on the sofa and started to cry along with Jonathan. After several minutes, she composed herself and called Josh. Through her tears she said, "You need to come home. Grandma has passed away." She hung up the phone and started to sob.

Josh worked only ten minutes away and arrived in less than five. He ran into the house and took control of everything. He called for an ambulance and arranged for her transport. He took Jonathan from Jennifer, put on a clean diaper, and fed him a bottle to stop him from crying. Then he made the hardest phone call to Robert, Grandma's husband.

Robert arrived as Grandma was being loaded into the ambulance. "Can I see her before you take her away?" A tear ran down his cheek. He kissed her good-bye. "I love you. Thanks for the time we had together."

Then, the door closed on the ambulance, and Grandma's body was taken away.

Jennifer walked up to Robert and gave him a hug as they consoled each other. He asked, "What happened?"

"She appeared to be peacefully sleeping on the recliner when I arrived home. She must have had a stroke or heart attack."

The next week was a blur of activity helping Robert plan the funeral. Many friends stopped by to give their condolences, along with the minister of their church.

It didn't sink in that Grandma was gone until Jennifer saw the coffin placed in the ground next to Grandpa's grave site. Everyone had left after the service, and she sat there staring at the ground where Grandma was laid to rest. She told Josh, "I just need a few minutes alone with her. Will you take Jonathan home? I'll catch up with you shortly."

She had no tears left as she sat there in a daze. "You helped me find happiness again during the darkest times in my life after Mom and Dad died, and then again after Hope passed away. You have no idea how much you mean to me. You showed me how to live again and find purpose from all the pain. I'll miss you so much."

Josh and Jonathan were the only family she had left now. She thanked God for the time she had with Grandma and asked for his strength and guidance.

Chapter Nineteen

"Though I walk in the midst of trouble, thou wilt revive me: thou shalt stretch forth thine hand against the wrath of mine enemies, and thy right hand shall save me." *(Psalm 138:7)*

Grandma provided Jennifer with some much needed financial support in her will. Jennifer placed a good chunk of the money in a college fund for Jonathan and the remainder in her savings account to be used for school emergencies. Grandma left her condo to Robert which only made sense. She had introduced Robert to so many of her friends in the condo complex. He would need those friends now to get over his loss.

Josh was very supportive in the weeks following Grandma's death. He helped Jennifer around the house and with Jonathan. Jonathan was the best medicine she had, though. He was such a happy baby it was hard to be sad for very long.

God was there for Jennifer again. Their church had just started a day care program at the first of the year, so she had somewhere safe to take Jonathan after spring break. There were seven volunteers that watched about twenty children. The cost was much cheaper than other day care centers in the area. There were two other boys about Jonathan's age, so he would have someone to play with. The first day Jonathan was to be left in the hands of the day care workers was harder on Jennifer than Jonathan. Thanks goodness Josh dropped Jonathan off on his way to work, so she wouldn't have to leave him.

At ten thirty, she called Josh. "How was Jonathan when you left him? Was he crying?"

"Jonathan immediately saw the other children and toys. He crawled over to play with them. He didn't even see me leave, he was having so much fun."

She smiled at the thought of Jonathan playing with the other children but anxiously waited for the day to end, so she could pick him up.

When she arrived at the church after work, several other mothers were picking up their children. She found Jonathan sound asleep in a crib. "Was Jonathan any trouble today?"

"He was a joy. He didn't cry all day until he started getting tired this afternoon. I rocked him, and he fell fast asleep."

She gently picked up Jonathan from the crib, carried him to the car, and placed him in his car seat as he continued to sleep all the way home. He slept soundly until Josh came in the door and announced he was home.

At the sound of Josh's voice, Jonathan woke up. Josh reached down and picked up Jonathan and started talking to him as if he could understand every word he said.

"Were you a good boy at day care today? Did you like Miss Teresa who took care of you? I bet you had fun playing with the other boys."

Josh chatted on as if expecting Jonathan to answer his many questions at any time.

"Could you place Jonathan in his highchair, so he can eat?" Jennifer asked.

Josh leaned over and gave her a kiss.

"How was your day?" Jennifer asked as she fed Jonathan.

"I am excited about a new surfboard design. I ordered some, and they are due to arrive tomorrow. It's made of new lighter, but stronger, material that is supposed to make it easier to surf. I'm hoping the waves will be good this weekend, so I can try one out."

"Jonathan and I can join you and make it a family day at the beach."

After dinner, she gave Jonathan a bath. Then, Josh read Jonathan a bedtime story as he fell fast asleep.

Josh joined her on the sofa. They were both beat. She laid her head on Josh's stomach as they watched television. She was lying there thinking how happy she was and how much Jonathan enjoyed his day care. She started teasing Josh by tickling his stomach like he does Jonathan's.

"You know you can't win this battle." Josh picked her up and threw her to the floor wrestling her, so she couldn't tickle him anymore. Josh pinned her to the floor and started kissing her all over. Before long, they moved to the bedroom and made passionate love.

As they lay in each other's arms, she told Josh, "I was thinking about having another baby before Grandma passed away. I know we are both busy and Jonathan is a handful, but I would like to give Jonathan a brother or sister before he's too old. I still want a large family, and I am not getting any younger. What do you think about making another baby with me?"

Josh answered by kissing her and making love to her again.

The next two months went by quickly and by the end of the school year, she was pregnant again. Her due date was in March the following year, around spring break. She needed to figure out how she would continue to operate the school after the baby was born.

She was so glad for summer break. It meant she could spend all day with Jonathan. He was turning one next week, and she was planning a big birthday celebration.

Jonathan just started to walk and could say a few words such as mama, dada and bye-bye. He was a normal, energetic boy, curious about everything.

She made Jonathan a chocolate birthday cake, and Harriet came to supper to celebrate with them. She laughed as she watched Jonathan eat his cake. There was more birthday cake on Jonathan's face than in his mouth. Harriet couldn't believe it had already been a year since Jonathan was born. She marveled at how much he had grown and how quickly he was learning new things.

Jennifer planned on spending the many beautiful, sunny, summer days with Jonathan on the beach watching Josh teach surfing lessons. Jonathan loved playing in the sand and wading in the surf. Every shell Jonathan found was a treasure he had to show her. Normally, by the time they left the beach, they were both covered in sand from head to toe.

It was the middle of summer now, which meant hurricane season in Florida. Ever since Jennifer rode out the hurricane in her apartment in Orlando, she always tensed as hurricane season approached. She religiously watched the weather report each day to make sure no hurricanes had formed and the ones that did were no threat to them.

In August, the weather stations started reporting on a storm which had formed out in the Atlantic. It was still several days away, so she cautiously watched the weather each day to make sure it was not heading in their direction. This particular storm had grown into a monster with winds measuring one hundred forty mile per hour. It was headed toward the Bahamas, but to her relief, the weatherman predicted it would turn north before it hit Florida.

Josh was just the opposite of Jennifer. He lived for hurricanes and the waves they would bring. He eagerly watched the storms to determine when the waves would reach their peak. Hurricane season meant bigger waves to surf.

The swell was supposed to start increasing the next day as the hurricane turned north. Josh had already coordinated the schedule at work to allow the other two employees time to surf as well.

The next morning Josh arose from bed early. "I'm headed to the beach to check the surf conditions. Why don't you join me after Jonathan wakes up?"

"Be careful. There is supposed to be strong rip currents with the increase in wave height. I will join you in about an hour."

When Jonathan woke, she told him. "Daddy is surfing this morning. Do you want to go to the beach and watch?"

As if he understood her, he started repeating the word, "Surf." She fed him breakfast, put on his swim trunks, lathered them both in sunscreen, and grabbed a chair and some blankets.

They walked down the sidewalk to the beach and then onto the boardwalk over the dunes. She came to a sudden stop. The waves were enormous. The surf was roaring with fury as the gigantic waves crashed against the shore. They pounded the beach one after another, taking sand as they retreated back into the ocean. The sound was deafening as the waves came barreling ashore and it reminded her of the roar of a large waterfall.

She anxiously looked out over the ocean, searching for Josh. After several minutes, she finally spotted him on his board waiting for the next large wave. As the swell approached, Josh started paddling hard to reach the crest of the wave. He jumped up on his board as the wave crashed behind him. Josh squatted down to lower his center of gravity to keep from being washed off his board. He flew down the face of the wave like a race car rounding the curve at a racetrack. All of a sudden, Josh's board came out from under him. Josh disappeared into the murky water. She watched for Josh to reappear after the wave passed over him, but all she saw was his empty board. Frantic, she dropped everything she was carrying, picked up Jonathan, and ran down to the edge of the surf. She yelled for help. Several surfers approached, and she pointed to where Josh had disappeared. They paddled out quickly, searching, and diving underneath the water to try to find Josh. After what seemed like an eternity, one of the surfers emerged, pulling Josh onto his surfboard. He paddled to shore, and Jennifer ran down the beach toward him.

Several people helped lift Josh onto the beach. He was not breathing. A guy raced up and said, "I'm an EMT." After checking for a pulse, he started mouth to mouth resuscitation and CPR.

Jennifer knelt down beside Josh, grabbed his hand, and yelled, "Josh stay with me, breathe!" Someone must have called 911 because an ambulance pulled up to the beach, and they started working on Josh, trying to bring him back to life.

After what seemed like forever, but in reality was only about five minutes, they finally felt a pulse. Josh was placed on a stretcher and rushed to the waiting ambulance. The ambulance door slammed shut and with sirens blaring, headed to the hospital.

She stood there dazed and trying to get her head around what she had just witnessed. Josh couldn't die. Jonathan started to cry, which brought her back to the present.

With Jonathan hugging her tightly she ran back to the house, grabbed her purse and car keys, strapped Jonathan in his car seat, and drove as fast as she could to Cape Canaveral Hospital.

She rushed into the emergency room. "My husband was just brought in by ambulance. Do you know where they have taken him?"

"The doctors are with him now. Take a seat and a doctor will be with you shortly."

The nurse's words kept going through her head. Josh was not dead if they were still working on him. She couldn't sit. She started to pace with Jonathan in her arms, just to be doing something. She prayed to God, "Do not let Josh die."

Finally, a doctor appeared and asked for her. "Josh has regained consciousness and is breathing on his own. His pulse is still a little weak but is getting stronger."

She breathed a sigh of relief and thanked God under her breath.

"I want to perform a CAT scan to make sure Josh doesn't have a concussion. I also want to examine Josh's lungs to make sure they are clear. If you follow me you can visit with him for a few minutes."

She followed the doctor to the exam room. She walked in and rushed to Josh's side. She reached for his hand as tears of joy ran down her face.

Josh had an oxygen mask over his face. He lifted it off and smiled up at Jonathan and her. He tried to sit up, but she pushed him back down. "You need to stay down and rest. Your body has gone through a traumatic event."

He joked, "Don't worry. You are always telling me what a hard head I have. I am sure I will be fine."

"This is not funny! You almost died." She wiped the tears from her face. "If the EMT hadn't been at the beach to perform CPR, you may not be here talking to me now." She leaned over to kiss Josh and grabbed her stomach as a sharp pain hit her.

"Are you all right?"

Before she could answer, Josh yelled for the doctor. "My wife is pregnant and experiencing abdominal pain! Can you make sure she is all right?"

The doctor motioned for her to sit down in a chair by the wall while a nurse left to get a wheelchair.

She tried to reassure Josh. "It's nothing. I probably just strained a muscle lifting Jonathan."

He was not convinced. A nurse arrived with the wheelchair.

"Sit and let the nurse take you to your doctor to make sure everything is all right."

The nurse took Jonathan from her arms and held him while she sat in the wheelchair. She was pushed to OB/GYN office located in the same building as the hospital.

The doctor took her right away. His nurse held Jonathan while the doctor examined Jennifer.

The doctor felt around her stomach and listened to the baby's heart beat. "Describe the pain to me."

"It was just a sharp pain in the lower part of my belly." She pointed to the area. "It seems to have gone away now, though."

"Let's take a look at the baby just to make sure the fetus is not in any distress." He placed the sonogram paddles on her stomach. The doctor spoke to her calmly. "Now try to relax."

"I arrived at the emergency room with my husband just a little while ago. He almost died in a surfing accident. That is when the pain started."

"The baby appears to be fine, but I want you to stay in bed for a couple of days. Take it easy and do not lift anything heavy. Is there someone who can take care of Jonathan for you until Josh is released from the hospital?"

Thoughts of Grandma entered her mind. She wished she was here with her now. "Yes, Jonathan's grandmother can watch him for me."

A nurse wheeled her back to where Josh was being examined. As soon as she entered the room, Josh sat up and asked. "What did the doctor say? Is the baby in any danger?"

She explained, "The baby is fine. The pain has stopped. I was instructed to stay in bed for a couple of days just as a precaution. Do you think your Mom would mind watching Jonathan for me?" It suddenly dawned on her. "I forgot to call your Mom to let her know you are in the hospital."

A nurse entered the room to take Josh for additional testing.

"I am sure Mom would love to watch Jonathan for a few days," Josh said before he was wheeled out of the room.

Jennifer called Harriet from her cellphone. She was understandably upset, to say the least, after she learned what had happened to her son and was eager to help in any way she could. Harriet arrived at the hospital within an hour. She lifted Jonathan into her arms and gave him a big kiss on his chubby cheek.

"How would you like to spend a couple of days with Nana?" Without waiting for an answer she asked, "How is Josh doing?"

"I'm still waiting for him to return from having some tests run to make sure he doesn't have a concussion and that his lungs are clear. Hopefully he will be back soon."

A nurse appeared and notified them that Josh had completed his test. He had been moved to a hospital room for the night. She gave them the room number. They found the room on the second floor and quietly opened the door so as not to disturb him. Josh was sitting up in bed trying to find a comfortable position.

"How do you feel?" Harriet asked.

"Other than a killer headache, I am fine. The doctor is supposed to stop by shortly to share the results of my test."

"I was always worried something like this would happen with you surfing. I just figured it would be a shark bite though," his Mom scolded him.

"It was just a freak accident, Mom. You don't have anything to worry about."

The doctor appeared at the door. "The CAT scan shows Josh has a mild concussion from where the surfboard hit him on the head. I want to keep him overnight for observation to make sure there are no complications. I am also starting him on antibiotics to prevent him from developing an infection in his lungs due to the sea water he inhaled.

Other than a headache and sore ribs from the chest compressions, he should be as good as new in a couple of days."

Jennifer thanked the doctor as he left the room.

Harriet leaned over and kissed her son on the cheek. She brushed his hair from his forehead like when he was a child.

"Thanks for helping out while I am in the hospital, Mom."

"I was hoping to get to spend more time with my grandson, but I wish it was under better circumstances." She tickled Jonathan, cradled in her arms, and listened to him giggle. "I am thrilled to be able to help."

"Is there anything I can get you?" she asked Josh.

"I'm very sleepy. The doctor must have given me something to help with the pain. I am having a difficult time staying awake."

"The sleepiness is probably from the concussion. You should probably not fall asleep just yet," she said.

Jonathan started to fuss, and Jennifer told Harriet, "It's way past Jonathan's meal time. Can you take him home, feed him, and change his diaper while I stay here with Josh?"

"Yes, then I will lay him down for a nap. Don't worry."

"I want to stay with Josh at the hospital tonight if you can handle Jonathan on your own."

Josh started to protest, "You heard the doctor's orders. You need to go home and get some rest."

"I won't be able to rest at home as long as you are in the hospital. I would just be worrying about you and how you are doing."

"You stay as long as you need. I will make sure Jonathan has everything he needs. I will come back later this evening with Jonathan to check on how you are doing," Harriet said.

Jennifer was still in her beach attire and asked, "Can you bring Josh and me some clean clothes when you come back?"

Harriet left with Jonathan, and Jennifer crawled in bed with Josh. She laid on her side and Josh wrapped his arms around her stomach.

"Are you sure the pain has stopped?"

She placed her hands on top of Josh's, laying across her stomach and told him, "I am fine as long as we are together."

A nurse brought a fold-out bed for Jennifer to sleep in. As evening approached Harriet returned with some clean clothes for them. Jennifer changed out of her beach wear and into jeans and a loose fitting blouse. The day's events had taken their toll, and Jennifer was exhausted. She laid on the fold-out bed, which was placed next to Josh's bed. She fell fast asleep, holding Josh's hand.

She awoke to the sound of the doctor talking to Josh. He was shining a light in Josh's eyes to check his responsiveness. Then, he put the stethoscope to Josh's chest and listened to his heart, "Breathe deeply," he said.

Josh coughed as he breathed in. The doctor listened some more and then told Josh, "You seem to be doing well, but I want you to rest for at least another week before returning to work. I will get the paperwork started to release you today."

After the doctor left, Josh asked, "How did you sleep? Have you experienced any more pain?"

"I slept surprising well. I am feeling much better."

Josh laughed. "You are the only person I know that can actually sleep in a hospital."

"Being pregnant makes me more tired, so I can sleep just about anywhere. My body needs to rest while it can because after the baby is born there will be no time for sleep."

Jennifer called home to check on Jonathan. Harriet answered the phone right away. "We are having a blast together playing in the living room."

"The doctor examined Josh this morning. He is doing good. The doctor plans to release him after lunch."

"That is great! Do you need me to bring anything to the hospital?"

"No, just kiss Jonathan for me and tell him how much I miss him." She hung up and shared Jonathan's status with Josh. This was the first time they had been separated from him over night since he was born.

Josh's whole body ached, but other than that he was feeling fine. He changed into his street clothes and anxiously waited to be released. Jennifer retrieved her van and met Josh sitting in a wheel chair at the entrance to the hospital.

When they arrived home Jonathan ran into Josh's arms and he lifted him into the air, forgetting about his injured ribs. A sharp pain pierced his chest. He quickly put Jonathan down, holding his ribs, becoming dizzy. Jennifer took Josh by the hand and led him to the chair. "Sit down and take it easy. You heard the doctor. He said not to overdo it."

She walked over to Jonathan and kissed him on the forehead. "Daddy will play with you later. Right now he needs to rest. Did you have a good time with Nana?"

Jonathan proceeded to chatter on in his own language, telling her how much fun he had with Nana. Harriet stayed another night to help with Jonathan so Jennifer and Josh could rest.

By the next morning, they both felt stronger. Josh called the surf shop, "How are the new surfboards selling?" she heard him ask. She could tell by his smile they were selling well.

After breakfast, she thanked Harriet for all her help and invited her to supper later in the week, so she could spend some more time with Jonathan.

A week later, Josh was back to normal, but he was still concerned about Jennifer and the baby. He accompanied Jennifer to the doctor's office to make sure everything was fine. He held Jonathan as the doctor examined her and the baby.

As the doctor performed the sonogram, Jennifer could tell by the look on Josh's face that he was nervous.

Josh asked the doctor, "Is the baby all right?"

The doctor pointed to the screen and said, "The baby appears to be developing on schedule." He directed them to the baby's fingers and toes. "There is another part of the anatomy that you might be interested in," and pointed to the penis.

Josh smiled and asked, "We are having another boy?"

"You most certainly are," the doctor responded.

Josh grabbed Jennifer's hand and squeezed it to let her know how excited he was.

"You should continue to get as much rest as you can, and let me know if you experience any more pain," the doctor instructed Jennifer.

On the drive home, she told Josh, "I am thrilled we are having another boy. Jonathan will have a little brother to grow up and play with." It couldn't be more perfect. She thanked God for watching over them and for protecting her unborn baby and husband.

Chapter Twenty

"When thou passest through the waters, I will be with thee; and through the rivers, they shall not overflow thee: when thou walkest through the fire, thou shalt not be burned; neither shall the flame kindle upon thee." *(Isaiah 43:2)*

The summer was over before Jennifer knew it. She hired another teacher at Hope Academy to assist in teaching her class and to take it over when she left on maternity leave in March. Until then, the new teacher would help reduce her load by helping to teach her class. She was a little nervous about this pregnancy after having the premature pains when Josh was in the hospital. She didn't want to risk losing the baby.

The school's third year was starting, and she looked forward to seeing the children again. Their strength and endurance always inspired her. She met with the teachers prior to the student's arrival to prepare for the next school year. The lesson plans were loaded into the computers along with the activities planned for the children during the year. She was confident they were ready to face the challenges of another year, or so she thought.

She arrived early the first day of school, as always, to open the school and make sure everything was ready for the students. She immediately knew something was wrong when she noticed the lock on the door had been cut off. She had a bad feeling as she walked into the school. She looked into the classrooms and found all of the computers had been stolen.

She went to her office to call the police as the other teachers started to arrive. While she waited for the police to arrive, she met with the teachers to discuss how they were going to operate without computers to aid them. Jennifer was lucky there was a hard copy of the children's medical needs for the day. The teachers agreed they could mange teaching the old fashioned ways with a black board, pencils, and paper until Jennifer could replace the computers that were stolen, or they were returned.

The children started arriving with their parents, and Jennifer put on a brave face as she explained the situation to the parents. She watched as the children paraded down the hall. Some struggled to walk, but they were all smiles the first day of school. Many of the children were returning from last year and were familiar with their routine.

The teachers made a game out of using pencils and paper. One teacher joked, "We are going to demonstrate how your parents were taught at school. You will see how challenging school was for them. Also, how teaching and learning has changed."

Stephanie, the new teacher she hired, took her class while she talked to the police.

"In many cases like this, the criminals transport the computers to another state. They are sold before we have a chance to find them. I do not have much hope that the computers will be returned, but hopefully we will catch the culprit before they vandalize someone else. You might want to install a better security system to help deter whoever broke in from breaking in again."

"Thanks for your help, officer."

After the police left, she contacted a locksmith to fix the lock on the door. Then, she called her insurance company to determine if her coverage would pay to replace the computers. Unfortunately, she had a ten thousand dollar deductible to reduce her premium. The cost to replace the computers would be about ten thousand dollars, so she would be responsible for the replacement cost. She didn't want to have to dig into her emergency fund, created from the money Grandma had willed her, to buy the new computers. She prayed for guidance from God to show her what she should do to solve this problem.

The locksmith arrived to fix the broken lock on the door. As he worked on the door, she told him about being robbed and asked, "Do you happen to know the name of a good security company in the area?"

"As a matter of fact, my cousin owns a security company locally. I am sure he would be more than happy to inspect your building and suggest a security system for you." He wrote down the name and number of his cousin and handed her the slip of paper.

As soon as the locksmith left, she called the number and explained the situation. It was a small company. The owner agreed to stop by after lunch to discuss options for installing a security system for the school.

When he arrived, she was surprised to see how young he was. The man looked to be about ten years younger than her, in his twenties. She introduced herself and asked, "Would you like to tour the school first?"

"That would be a good place to start."

As she showed him around the school, he explained, "The company has been in business for over thirty years. We provide many options for protecting homes and businesses." He pointed toward the doors and windows. "These areas are where you are the most vulnerable and I would recommend installing an alarm system and cameras."

"I am looking for something affordable."

"I happen to have a security system in stock that we are no longer using, that I could install at cost. The only reason it's no longer being used is the camera clarity is not as clear as the newer models. Since we upgraded our equipment, no one has bought the older model, so I need to move it out of my inventory."

"That sounds perfect, but how much money are we talking about?"

"I will install it for free and only charge you the cost of the equipment which is nine hundred fifty dollars, plus tax. That cost includes two cameras, one placed at each door, and the alarm system."

"That sounds great! When can you have it in place?"

"If you like, I can come back at the end of the school day. That way I don't disrupt any of the classes in session."

"That would be perfect; I will see you around three."

As promised, he arrived as the last student was leaving, and installed the system within a couple of hours. With new locks on the doors and a security system in place, Jennifer felt a little safer when she left for the evening. The teachers did an outstanding job improvising without computers and using what they had available to them. But she knew they couldn't operate without computers for very long.

She picked Jonathan up from day care and her mood immediately improved. He was talking a mile a minute telling her everything he had done and about a new friend he met. She made Jonathan a snack to hold him over until she could fix supper. Josh would be home in about an hour, so she changed into some comfortable clothes and made ravioli, Jonathan's favorite.

When Josh came home, she told him about the burglary.

"I am more concerned about your well-being and safety than I am on how you are going to replace all those computers." He placed his hand on her tummy and asked, "How is our son doing?"

"We are definitely going to have a football player with as much kicking that is going on!"

Josh smiled as he felt a thump against her stomach.

Jennifer went to bed early but didn't sleep much, as she tossed and turned, worried about the thief of the computers and replacing them. She never considered anyone would want to steal from the school. She realized she should have notified the school board about what happened to see if they had any funds set aside to replace the computers.

She arrived at school the next morning and looked up to see the camera still in place and the door not tampered with. She opened the door and everything was as she had left it the day before. When the teachers arrived, she asked for their patience in finding a solution to their problem.

After helping the students to their classrooms, she called the county school superintendent to ask for his advice.

He reiterated what she already knew, "School funding was cut this year, and there are no additional funds available to allocate to you."

"Thanks for you help anyway. I guess I will have to use my emergency fund to replace the stolen computers if they are returned."

She prayed silently asking God to help the authorities find her computers when the phone rang. It was the police officer she had talked to yesterday.

"I've been checking all the pawn shops in the area hoping someone may have tried to sell your computers. One of the pawn shop owners notified me last night that someone stopped by and asked if they bought used computers. This person had several computers he needed to sell. The pawn shop gave me the name of the man that had inquired about selling the computers. An officer stopped by the man's residence this morning and found a living room full of computers."

She couldn't believe what she was hearing. It was too good to be true.

"Can you come down to the station today to verify whether the computers found were the ones taken from your school?"

"Yes, I will stop by during lunch." She hung up the phone, elated that her computer problems may be fixed. She yelled with joy, "Thank you God!"

When she arrived at the police station, she found they were indeed her computers.

"Once we finish processing the stolen goods, I can have someone load them into the police van and deliver them back to the school. We also have a computer wiz who can help set them back up for you if you like," the police officer offered.

"Thanks you so much for your help. You have no idea how much I appreciate your effort in finding the computers."

She couldn't wait for Josh to get home to share the good news with him. When he walked in the door, she was so excited she threw her arms around his neck and gave him a big kiss.

"What did I do to deserve that?"

"My prayers have been answered once again. The school's computers have been recovered. I am amazed that every time I find myself in need, the good people in this community always come to my aid."

Josh reminded her. "Striving to help our fellow neighbor and putting others first before our own desires is what the holy spirit wishes of us." Josh kissed her on the nose and quickly changed the subject. "What's for supper? I am starved!"

Josh was right. God had always put people in her life who put her needs before their own. She would just have to continue to pay forward for all the good deeds she had received.

Chapter Twenty-One

"Man's goings are of the Lord; how can a man then understand his own way?" *(Proverbs 20:24)*

This pregnancy seemed to be wearing on Jennifer, as she was tired all the time. She was also starting to have shortness of breath at times when she overworked herself. She was still eight weeks from her due date and didn't know how she would physically be able to work until she gave birth. She discussed this with her doctor during her monthly checkup.

He ran some test and told her, "Your blood sugar and blood pressure are high. I am ordering you to bed until your due date."

Stephanie, the new teacher she hired, had been helping her teach class all year. She gave Stephanie a call and asked, "Can you take over my class full time for me immediately? My doctor has ordered me off my feet and in bed until I deliver."

"No problem, I am sure the students will miss seeing you, but don't worry. I am very comfortable teaching your class. The students and I get along well."

She thanked Stephanie and then called the other teachers to let them know her predicament. She told them, "Call me if you need anything. I will work from home as needed."

They were all very supportive and understanding. They told her to relax and not to worry about the school. They assured her they could handle whatever arose for a couple of months without her.

Josh treated Jennifer like an invalid and wouldn't let her out of bed for any reason other than bathroom breaks. After lying around for one week, she was going stir crazy watching TV all day long while Josh was at work and Jonathan was at day care. She felt so guilty making Josh take care of everything on his own. How was she ever going to do this for seven more weeks?

After three weeks, she started to feel pain in her stomach again. She frantically called Josh, and he immediately took her to the doctor. Her blood pressure was still elevated. The doctor was concerned for her and the baby. He admitted Jennifer into the hospital so he could monitor her until her blood pressure could be reduced.

Josh called his Mom. She took care of Jonathan, so Josh could spend the night at the hospital with Jennifer.

The next morning she was not feeling any better. She was still experiencing sharp pains and feared for her baby's life.

The doctor arrived and examined her and the baby. With a concerned look on his face he said, "I am going to schedule a c-section for you today. Your blood pressure is still too high and the baby's heart beat is elevated, which indicates he is also under stress."

As they prepared her for the surgery, Josh held Jennifer's hand and told her, "I will stay by your side during the surgery." Josh prayed with her, "God please watch over Jennifer and the baby during the procedure. Guide the doctor's hands during delivery to keep my son and wife safe and healthy." Josh leaned down and kissed Jennifer. "Don't worry, everything will be okay," Josh tried to reassure her.

She was moved into the operating room. Medicine was administered to numb her from the chest down as they had done before when Jonathan was born. This time, though, she was having a difficult time staying awake. The doctor started the operation and she could hear Josh talking to her, "Stay with me Jennifer," as he held her hand. Then, everything went dark.

The heart beat monitor made a shrill noise as it flat lined. Josh yelled, "Do something!"

The operating room was suddenly filled with commotion. Josh was escorted out of the room as he called out to Jennifer. Josh collapsed in the hall by the door with his head in his hands.

Jennifer heard a soft voice calling out to her and she strained to hear the words being said. "Your work is not done. You must go back." Go back where? She tried to open her eyes but they were so heavy. She was so tired and just wanted to sleep.

Jennifer heard her name being called. She slowly opened her eyes and tried to focus. The room was so bright and she squinted in pain.

Josh held Jennifer's hand. Her normal tan skin was very pale and ice cold. He placed both of his hands around hers to warm them. "Jennifer, I am here," Josh said softly as he rubbed her hands.

"Everything is going to be all right. You gave birth to a healthy baby boy."

When Jennifer heard the word baby she suddenly remembered. She was delivering her baby. She tried to talk. "Baby, where?"

"Take it easy. You had a difficult delivery. The baby is in the nursery with the other newborns. He is a little smaller than Jonathan was when he was born. He weighs just six pounds but is in perfect health." Josh kissed her hand.

She whispered, "Can I see Jesse?" That was the name they had chosen for their son.

"You have been through a lot and need to rest."

"What happened?"

"You started to hemorrhage during the c-section, which caused your blood pressure to plummet and you to lose consciousness. The doctor managed to control the bleeding and gave you a pint of blood. Jesse was not affected by your condition. He was given a thorough exam and was transported to the nursery. He is just perfect. He has all his toes, fingers, and your brown eyes." Josh smiled down at Jennifer.

"When can I see him?"

"If it will make you rest, I will ask the nurse to bring Jesse to you for just a little while."

Josh left the room and returned a few minutes later with the nurse holding Jesse in her arms. Jennifer's eyes were closed, so Josh sat quietly in the chair and the nurse handed him his son. Josh stared in awe at the baby sleeping in his arms. He looked over to Jennifer and watched as her chest rose up and down. She was sleeping soundly. Josh whispered under his breath, "Thank you God for not taking Jennifer. We still need her."

Jesse yawed in Josh's arm. Josh peered into his son's deep brown eyes and smiled.

Jesse started to cry, and Jennifer opened her eyes. Josh laid Jesse gently in Jennifer's arms.

"Hush my little boy. Mommy is here." A tear ran down her face at the sight of her son.

"You are such a beautiful boy." She cradled Jesse, and he stopped crying. She kissed his forehead and told him, "I love you."

"It's time for you to rest." Josh reached down and picked up Jesse. Jesse started to cry again after being removed from his mother's warm clutch. Josh started to rock Jesse in his arms. "It's all right. Don't cry." At the sound of Josh's voice, he stopped crying.

Reluctantly, Josh handed Jesse to the nurse.

"Close your eyes and I will be here when you wake up."

"I am fine," Jennifer tried to protest.

"How is your pain level?" the nurse asked.

"I am a little sore and I have a headache."

"This should help you rest." The nurse administered some medicine to help ease her pain.

She quickly drifted off to sleep.

"She will probably sleep for a while, if you want to get something to eat," the nurse told Josh.

"Thanks, I want to stay with her a little longer to make sure she is comfortable."

Josh watched as Jennifer slept soundly and realized how lucky he was. With all the excitement he forgot to call his Mom to give her the good news that she had another grandson. He stepped out in the hall so as not to disturb Jennifer.

"Hi Mom. I'm sorry I didn't call sooner." Josh explained what had occurred the last few hours.

"I am just relieved Jennifer and the baby are all right. I was worried something had gone wrong, since I hadn't heard from you. Jonathan is fine. I will plan on keeping him until Jennifer is well enough to come home."

It was getting dark. Josh checked in on Jennifer before leaving the hospital to go home, shower, and get something to eat. He was exhausted but didn't want to leave Jennifer alone for very long.

When Josh returned, the doctor was in the room with Jennifer. Josh held Jennifer's hand and stayed by her side as the doctor explained what happened.

"Your blood pressure has returned to normal. You should be able to go home in a day or two."

"Can you tell me what caused me to hemorrhage during delivery?"

The doctor explained, "You have a condition that some women experience during delivery where your blood does not clot normally, so during your c-section, you started to bleed uncontrollably. I immediately administered a blood clotting agent to help stop the bleeding, but due to the large amount of blood lost, you had to be given an additional pint of blood. You are a very lucky girl. This condition has resulted in death for many women."

Jennifer hesitated and then asked the doctor, "Will I be able to have any more children?"

"I would advise against getting pregnant again, due to the nature of your condition. You may not be so lucky next time."

The doctor left the room, and Josh tried to comfort Jennifer. "God has given us two healthy beautiful boys. We don't need any more children."

"I know, I just thought…" She ended her sentence in mid stream. "I'm just tired. Why don't you go home and get some rest while I sleep?" Jennifer closed her eyes and pretended to sleep, so Josh would leave.

Josh had no intention of leaving Jennifer alone. He kissed Jennifer and told her quietly, "I love you."

A tear ran down Jennifer's face as she struggled to comprehend the fact that she couldn't have any more children. She turned away from Josh so he wouldn't see her crying. She eventually drifted off to sleep.

Josh made himself comfortable in a chair in the corner of the room. He finally fell asleep listening to Jennifer's rhythmic breathing.

Jennifer and Josh were woken in the middle of the night when a nurse came in to check on her. Josh looked at his watch; it was 3AM. He had a crick in his neck and was stiff from sleeping in the chair. He got up to stretch as the nurse checked Jennifer's vital signs.

The nurse asked, "How are you feeling?"

Jennifer looked at Josh and smiled. "I am doing fine."

"Just press the button by your bed if your pain level gets too bad."

The nurse walked out of the room and Jennifer asked Josh, "What are you doing here? You should be at home in bed."

"I didn't want to leave you alone in case you needed something during the night." He leaned over and kissed her gently on the lips. "How are you really feeling? You gave me quite a scare. I thought I lost you."

"Now you know how I felt when you disappeared in the ocean after your surfboard hit you over the head. I will be fine. I just need a few days to get my strength back. Now go home and get some rest, so you can help take care of Jesse when I get home."

Josh smiled and said, "You must be feeling better, since you are bossing me around again."

Jennifer slapped his hand and then kissed it. She suddenly became very serious, "Josh, I think I died. I remember not being able to hold my eyes open. They were so heavy. I closed my eyes and started drifting away from my body. I could hear you calling my name as I was being pulled toward a bright light. It was so peaceful. Then, I heard a voice telling me I had to return. The next thing I remember is waking up here."

"Your heart stopped beating, and I frantically called your name while I was being escorted out of the operating room. I sat in the hall praying for God to save you. He answered my prayers."

Chapter Twenty-Two

"My son, keep thy father's commandment, and forsake not the law of thy mother." *(Proverbs 6:20)*

Jennifer took the rest of the school year off to recover from her ordeal and spend time with her new baby boy. She was not prepared for how much work one more child added to her day. At first, Jonathan was jealous of Jesse and wanted her undivided attention every time she fed Jesse. Over time though, he started to understand his role as a big brother and helped take care of and watch over his little brother.

Over the summer, Jonathan turned two years old and his vocabulary was increasing every day. His new word this week was "fish" as they watched the dolphins playing in the surf one day while they were at the beach.

She hoped during the summer to reduce her diaper changing load by potty training Jonathan. It was not as easy as she thought it would be. Jonathan knew when he had to go, but couldn't quite figure out how to hold it until they reached the commode. The laundry duty increased, having to clean multiple pairs of underpants for Jonathan each day. She started taking Jonathan to the bathroom every couple of hours in an effort to get him to use the commode. Her logic didn't prevail at first, but Jonathan was slowly starting to learn. By the end of the summer, her effort had paid off. Jonathan was potty trained.

The first day of school arrived, and it was time for her to resume teaching. Josh agreed to take Jesse to day care for the first time, along with Jonathan. Jesse was not as cooperative as Jonathan and started screaming as soon as Josh handed him over to the day care worker. Jonathan walked over to his little brother. He held his small hand and told him, "I am here with you. You will like it here."

The day care worker placed Jesse on the floor with Jonathan, and he stopped crying. Josh quietly snuck out while Jesse was busy watching Jonathan play.

Josh and Jennifer fell back into their routine, and the weeks quickly passed. Before they knew it, the holidays were upon them. This was Jesse's first Christmas.

Christmas was always a special time for their family. She bought the boys a toy from Santa Claus each Christmas, along with a few other small gifts. She didn't want to spoil the boys too much so she refrained from spending a lot. Christmas was a time to spend together as a family. Josh enjoyed competing in the Surfing Santa Contest every year. He dressed in a Santa hat, fake beard, and wore a red outfit over his wetsuit. Then he rode the waves with the other Santas. The boys and Jennifer would cheer Josh on. It was always a day filled with plenty of laughs.

They would also attend the Christmas boat parade. They had a secret pristine viewing spot along the Banana River. About an hour before the boats left the marina, they would drive down to the river, place their beach chairs along the shoreline and enjoy a picnic feast while they waited for the boats. Once dark, the boats started parading by with mast and decks ablaze with Christmas lights and Christmas music blaring.

Every Christmas Eve, they attended evening church service. Following the service, Jennifer begged Josh to take them around the neighborhood, so they could view the Christmas lights. As the boys grew older, they would try to convince Jennifer they didn't want to go by saying, "Oh Mom do we have to? We want to get home so we can watch TV." She always believed, though, that they enjoyed it as much as she did, and would ignore their complaints.

New Year's Eve was spent celebrating on the beach. They watched the fireworks as they were launched from a platform anchored right offshore. The boys covered their ears as the fireworks exploded above them with a loud boom. Their eyes lit up as the many colors flashed through the sky.

The years were passing by too quickly. The boys had grown up to be just like their father. Both boys loved to surf, kayak, and anything to do with water. Jesse was on the swim team and Jonathan was on the row team. They were both fiercely competitive, always trying to one up the other to see who was the best.

Jonathan was now sixteen and Jesse was fifteen years old. These were the years Jennifer feared the most. Jonathan had just received his driver's license and Jesse had his learner's permit. She now realized how terrified her parents must have been when she had started driving. The fact that she lost both of her parents in a car accident didn't help. Any time the boys drove anywhere without her, she made them call her as soon as they arrived at their destination. Thanks goodness for cell phones.

Jonathan had just started dating Taylor, a sixteen year old girl he met at his high school. She was very pretty, a tall brunette, with big brown eyes, who seemed to make Jonathan very happy. Josh and Jennifer always instilled in their boys how women were to be treated. Jennifer never had to worry about their behavior.

It was a Saturday night, and Jonathan was taking Taylor to the movies. It was winter time, so the tourists and snowbirds clogged the roads no matter what time of day or night you were out.

Jonathan had been gone about thirty minutes when Jennifer turned on the television. The program being broadcast was interrupted with a news alert. "The Merritt Island Causeway is shut down due to a car crash which has blocked all lanes. We have a news crew en route and will provide more details as soon as they become available." She could hear the sirens from the emergency vehicles on A1A heading to the crash sight.

She immediately tried to reach Jonathan on his cell phone. It rang and rang, then went to voicemail. Frustrated at not being able to reach Jonathan, she called Josh, who was still at the surf shop. "Did you hear about the crash on the causeway? I tried calling Jonathan's cell phone, but he is not answering."

"I am sure Jonathan is fine. He has probably already arrived at the movie theatre and has turned his cell phone to silent so as not to bother the other patrons," he rationalized. "I will be home in about an hour."

She could tell Josh was busy with a customer and didn't have time to deal with her possibly unwarranted concern. She was not convinced, though, that Jonathan was not in trouble. She had a bad feeling. Consider it mother's intuition, but she had to make sure Jonathan was not involved in the accident. She drove toward the causeway, trying to get close enough to the wreck to determine if Jonathan's truck was involved. She took the back roads to avoid the traffic, but when she arrived at the causeway, traffic was at a standstill. She decided to park her car at a restaurant located on the Banana River and run the mile or so to where the wreck was located. She arrived at the crash scene out of breath. It was now dark and the emergency vehicle lights blinded her, so she couldn't see the vehicles involved in the crash. She finally flagged down an officer and asked, "Was there a black truck involved in the accident? I am just trying to make sure my son was not involved."

Her worst nightmare came to life as the officer said, "There was a black truck with two teenagers inside, a boy and girl. They have been transported to Cape Canaveral Hospital. You can check with the hospital to determine if your son was one of them."

The hospital was only about a half mile away. She ran as fast as she could to the emergency room. Breathless once again, she entered the emergency room and gave the woman behind the desk her name. "Can you tell me if my son, Jonathan, just arrived by ambulance from the car accident down the road?"

The nurse checked her computer and motioned for her to follow. Jennifer entered the exam room and found Jonathan lying on the table. A doctor was examining him. She rushed to Jonathan's side.

Before she could ask Jonathan how he was, he said, "I'm fine Mom, but I am not sure about Taylor. Can you find her for me?"

The doctor explained, "Jonathan has a broken leg, but I want to run more test just to make sure he does not have any internal injuries and does not have a concussion."

"Mom, please just find Taylor for me, and let me know how she is doing."

"Thanks for taking care of my son. Do you know where I can find Taylor?" Jennifer asked the doctor.

"She was taken to x-ray." The doctor motioned for her to leave Jonathan's room as he followed her out of the room.

"Taylor may have a spinal cord injury. She was unable to feel anything from the neck down and had to be put on a respirator. She is still being evaluated to determine the extent of her injuries."

"Have Taylor's parents been contacted?"

"You can speak to the nurse at the front desk." The doctor returned to Jonathan's room to finish his exam.

Jennifer walked back to the emergency room nurse's station feeling better knowing Jonathan was not severely injured, but was now very concerned about Taylor. The nurse was busy with another patient that had just arrived. She sat down and waited until the nurse was free, then stepped up to the counter. She explained once again who she was and asked, "Do you know if Taylor's parents have been contacted?"

"I am not sure. A police officer was going to contact them." The nurse went back to pecking away on the computer keyboard.

156

Jennifer thought to herself, If it had been the other way around, she would want to know as soon as possible if her child had been injured. She decided to call Taylor's parents just to make sure they had been notified. She tried to calm herself, breathing in and out deeply, as she dialed their phone number. As she waited for Taylor's parents to answer the phone, flashbacks of the police officer standing at Elaine's front door to notify Jennifer of her parents death popped into her head. Taylor's Mom suddenly answered the phone, and Jennifer was brought back to the present. "Hi, this is Jennifer, Jonathan's Mom. I wanted to make sure you were aware that Jonathan and Taylor were in a car accident tonight."

"Are they all right?" Taylor's Mom frantically asked.

"They are currently being examined to determine the extent of their injuries at the hospital. I am in the emergency room now waiting to hear how they are doing." Jennifer didn't have the heart to tell them that Taylor may be paralyzed.

"We are on our way." Taylor's Mom said as she hung up.

Next, Jennifer called Josh to explain what little she knew.

Josh was shocked at the news and indicated he would leave immediately to pick up Jesse from his friend's house and meet her at the hospital.

It had been fifteen years since Jennifer was last in this hospital giving birth to Jesse. Memories of almost dying came back to her and the words she thought she had dreamed, *"Your work is not done."* She walked to the hospital chapel and started to pray. She asked God, "Please be with Jonathan and Taylor. Help them heal from their injuries. Give them the strength to get through this ordeal." She felt more at peace knowing God was by her side to guide her and give her the strength she needed to face whatever lay ahead. She returned to the emergency room area and sat waiting for news on Jonathan's test results.

Taylor's parents rushed through the door. "Hi, I'm Jennifer. I wish we were meeting under better circumstances. I think Taylor is still being examined."

"Do you know how bad Taylor's injuries are and what happened?"

She hesitated and then repeated what the doctor had shared with her, "Taylor's spinal cord may have been injured and they are running tests now to determine the extent of her injuries."

"Do you know where we can find her?"

"The nurse should be able to tell you where Taylor is." She pointed to the front desk.

Jennifer worried that Taylor's parents may blame Jonathan for their daughter's injuries. She was not sure who caused the accident but knew it couldn't have been Jonathan's fault. He was a very careful driver knowing how much she worried about his safety when driving. A doctor approached Taylor's parents and motioned for them to follow him. Jennifer felt so bad for them and hoped the news was better than the initial exam indicated.

Josh and Jesse came rushing through the door next. "How is Jonathan doing?"

"I'm still waiting for his doctor to return and provide the results of the test. All I know for sure is that Jonathan has a broken leg."

Josh pulled Jennifer to him, hugging her. "I apologize for not taking you more serious earlier when you called about the accident. Why don't you sit down. I'll get you some coffee and something to eat while we wait for more news."

"No, I couldn't possibly eat anything."

Josh reached for her hand and held it while they waited together. At last, Jonathan's doctor entered the waiting area.

"Other than a broken leg and some bruised ribs there appears to be no additional injuries. If you would like to stay with Jonathan while his leg is being placed in a cast, I can show you to his room."

They followed the doctor down the hall and joined Jonathan.

"Hey buddy. How are you holding up?" Josh asked.

"I don't feel any pain."

The doctor explained, "Jonathan was given some pain medicine to help reduce his discomfort from the break."

"Mom, did you find Taylor? Do you know how she is doing?"

She took Jonathan's hand and looked him in the eyes. "Taylor's spinal cord may have been injured. The doctors are still running tests."

Jonathan released her hand and angrily put his hands to his head. "No, it just can't be. We were just going to the movies. This can't be happening!"

"Do you remember what happened?" she asked.

"I was driving on the causeway headed toward the mall, talking to Taylor, when all of a sudden this car appeared in front of me coming from the opposite direction. It had crossed over the center line. Before I had time to react, it hit us head on. I remember being slammed in the face when the airbags deployed. I was a little disoriented. Once I came to my senses, I realized we had crashed. I looked over at Taylor and she was slumped over in her seat. I called her name, but she didn't respond. I was pinned under the steering wheel and couldn't reach her. Then, there were people yelling at me as they tried to open the truck door to get me out. I may have blacked out from the pain. That is all I remember until I got to the hospital."

"I am so glad a broken leg is all you have. It could have been so much worse. As soon as the doctors are finished with you, we will find Taylor."

It took another hour before Jonathan was able to leave. He was given strict orders to rest and elevate his leg to reduce the swelling. He was provided crutches and placed in a wheelchair. It was now past ten o'clock. They went to the front desk to ask about Taylor.

The receptionist informed them that visiting hours were over. Since they were not Taylor's immediate family, she couldn't give them any additional information on Taylor's condition, other than the fact that she was stable.

Jonathan was visibly upset and asked, "What time do visiting hours begin?"

"At nine."

By the time they arrived home, the pain medicine Jonathan was given at the hospital had worn off and his leg was throbbing. Jennifer gave him another pain pill and Josh helped Jonathan get into bed.

Jennifer checked in on Jonathan to make sure he didn't need anything before she went to bed. He was still awake so Jennifer sat with him for a while. "Don't worry, there is nothing more you can do tonight but pray. God will watch over Taylor and help her make a full recovery. Now get some rest, and you can see her in the morning." She pulled the covers up and tucked Jonathan into bed like she used to when he was a child. The pain pill was quickly taking affect. Jonathan tried to act like he was all grown up and was embarrassed when she fussed over him. She watched as Jonathan fell asleep. He would always be her baby no matter how old he was.

Jennifer climbed into bed, and even though she was exhausted, couldn't sleep. "Josh, are you still awake?" she quietly whispered.

Josh rolled over and put his arms around her. "What's troubling you?"

"Do you think God is testing my faith? I don't know what I would have done if we lost Jonathan tonight. I know I can't live my life in fear, but after losing my parents and Hope, it's hard not to think the worst could happen."

"The worst has already happened to you and you survived. You must know by now that God is by your side making sure you stay on your chosen path. Now get some rest."

She woke Sunday morning feeling less anxious and ready to face another day. Jonathan was still sleeping when she left to attend the early service at church. She needed some time with God to thank him for protecting Jonathan and to pray for Taylor to make a full recovery. Josh stayed at home with Jonathan in case he needed anything.

Jennifer arrived home at nine thirty to find Jonathan awake and trying to walk, using his crutches.

"It's about time, Mom. Dad didn't want to go to the hospital without you," Jonathan impatiently said.

"Well, I am here now, so we can go. Jesse, do you want to stay at home or go with us to the hospital?"

"I will wait here."

They stopped at the front desk of the hospital and were given Taylor's room number. Upon arriving at Taylor's door, Jennifer knocked quietly in case Taylor was trying to sleep. Taylor's Mom opened the door and motioned for them to enter.

Jennifer could tell Taylor's Mom had been awake all night, but smiled when she saw them. "Taylor has been asking about Jonathan and will be glad to see you."

Jonathan hobbled over to Taylor's bedside using his crutches to support him. He immediately noticed she was wearing a back brace. Leaning on his crutches, he reached for her hand. Jonathan smiled when he felt Taylor's fingers move.

Taylor's Mom explained, "Taylor's back is just fractured. The doctor examined Taylor this morning. She is starting to regain some movement now that the swelling is going down. The respirator was removed a few hours ago. Her throat is sore, but she can talk."

With a horse voice Taylor whispered, "I was so worried about you. How bad is your leg?"

"I have to wear this cast for about ten weeks, but the doctor said I should be able to return to the rowing team by spring."

Jennifer asked Taylor's Mom, "Would you like to have a cup of coffee with us so Taylor and Jonathan can spend some time alone?"

She understood her intentions and smiled at Taylor. "I will be right back honey."

Over coffee, Jennifer explained to Taylor's Mom what Jonathan had remembered about the crash.

Taylor's Mom told them, "I don't blame Jonathan. Taylor told me what happened. There was no way for Jonathan to avoid the car that hit them. I am grateful that their injuries were not worse. I know it may take several months for Taylor to fully recover, but I realize the alternative could have been much worse."

They returned to Taylor's room and had to pry Jonathan away so Taylor could rest. Jonathan returned frequently over the next four days to keep Taylor company. When Taylor was released from the hospital she was able to walk on her own, but would have to wear the back brace for another twelve weeks to give her back a chance to heal. Taylor returned to school after recovering at home for two weeks.

The accident seemed to bring Taylor and Jonathan closer together. They talked every day in person or on the phone. Their relationship continued to grow, and Jennifer became concerned about what would happen when they graduated from high school. She didn't want Jonathan to go through what Josh and her did when she left for college. She feared the same thing might happen to them. The only difference was Taylor and Jonathan both planned to attend college, unlike Josh and her.

Jonathan wanted to study engineering like her and had applied at several colleges in Florida. He was hoping to receive a rowing athletic scholarship. After Jonathan's broken leg healed, he worked even harder to prove that he was fit to compete. His high school rowing team had come in first place the last two years, and he hoped that might improve his chances for an athletic scholarship.

Jonathan received several acceptance letters and one offered him a full athletic rowing scholarship. Josh and Jennifer were thrilled when Jonathan told them about the scholarship opportunity. Jonathan, on the other hand, didn't seem so excited.

"The college that is offering me the scholarship is in Gainesville, Florida. Taylor is planning to attend school in Orlando. Her parents want her to attend a college closer to home."

"I know this decision will be difficult for you. Dad and I will stand by whatever college you decide to attend. We have a college fund for you, so money is not a factor. You need to discuss this with Taylor and decide what will be best for you."

She knew in her heart Taylor would tell Jonathan to attend college in Gainesville. She would want what was best for him just like Josh wanted what was best for her when she left for college. Taylor wouldn't want Jonathan to miss an opportunity to be on a college level rowing team.

A week later Jonathan announced, "I've accepted the offer to go to college in Gainesville."

They congratulated him, but Jennifer knew the hard part was yet to come. Saying good-bye to Taylor when he left for college would cause him a lot of heartache.

History didn't repeat itself, though. Taylor and Jonathan continued to see each other while they both went to separate colleges. It was not easy for them to be apart for such a long time, but they made it work. They made the most out of their weekends and holidays together. During spring break their senior year, Jonathan asked Taylor to marry him. They had been dating for almost five years and their love for each other continued to grow stronger every year. They planned to get married right after graduation.

Taylor graduated and received her teaching certificate. She studied early child development and wanted to teach elementary school. Jennifer was very proud of her for picking that profession. She couldn't have asked for a better daughter-in-law.

Jonathan graduated with a degree in software engineering and was offered a job locally supporting the space program.

Jennifer was truly blessed that Jonathan found someone like Taylor to spend the rest of his life with. They were both fortunate to find jobs locally after graduation. She couldn't have been more thrilled when she heard they were moving into a condo in the same building where Robert still lived in Grandma's at the beach. They could afford the rent, and it would keep them close to family.

Chapter Twenty-Three

"But the Lord said unto Samuel, Look not on his countenance, or on the height of his stature; because I have refused him: for the Lord seeth not as man seeth; for man looketh on the outward appearance, but the Lord looketh on the heart." *(1 Samuel 16:7)*

Jesse was not like his brother. He was more like Josh, an introvert who enjoyed spending time on the beach surfing. Jesse loved the solitude of surfing, sitting on his board, floating up and down as the waves passed underneath him while he waited for the next wave to ride to shore. He also loved wildlife and was always bringing home injured or lost animals that needed help.

When he was thirteen years old, Jennifer came home from work one day to find a pelican sitting on her living room floor. Jesse had been walking on the beach when he noticed the pelican had something wrapped around its wing. It had gotten tangled in fishing line. The line was tightly wound around the bird's wing, so it couldn't fly. Jesse somehow managed to carry the pelican home without being pecked to death. Jennifer watched as Jesse cut the line from around the pelican's wing while he quietly talked to the bird to keep it calm. It was as if the pelican sensed Jesse was trying to help and not hurt him.

Once the line was removed, Jesse discovered a deep gash where the line had cut through the skin. Jesse asked, "Can you hold the bird while I rub some antibiotics on the cut and gently wrap the wing?"

Jennifer looked at Jesse as if he was crazy. "You want me to hold the bird while you poke at the wound, putting medicine on it?"

"Come on, Mom. He won't hurt you. Just hold him like this." Jesse showed her how to hold the pelican's large beak securely so she wouldn't get injured.

Jennifer slowly kneeled down beside the pelican and cautiously held the bird while Jesse continued to treat the injury. The pelican stayed part of the family for two weeks. Jesse housed the pelican in a large cage he built in the back yard. Jesse caught bait fish for the pelican to eat each day, using a large throw net. He kept the pelican until the wing healed and it could fly again. Jennifer had tears in her eyes the day Jesse removed the bandage from the pelican's wing and released it back into the wild. It was such a beautiful sight to watch as the pelican soared overhead for a few minutes, as if to say good-bye. Then it turned offshore to join the other pelicans floating above the crest of the waves.

The injured pelican was followed by a baby squirrel, a turtle with a cracked shell, a baby raccoon, and a dog that had been hit by a car. Walking home from school one day, Jesse saw a dog limping on the side of the road. Jesse slowly approached the dog and saw his leg had been broken. The dog was whining in pain. Jesse called Josh and asked if he could leave work early to take the dog to the vet. Josh, an animal lover at heart, left immediately to help Jesse. The veterinarian took x-rays. The leg and hip where badly damaged from the impact with the car. The dog needed surgery to repair his injuries. Josh and Jennifer knew how much this meant to Jesse and didn't want the dog to suffer. They paid the fifteen hundred dollars to save the dog. Jesse promised he would pay them back one day. The dog came home with them to recover and joined their family. The dog weighed about forty pounds and had short, black and white hair. He looked to be part lab and part hound dog with big, floppy ears. The vet estimated the dog to be about six years old.

Jesse nursed the injured dog back to health. He had a new best friend. Jesse decided to name the dog Lucky after surviving his misfortune. Since they had a small yard, Jesse walked Lucky every morning before school and in the afternoon when he got home. Lucky would wait by the door after Jesse left for school and would stay there until Jesse returned home. They were inseparable.

The day came for Jesse to leave for college. It was harder for him to leave Lucky than it was to say good-bye to his Dad and Mom. Lucky was no longer a young dog and was not very active anymore. Arthritis had started to affect his joints.

"I'm worried he will just lie down and die if I am not here to make him get up," Jesse said with concern in his voice.

"I will take good care of Lucky. I'll bring him to the surf shop with me, so he won't be lonely. I am sure he will get plenty of attention from the customers," Josh assured him.

Jesse patted and kissed Lucky on the head before saying his good-byes to leave for college. It was not surprise when Jesse announced he wanted to become a veterinarian.

The first few weeks after Jesse left for college, Lucky lost his appetite and wouldn't eat. Jesse called every day to see how Lucky was doing. Jennifer would lie and say, "Lucky is just fine. You have nothing to worry about. Just concentrate on your studies." She felt bad for lying, but she knew telling Jesse the truth would only make him worry about something he had no control over.

Lucky had always been fed dog food, but Josh and Jennifer decided to make an exception and feed him people food in hopes of getting him to eat something. For dinner, Jennifer cooked an extra chicken breast and slowly hand fed it to Lucky. He finally ate. She started mixing his dry dog food with leftovers and Lucky slowing gained some weight back.

After being away at school for two months, Jesse came home to a very happy dog. Jennifer had never seen a dog so excited to see anyone before in her life. Lucky became a puppy again, jumping around and licking Jesse's face.

Eventually the day came, though, that Jennifer had to tell Jesse, "It's time to let Lucky go. His arthritis has worsened to a point where he can no longer walk, and he is in so much pain he won't eat. It's the humane thing to do, to put Lucky out of his misery."

"I want to be there with Lucky. I will arrange to have the vet come to our home, so Lucky will be as comfortable as possible. I don't want Lucky to think I deserted him."

Jesse came home from college on Friday afternoon. While Josh and Jennifer were still at work, he met the veterinary at the house. Jennifer knew how hard it would be for Jesse and could hardly concentrate on teaching her class. When she arrived home, the house was notably quiet. Jesse left a note on the refrigerator that he had gone to bury Lucky and would be home later. A tear ran down her face knowing how much Jesse must be hurting. Jesse kept himself busy with school after that, and he didn't come home again for several months.

During Jesse's summer breaks, he always volunteered at the Humane Society, and worked part time at a veterinary office. He graduated with his bachelor's degree and was accepted into a veterinary school. Jesse moved to a farm not far from the school. He rented a room at the farm, so he could gain experience treating many different types of animals while finishing his education.

During college, Jesse never dated much and always made excuses that he was just too busy with his studies when asked about it. Jennifer started to worry, like all mothers do, who want their sons to be happy. She prayed that Jesse would find someone special to share his life.

After completing veterinary school, Jesse was hired by a local vet to receive the additional training he needed to obtain his license. Jennifer, concerned about her son's well-being, called to see how he was doing.

"Everyone in the office is very friendly. Alex helps me take care of the animals and follow up on their treatments."

Now her interest was peaked. "Who is Alex?"

"Alex is the veterinary assistant that has been assigned to work with me. She loves animals as much as I do and has a habit of bringing patients home that have been abandoned."

"She sounds wonderful. When do I get to meet her?"

"Mom, we are just friends, nothing more. Quit meddling."

Two months later Jesse called home. "I would like both of you to meet Alex. Can I bring her to supper one night?"

"Why don't you stop by on Saturday? Is there anything in particular you would like me to make?"

"You know I love your lasagna," Jesse answered. Before Jennifer had a chance to ask any more questions, Jesse spoke up. "I have to go. I will see you on Saturday."

Jennifer wanted to make the evening special for Jesse's new girlfriend and make her feel at home. She cooked lasagna with fresh garlic bread and a salad, along with chocolate cheesecake for dessert.

Josh teased Jennifer as she nervously paced waiting for Jesse to arrive. "Don't start your match-making. We don't know how serious this is, so don't embarrass Jesse."

"I would never embarrass my son." Jennifer ran to the window at the sound of a car pulling into the drive way. "They're here! How do I look?"

"Like an overprotective mother," Josh laughed.

Jennifer opened the front door before they even had a chance to get to it and eagerly introduced herself to Alex. Alex was a petite girl with blond hair, big blue eyes, and a tan complexion who didn't wear or need much make-up.

Alex shyly said, "I am so glad to meet you."

Jennifer could tell she was nervous and wanted to make a good impression. To help Alex relax and so Jennifer could find out more about her, she asked, "Would you like to help me in the kitchen?"

"Sure, how can I help?" Alex asked as Jennifer showed her to the kitchen.

"Can you set the table, while I finish the salad? The plates and glasses are in this cabinet." While Alex set the table Jennifer nonchalantly asked, "Are you from a large family?"

"Yes, I am the youngest of four children. I was raised on a farm, which is how I became interested in caring for animals."

"How long have you and Jesse been dating?"

"Almost three months now."

Before Jennifer could ask another questions, Jesse walked into the kitchen. "Everything smells wonderful. I am starved. Is supper about ready?"

"Yes, why don't you get your father while we finish putting everything on the table."

After everyone was seated, Jennifer gave the blessing. "Thank you God for our special guest tonight, and bringing Alex into our lives. Bless this bounty to nourish our bodies and souls. Amen."

Everyone hungrily filled their plates and started eating. To break the silence at the table, Jennifer asked Jesse, "Have you had any unusual patients recently?"

He shared with them some of his more challenging cases and how much he enjoyed working with the different animals. "I hope soon to be able to open my own veterinary practice. Alex has been so helpful, maybe I can talk her into joining me."

Alex blushed at Jesse's compliment.

Jennifer could tell Jesse had fallen in love with Alex. After supper, Alex helped Jennifer clear the table and clean up the dishes, which gave Jennifer more time to probe her for information.

Jesse walked into the kitchen and asked Alex, "Do you want to take a walk on the beach?"

"I could definitely use some exercise after that food." Alex put down the dish towel and grabbed Jesse's extended hand.

After they left, Jennifer told Josh, "I really like Alex and hope she is the one that Jesse marries."

"There you go meddling again," he laughed. "I hate to agree with you, but she does seem to be a perfect fit for Jesse." Josh leaned over and gave Jennifer a kiss and said, "Just like us."

After all these years, Josh could still make her feel like a giggling school girl.

A month later, Jesse and Alex dropped by the house unexpectedly. Jesse walked in holding Alex's hand and said, "I've something I want to share with you. Alex and I are getting married."

Alex held out her hand to show the engagement ring that Jesse had given her.

Jennifer tightly hugged Alex. "I am so pleased you are becoming part of our family."

Jennifer thought to herself, My prayers have been answered once again. God has given Jesse someone to share his life with and make him happy.

Chapter Twenty-Four

"That thine alms may be in secret; and thy father which seeth in secret himself shall reward thee openly." *(St. Matthew 6:4)*

Not long after Jonathan and Taylor were married, he called with a surprise. "You are going to be a grandmother!"

"Taylor is pregnant!" Jennifer yelled to Josh while still on the phone with Jonathan.

"Her due date is the second week in May."

"I am so happy for you. How is she feeling?"

"She is having a little morning sickness, but other than that, she seems to be fine."

"Let me know if there is anything I can do to help. I still have some things in storage from when you were a baby. I'll sort through your old baby stuff to see if there is anything you could use."

"That would be great, Mom."

"You and Taylor will have to come to dinner one night so we can celebrate."

"I'll ask Taylor what day would be good for her. I have to run."

Jennifer prayed that their child would be healthy. She thought about the difficult time she had when she was pregnant with Jesse. "God, watch over Taylor and give her a healthy baby," she prayed.

Taylor was plagued with morning sickness for the first three months. She missed several weeks of teaching and ended up in the hospital due to dehydration. The doctor kept her overnight and told her she needed to remain in bed for at least a week. Taylor ate nothing but bland food, hoping the nausea would pass. After a few more weeks her stomach settled down and she was finally feeling better.

Jonathan called after Taylor's latest doctor's appointment to share, "We are having a girl!"

"That is wonderful! I hope you are not disappointed that it's not a boy."

169

"No, Taylor really wanted a girl, so I am happy for her."

Taylor's pregnancy brought back memories of her first pregnancy with Hope. Hope was always in her heart, but she hadn't thought about her for some time now. She remembered how happy she was when she found out she was having a girl. She pictured them going shopping together, showing her teenaged girl how to put on make-up, talking about boys, and helping her plan her wedding. She imagined how beautiful she would have been in her wedding dress, walking down the aisle to be married. She was never able to experience any of that, of course, but was happy Taylor would have the opportunity.

The remainder of Taylor's pregnancy progressed normally. As her due date approached, Jennifer called Jonathan every day to check on how Taylor was doing. Jennifer was more nervous about her first grandchild being born than Jonathan was.

Finally, on May twelfth the sound of the phone ringing woke Jennifer up around midnight.

"Taylor's water broke and she is in labor. We are at the hospital," Jonathan blared over the phone.

Jennifer shook Josh to wake him up, "Get dressed. Taylor is in labor."

Taylor was giving birth at the same hospital where Jonathan was born twenty-three years earlier. Josh and Jennifer located Taylor's hospital room and quietly entered. They found Jonathan pacing nervously by Taylor's bed, waiting for her next contraction.

"The doctor just left. Taylor and the baby are doing well," Jonathan nervously said. "Taylor is still a long way from being fully dilated, though. She has several more hours before she will give birth."

"Can I get you some coffee or something to eat?" Jennifer asked Jonathan.

"I am too excited to eat. I am fine for now. I will come find you in the waiting room once the baby is born."

Jennifer understood Jonathan wanted this time alone with Taylor. Josh and Jennifer walked down to the cafeteria for some breakfast. While eating, they reminisced, "Do you remember when I was here giving birth to Jonathan? You were just as nervous as Jonathan is today."

"All I can remember is how happy I was to hold our son for the first time. The feeling of ultimate, unconditional love for him was amazing." He reached across the table and held Jennifer's hand. "How are you doing?" He instinctively knew she would be thinking about Hope.

She smiled and told him, "Even though Hope's death brought me so much sadness, her life taught me so much more. I learned that life is a precious gift from God which should be lived as each day may be your last, and never wasted."

After breakfast, Josh and Jennifer returned to the waiting area. After what seemed like an eternity, Jonathan reappeared with a status report. "Taylor's contractions are much closer together now. It should not be too much longer," Jonathan explained.

Jennifer couldn't sit still any longer, and stood up to pace while she waited for news of their granddaughter. She had been thinking about what she could do to help Taylor after the baby was born, but hadn't found the right time to share her idea with Josh. Jennifer decided now was as good a time as any as she sat back down next to Josh.

"I remembered how overwhelmed I felt when Jonathan was born. Grandma stepped in when I needed it most. I've an idea I want to share with you."

"What are you meddling in now?"

"It's not like that. I only have a few weeks left before summer break at Hope Academy. I have been running the school now for over twenty years, and I am not getting any younger. As you know, I am now in my fifties, and have been considering reducing my role at the school. I think Taylor would make a perfect replacement for me. Taylor is an excellent teacher and is trained in teaching special needs children. She will be off from work until August to take care of the baby. When school resumes in the fall, I could train Taylor to take my place at Hope Academy. I could provide consultation support as needed. That way operation of the school will remain in the family, and I can offer to babysit for Taylor and Jonathan." Jennifer had talked nonstop, without taking a breath. She took a deep breath and asked Josh, "What do you think?"

Josh was silent for a moment while he considered her idea. "Are you sure this isn't just a scheme so you can spend more time with your granddaughter?"

She slapped Josh across the arm and told him, "I would never do that!"

"In that case it sounds like you have given this a lot of thought. I didn't realize you were ready to stop teaching. I guess I knew one day you would have to pass operation of Hope Academy over to someone. I agree Taylor is perfect for the job. She is smart and personable. She works well with everyone and has the teaching background you need. At the same time, she is confident and outspoken. She would make sure the school continues to succeed and provide the necessary care for the special needs children in our community. Have you discussed your idea with Taylor yet? Is she interested in taking over such a big job right after having her first child?"

"I didn't want to put any additional stress on Taylor while she was pregnant. I know Taylor will need to give notice at her current school if she plans to leave, so I need to broach the subject soon with her. I will give her a chance to recover from her delivery before discussing my job offer with her and Jonathan."

Josh smiled, "I know you would hate spending every day with your granddaughter while Taylor and Jonathan were at work."

"Be nice or I won't bring your granddaughter to the surf shop to visit you. I know you are already trying to figure out when you can teach her how to surf."

Jonathan suddenly appeared through the doorway with a big smile on his face. "Taylor gave birth to a beautiful baby girl. We named her Abigail Jennifer and plan to call her Abby for short."

"You named her after me?" She hugged Jonathan, with tears in her eyes.

"Abby is in the baby viewing area if you want to see her."

They walked to the viewing area and searched for Abby through the glass. Jonathan pointed her out to them. She was wrapped in a pink baby blanket all snuggled and warm, sleeping. She looked so peaceful, like an angel from God. She reminded Jennifer of how Hope looked when she was first born.

"I need to get back to Taylor to make sure she is resting and doesn't need anything."

Josh and Jennifer stood gazing at Abby through the glass, mesmerized by their new granddaughter.

Jonathan returned a short while later. "Taylor is resting. I'm in much need of a shower and something to eat. I am going to run home while Taylor is asleep."

"I can stay with Taylor to keep her company if you like. That way if she wakes while you are gone I will be there in case she needs anything."

"That would be great, Mom. I will return in about an hour."

"I need to check on the surf shop. Call me when you are ready to go home, and I will pick you up," Josh said.

Jennifer stood at the window to the baby viewing area and watched Abby sleep in her bassinet for a little while longer. She prayed for God to watch over her and to let her grow up to live a long and healthy life.

Jennifer quietly entered Taylor's room trying not to wake her. Taylor slowly opened her eyes.

"I didn't mean to wake you. Jonathan ran home to shower and get something to eat. I can stay with you while he is gone. Just relax and get some rest."

"I am too happy to sleep. Can you ask the nurse to bring Abby to me, so I can hold her for a while?"

Jennifer left the room and returned with a nurse carrying Abby in her arms. The nurse gently laid little Abby in Taylor's arms. A tear ran down Taylor's face as she kissed her precious little girl on the nose. Abby slept peacefully for a while and then started to cry, to let everyone know she was hungry.

Jonathan walked into the room. "What's all the noise about?"

"We have one very hungry little girl." Taylor started to breastfeed Abby, and she stopped crying.

Jennifer left the room so Jonathan and Taylor could have some time alone with Abby. She walked outside as the sun was just starting to set. The air was warm, and there was a slight breeze blowing from the east across the Banana River. The water in the river glistened as the sun sunk down below the horizon. While she waited for Josh to pick her up, she thought about her life and marveled how the love of two people created such a miracle. It seemed to all fit as if it was God's plan all along. God knew it would be too painful for Jennifer to give birth to another girl after losing Hope, so she was blessed with two boys instead. Then, Jonathan just happens to marry someone that would be perfect to run Hope Academy, who gave birth to a beautiful girl. God works in mysterious ways. God had always been by Jennifer's side even when she thought he had abandoned her. Now He has given her another gift, a granddaughter to spoil.

***

Taylor was thrilled with the idea of overseeing the operations at Hope Academy while Jennifer watched Abby for her. During the summer, Jennifer showed Taylor the business plan for the academy and introduced her to the other teachers. She was afraid the teachers wouldn't approve of her transferring operations to Taylor without consulting them first. Her fears were unwarranted though, because after they met Taylor, they understood her choice and welcomed Taylor to the team.

Taylor quickly learned the business and made a seamless transition to Hope Academy. After Taylor's first week Jennifer received several phone calls from the teachers and parents praising Taylor for how well she handled the students. Any fears she had that Taylor wouldn't be able to handle the responsibility soon vanished.

Jennifer loved staying at home and spending time with her granddaughter. It was amazing how having a baby in the house turned her into a kid again. While Taylor was busy at Hope Academy, she enjoyed getting to know her granddaughter. At first all Abby pretty much did was sleep, waking up periodically to eat. But within a few months, she was crawling and getting into everything. Jennifer took her to the beach to play in the sand, the library to pick out children's books to read to her, and the local park to play almost every week.

When Abby turned two years old, Jonathan announced Taylor was pregnant again. She was already three months along and was due to give birth around Thanksgiving. This due date was ideal because Taylor would only miss about two weeks of school between Thanksgiving and Christmas break.

Taylor had a much easier pregnancy this time and was able to maintain her work schedule right up to her due date. Matthew was born the weekend before Thanksgiving. He looked just like Jonathan when he was a baby with sky blue eyes and a few strands of blond hair. Jennifer hoped Abby wouldn't be jealous of her little brother and that they would grow up as close as Jonathan and Jesse still were.

When Taylor returned to work after the holidays, Jennifer was more than happy to watch Matthew and Abby. She had forgotten how much work it was to raise two infant children, never having a second to herself. At first, having a two year old and a newborn around the house seemed a bit overwhelming, but they soon got into a routine of nap time, feeding time, and play time.

Abby was a proud big sister. She would gently rub Matthew's head and talk to her brother about their Mom, Dad, and grandparents.

Abby was two and a half years old and a very bright girl. She already knew her alphabet and spoke clearly. She couldn't wait to go to school like the big kids.

Matthew was like Jonathan when he was a baby. He rarely cried or was fussy and smiled at everything.

Life couldn't get any better. Jennifer had a loving husband, two wonderful kids, and now two grandchildren that she was blessed to spend time with almost every day.

Chapter Twenty-Five

"Now faith is the substance of things hoped for, the evidence of things not seen." *(Hebrews, 11:1)*

Jesse finally completed his veterinary internship. He wanted to start his own veterinary clinic, but soon realized he would need to save a lot more money or take out a big loan to do so. Alex already had a good job at a veterinary clinic in Cocoa. Jesse started looking locally for openings at existing animal hospitals. He hoped to find a position with a high enough salary so he could save toward opening his own practice one day. He was not having much luck, though. No one was looking to hire a vet with his experience.

After church on Sunday, Jennifer stopped to talk to a friend. "Jesse completed his veterinary training after eight years," she shared. "He is now looking for a job. You wouldn't happen to know anyone who needs a good veterinarian do you?"

"As a matter of fact, I do. A friend of mine has been thinking about retiring and needs someone to take over his practice. He has a well established veterinary practice and is looking for someone to share his practice and eventually take over the business."

"That sounds perfect!" Jennifer excitedly wrote down the information about the vet so she could pass it on to Jesse.

As soon as Jennifer arrived home she called Jesse, all excited with the news about the possible position. She tried not to get her hopes up, but prayed that Jesse would be hired.

Jesse called the vet first thing Monday morning to inquire about the job. He discovered the vet had already interviewed several candidates. Jesse thought he had hit another dead end. But just as he was about to hang up, the vet suggested he stop by in the morning at eight o'clock before the office opened.

Jesse called his Mom to share the good news about the interview. Jennifer could tell Jesse was worried. "You don't need to worry. I've watched you with animals and know you are the best person for the job. Just be yourself and I am sure you will be hired."

"I hope you are right Mom. I am sure I don't have near the experience of the other candidates."

After Jennifer hung up the phone she prayed Jesse could convince the doctor he was the best person for the job. She hoped now that he had completed eight years of school and training he would get to do what he loved for a living, helping animals.

Jesse didn't sleep much that night, worried about his interview. He was very comfortable treating many different kinds of animals, but when it came to dealing with people he was not near as at ease. Unable to sleep, he got out of bed at six Tuesday morning.

Alex tried to get him to eat something before he left, but he was too nervous. Jesse put on his only suit and Alex helped him with his tie. Alex kissed Jesse for good luck before he walked out the door.

Alex didn't have to go to work until lunch, so she tried to stay busy around the apartment while she waited for Jesse to call after his interview. She wanted very badly for him to be hired for the job he worked so hard for.

Jesse arrived at the animal hospital and sat in the waiting area until the doctor was ready to see him. The office didn't open until nine, and he could hear dogs barking wildly behind the closed doors. He figured the vet was probably checking on his overnight patients.

A woman dressed in scrubs with her long hair tied in a ponytail stepped out from the back to let Jesse know, "Dr. Eadenton will be with you shortly. Would you like to take a tour of the facility while you wait for the Doctor?"

Jesse thought anything was better than sitting around worrying about the interview. "Yes, I would like that," he eagerly accepted.

"I am Sam, Dr. Eadenton's veterinary assistant. The examination rooms are along the main hall. The operating room and kennel area are located in the back of the building."

Jesse followed Sam, looking in each room, impressed with the cleanliness and how organized everything appeared.

They walked to the back of the building where several cages lined the wall. "We currently have just a few dogs staying with us," Sam explained.

One cage had a sickly looking dog that caught Jesse's attention. He stopped to look at the dog. It was very thin with bare patches of skin showing where hair was missing, and he was covered in scars. The dog appeared to only weigh about forty pounds, but should have weighed around eighty pounds. Jesse asked Sam, "What is this dog's story?"

"Someone found him two days ago along the side of the road. They brought him to us to examine and try to save. It's obvious the dog has been mistreated. We have been giving him fluids and trying to get him to eat something, so we can fatten him back up. Unfortunately, he doesn't seem to have the will to live. He was covered in fleas, so we bathed him and treated his open wounds. He has not barked or whined since he was brought in. He just lies quietly in his cage."

"Can I open the cage and look at the dog?" Jesse asked.

"Sure, maybe you can get him to eat something."

Jesse gently opened the door to the cage, squatted down, and held out his hand so the dog could sniff him. The dog didn't even lift his head. Jesse started to talk to the dog quietly while gently patting his head and tummy. Jesse slowly moved his hands around the animal's body, feeling for anything that might be causing the animal discomfort. He peered in the dog's mouth and discovered the dog was missing a few teeth which might make eating painful. He asked Sam, "Do you have any soft treats available?"

"We have some bacon favored treats in the exam room that I give the dogs after being treated." She returned with the container and handed it to Jesse.

Jesse continued talking to the dog quietly and held one of the bacon treats up to the dog's nose. The dog slowly reached for it and ate it. "What a good boy you are!" Jesse praise the dog and patted his head. After giving him two more treats, he asked Sam, "Do you have any chicken broth or cooked rice available that I can try to feed the dog?"

"Let me check the break area and see what I can find."

It was not long before Sam returned with a bowl of chicken and rice soup she had heated in the microwave. She handed the bowl to Jesse. "I heated it just to lukewarm, so it should not be too hot for the dog to eat."

Jesse set the bowl in front of the dog and placed a little soup in a spoon so the dog could try it without standing up. The dog sniffed then licked the spoon. "Come on boy, you can eat. Don't be afraid." Jesse encouraged the dog to stand so he could eat out of the bowl. The dog struggled to stand, so Jesse helped support the dog while he licked up all the soup in the bowl.

Just as Sam and Jesse were celebrating the dog eating, Dr. Eadenton walked up. Jesse had totally forgotten about his interview, and stood up to introduce himself to the doctor. Jesse reached out to shake the doctor's hand and realized it was covered in dog drool. He looked down at his suit which was now covered in dog hair and wrinkled from sitting on the floor.

Dr. Eadenton laughed, "We don't normally put our visitors to work. How is our patient doing? It looks like you were able to get him to eat something."

"After examining the dog's mouth, I thought it might be too painful for him to chew. Sam found some soup the dog was able to lick."

Sam took over the dog's care so Jesse and the doctor could talk privately.

Jesse was shown to the Dr. Eadenton's office after he had a chance to wash his hands. Jesse explained where he had gone to school, performed his internship, and how working on the farm had given him exposure to treating many different animals. After answering all the doctor's questions, Jesse asked, "What's going to happen to the dog in the cage?"

"The dog doesn't have an owner, so we are looking for someone to foster him until he is well enough to adopt."

"I'm currently living in an apartment and don't have much room, but I wouldn't mind fostering the dog. He seems to be comfortable around me, so maybe I can help nurse him back to health."

Dr. Eadenton smiled, "I will gladly let you have the dog. I am sure you will give him the attention and love he needs to heal."

Dr. Eadenton walked with Jesse back to where the dog was caged. "I'll make a decision about the position this week and notify you then." He shook Jesse's hand.

Jesse leaned down and opened the dog's cage. "Looks like you have a new home for now." The dog wagged his tail at the sight of Jesse. Jesse encouraged the dog to stand. He attached a leash to his collar and walked him to his truck. Jesse had some old blankets he always kept in his truck and laid one on the seat. He lifted the dog onto the passenger seat and made sure the dog was secure and comfortable.

On the way to his apartment, Jesse tried to think of an explanation to tell Alex of how he went for a job interview and ended up coming home with a dog. He knew that Alex was not going to be happy. They had agreed no animals until they could afford to buy a house.

Jesse parked his truck and helped the dog down. He slowly guided the dog toward his apartment. He hesitated as he opened the door.

As soon as the front door opened, Alex came running. She had been anxiously waiting for Jesse to return to hear how his interview went. She ran up to Jesse and gave him a hug. She looked down and asked, "What do we have here?" Alex kneeled down to pat the dog. "You look like you have had a rough life, boy. What happened to you?"

Jesse explained to Alex what he knew about the dog. "I just didn't have the heart to leave him there."

Alex kissed Jesse. "My big hearted husband has come to the rescue of another animal. Did you at least get the job?"

"I should hear something in a few days."

Alex leaned down and rubbed the dog behind the ears as he sat at Jesse's feet.

Jesse continued, "I know we agreed we wouldn't get any pets until we could afford to move into a house, but this dog looked so sad and afraid I couldn't bear to have him spend another night in that cage."

"What do you think we should name him?" Alex asked.

"So, you are all right with this?"

"It would have been nice if you talked to me first, but you know I could never turn away an injured animal." Alex went to the closet and pulled out an old blanket. She set it on the floor for the dog to sleep on.

"He looks like a Max to me," Alex said as she rubbed the dog's ears. "We need to fatten you up. Would you like me to make you both something to eat for lunch before I leave for work?"

"Do you have something soft we can feed him until his mouth has a chance to heal?"

"I've some left over chicken I can puree, along with some rice."

"He should be able to eat that."

Alex made Jesse a sandwich and placed a dog bowl in front of Max with his food. "Here you go, boy. You should be able to eat this," Alex said and she coaxed Max to eat.

After a quick smell of the bowl's contents, Max eagerly ate everything in the bowl. "That's a good boy," Jesse praised Max.

"I've got to run or I am going to be late for work," Alex said as she gave Jesse a quick kiss on the lips.

After lunch, Jesse and Max laid together in the living room resting. It was not long before Jesse fell asleep on the sofa. After being up all night worrying about his interview he was exhausted. Jesse woke to the sound of the phone ringing. He sat up and noticed Max sleeping on the floor beside the sofa. He hurried to grab the phone before the answering machine picked up. It was Dr. Eadenton from the animal hospital.

"After talking with you this morning and watching how well you interacted with the animals, there is no doubt in my mind that you are the best candidate for the job. Would you like to join my veterinary practice?"

Jesse couldn't believe his ears. He immediately accepted the offer and asked, "When do you want me to start?"

"If next Monday is not too soon, come to the office at nine. I will start familiarizing you with the business operations, and you can start seeing patients that afternoon."

Jesse hung up the phone and kissed Max on the head. He texted Alex and told her to call him as soon as she had a break. Then, Jesse called his Mom to share the good news.

***

Jennifer grabbed the phone on the first ring, hoping it was Jesse about the job. She was not surprised when Jesse shared that he had been offered the position. She was thrilled for him and couldn't be prouder of her son.

Jesse started his new job on Monday and began learning the business side of treating animals. Dr. Eadenton quickly became confident in Jesse's knowledge and skills. He was so comfortable in fact, that he decided to take a long overdue vacation just one month after Jesse started.

Max slowly put on weight and the bare patches slowly filled in with hair again. Jesse brought Max to work with him each day and left him in his office while caring for the other animals.

After six months, Jesse and Alex were able to save enough money for a down payment on a house. They wanted a small house with a large backyard, so Max would have room to run. Jesse told his Mom that they had started looking for a house. Jennifer remembered how much fun she had finding her first home with Dillon. She prayed they could find something within their price range.

It was not long before God answered Jennifer's prayers once again. Jennifer was grocery shopping when she happened to run into one of the parishioners. Jennifer made polite conversation and asked, "How is your mother doing?"

"I am afraid she is getting frail and she just moved into a retirement community. Her house was just too much work for her to keep up now that my father is gone. I just finished having my Mom's home refurbished, so it could be put on the market to sell."

"Really," Jennifer's interest was suddenly peaked. "I know someone that might want to buy your mom's home. Where is it located?"

"My Mom and Dad lived in the house for thirty years. It's located just west of Highway 95 outside of Cocoa. They built the house originally when no one was moving to the area. The house is on an acre lot and bumps up against a nature reserve so no one lives behind it. If you would like to see the house, I can give you the information."

"It sounds perfect." Jennifer jotted down the address on the back of her grocery list. As soon as she arrived home she called Jesse at work to share the details about the house.

"What are they asking for the house?" Jesse asked.

"I didn't think to ask that. Just take a look and if you want the house, make an offer. What do you have to lose?"

***

As soon as Jesse hung up the phone, he called to set up an appointment to tour the house. He scheduled to see it on Sunday around five since it was the one day that both Alex and him were off from work.

Alex and Jesse drove up to the house and couldn't believe their eyes. Before going inside, they knew it was perfect. The acre was fully fenced, with a small pond in the back yard. The landscape around the house had been well maintained. Flowers brightened the front of the house, with the azaleas in bloom, along with the many tropical plants. A flower garden lined the path to the front door. Jesse peered around the back of the house where large oak trees and palm trees shaded the yard.

"Max would love running around this yard," Jesse told Alex.

The three bedroom, two bath house was thirty years old with stucco siding. It was small, but much larger than their apartment. There was a family room and small kitchen. The carpet had been replaced and the house smelled of fresh paint. As they walked through the house, Jesse asked Alex, "Do you like the house?"

"Yes, of course I love it, but can we can afford it?" she whispered so the owner couldn't hear.

"There is no way to know unless we ask." Jesse approached the owner, "Alex and I love your home. How much are you asking for it?"

"Since the house is older, I realize it doesn't have all the modern conveniences of a new one. You seem like a real nice couple and remind me of my late husband and me when we were young. If you want the house I will sell it to you for one hundred and twenty-thousand dollars."

Alex and Jesse were fighting to remain composed after hearing the price. Jesse calmly replied, "That sounds like a fair price."

"Well then, I will send you a contract to sign. Just contact me when you are ready to close."

Jesse vigorously shook her hand with a big smile on his face and told her, "Don't worry, we will take good care of your home."

Driving home they could hardly control themselves, they were so excited. Jesse immediately called his Mom to share the good news. Jesse and Alex took out a thirty year mortgage, so the monthly payments would be manageable. At the end of four weeks they closed. It took them all day and several trips in Jesse's truck to move all their belongings into their new home.

Jesse hadn't seen his parents since he started his new job. He was thrilled when his Mom called and offered to bring supper the day they moved. Jesse was eager to show them his new home.

Currently, the house looked like a demolition zone with boxes everywhere. Alex didn't even know which box her pots and pans were located in to be able to cook anything if she had to at that point.

At 6PM the doorbell rang and Jesse dusted himself off from unpacking and opened the door for his parents.

"I've a chicken casserole that is still warm and carrot cake for dessert. Where do you want me to put it?" Jennifer eagerly asked.

Alex helped clear off the dining room table. "Set it here."

"Your father has a bag full of paper plates, cups, and silverware since I was not sure if you had unpacked yours yet. Oh, and a big jug of sweet tea." Jennifer smiled.

"Thanks so much. We haven't had a chance to start on the kitchen yet," Jesse said. "I am starved after moving all day. It smells great!"

Everyone found a seat around the table as Jennifer passed out plates and silverware. Jesse didn't hesitate and helped himself to a huge helping of casserole. He devoured it while Jennifer pried about his new job.

Jesse told them how much he had learned and enjoyed working with the staff and animals. "The days seem to fly by, I stay so busy."

Alex spoke up, "The owner has been so impressed with Jesse he left him in charge while he went on vacation." She was so proud of her husband.

Jennifer smiled, remembering what it was like when she started her first job as an engineer, hardly taking time to come up for air she was so busy. After dinner Jennifer surprised Alex with a housewarming gift of fancy bath soaps and towels to welcome them to their new home.

Jesse showed his parents around the house and property. Max had already made himself at home and was sprawled across the sofa in the family room. Even though the house was small, Jennifer could see a lot of potential. When Jesse showed them the bedrooms, he indicated that he was going to use one for an office and the other for a guest room.

Jennifer had hoped that Alex and Jesse would want to start having children now that they were more financially secure. The word nursery never came up though. Jennifer knew they still had plenty of time, but also knew all too well how fast time will slip away.

Chapter Twenty-Six

"To every thing there is a season, and a time to every purpose under the heaven" *(Ecclesiastes 3:1)*

Jesse started working longer hours at the animal hospital and frequently performed farm visits after hours. He treated farm animal such as horses, goats, and cows. Sometimes Alex would go along with him to help, when she had time.

One night they were visiting a horse with a lame leg. The horse had stepped in a gopher turtle hole and injured his leg. The owner feared having to put the horse down.

On the ride out to the farm, Jesse told Alex, "We have been so busy at work, Sam and I are having a difficult time keeping up now that Dr. Eadenton has retired. Would you consider quitting your job and joining my practice? It would be great working together again."

"I've been hoping you would ask, but I didn't know if we could stand spending every day together without driving each other crazy," she laughed.

"I always thought we made a good team. I think dealing with the daily crisis together will bring us even closer."

Alex leaned over and kissed Jesse on the cheek. "I will check with my veterinary office tomorrow to see when they can replace me."

When they arrived at the farm, Jesse entered the barn with the owner. He opened the horse's stall while Alex gathered up some supplies in the truck.

Alex walked into the barn and watched as Jesse tried to calm the agitated horse. The horse was skittish. Jesse calmly stroked his side and worked his way down the injured leg of the horse. "Your tendons are very swollen. I know this must be uncomfortable for you, but I am going to fix you up," Jesse said to the horse.

"It doesn't feel broken. Alex, can you hand me my bag?"

Alex approached and reached out her hand to give Jesse his bag when the horse suddenly bolted. Alex tried to step back, but stumbled. The horse came down on her stomach.

Jesse and the owner grabbed the horse's reins and pulled the horse away from Alex. Jesse hurried to Alex's side and told her not to move.

Alex grabbed her stomach and cried out in pain. Jesse dialed 911 and tried to keep Alex calm while they waited for the ambulance to arrive. He feared she might have internal bleeding. Since they were many miles away from the nearest hospital, it took the ambulance an excruciating twenty minutes to arrive.

The paramedic put an IV in Alex's arm before placing her in the ambulance. Jesse followed the ambulance to the hospital in his truck.

When they arrived at the hospital, Jesse tried to follow Alex into the exam room but was told to wait outside while they determined the extent of her injuries.

Jesse called his Mom, "Alex has been injured by a horse I was treating and has been taken to the Rockledge hospital."

"I will be there as soon as I call your Dad."

* * *

Jennifer frantically called Josh at work. "We need to get to the hospital. Alex has been injured!"

"I'll pick you up in ten minutes," Josh replied.

When they arrived at the hospital, they found Jesse pacing back and forth, waiting for news on Alex's condition. "I am so glad you are here. They won't tell me anything and won't let me see Alex."

"I'm sure they are just being thorough," Jennifer said, trying to reassure Jesse.

"It's all my fault. I should have known better than to let Alex approach an injured horse. I know injured horses are unpredictable. I should have had a better hold of his reins."

"It's not going to do Alex any good blaming yourself." Jennifer grabbed Jesse's hand. "Why don't we say a prayer for Alex?"

Jesse nodded and reached for his father's hand. It had been a while since he attended church due to his schedule, but he witnessed God's miracles in animals every day.

"God, Alex needs your help. Please guide the doctors in treating Alex and help her heal from her injures. In Christ's name we pray. Amen."

The doctor finally appeared. "Alex is bleeding internally and needs surgery to control the bleeding. You can visit with her just for a little while as we prep her for surgery."

Jesse was lead to Alex's room. She had an IV in her arm and was dressed in a hospital gown. Her eyes were closed, but she opened them when she heard Jesse approach.

"How are you doing?" Jesse asked as he grabbed Alex's hand?

"I am very sleepy. I think the doctor gave me something to help me relax."

"I will be waiting for you when you return from surgery. I love you so much. Mom and Dad are here. We are praying for you." With tears in his eyes, he kissed Alex. She was wheeled out of the room for surgery.

It seemed like an eternity before the doctor returned. Jesse jumped up from his chair and asked, "How is Alex?"

The doctor began by telling them, "The bleeding is under control, and Alex should make a full recovery." Then, he hesitated and asked Jesse, "Did you know that Alex was pregnant?"

"No, were you able to save the baby?"

The doctor calmly told them, "Alex was only about five weeks along, so she may not even have realized yet that she was pregnant. Unfortunately the baby couldn't be saved. Alex's uterus was damaged."

"Will she be able to have children?" Jesse anxiously asked.

"We will have to wait and see how she heals, to be able to determine if she can carry another child. She is currently in recovery. Once she awakes, you can see her."

After the doctor left, Jennifer tried to comfort Jesse, but he was inconsolable. He stood up, "I need some air," he said and walked outside.

"Should I go after him?" Jennifer asked Josh.

"No, just give him some time to think and absorb what has happened. You know how sensitive Jesse can be. Remember when he was a child and would take long walks on the beach to clear his head when he was worried about something?"

Jennifer remembered all those times she had done the same thing when she felt overwhelmed. "I just wish there was something I could do to ease his pain."

It was now after midnight, and Alex would be spending the night in intensive care where she could be monitored to make sure she didn't start bleeding again. Jesse refused to leave the hospital in case her condition changed. He insisted his parents go home to get some rest.

Jennifer felt so helpless, not being able to help ease Jesse's pain, but knew it was in Gods hands.

✱✱✱

It's the hardest thing in the world for a mother to see her son suffering. Instinctively women are wired to fix it when their children are in pain or need their help. But there was nothing Jennifer could do to fix this. All she could do was pray. "God, be with Jesse and give him the strength to deal with whatever the outcome of Alex's injury. Also, help him to find a purpose for his sorrow and guide him as you have done so often for me."

Josh had to leave for work the next morning. Since it was Saturday, he had surfing lesson scheduled until two. "Call me when you find out how Alex is doing. If you need me I can meet you at the hospital as soon as I am finished with my last lesson."

Jennifer didn't have to watch Abby and Matthew, so she gathered up a pair of Josh's jeans and t-shirt that should fit Jesse and left immediately for the hospital. She arrived at the Intensive Care Unit and found Jesse still sitting in the waiting area with his head hung low.

"How is Alex?"

"I had a chance to visit with her and her doctor this morning. There were no signs of bleeding overnight, so they are moving her to another room this morning."

"That's good news." Jennifer tried to sound positive to cheer Jesse up. She handed Jesse the clothes she brought. "Do you want to change into something clean, then go down to the cafeteria with me to get some breakfast?"

"As soon as Alex is settled into her room and I am sure she doesn't need anything, I'll change and get something to eat."

Jennifer hated to bring up the topic but asked, "Does Alex know about the baby yet?"

"Alex didn't know she was pregnant, but she was very upset to know she lost our baby and may not be able to get pregnant again."

A nurse appeared, "Your wife is being moved to room 312. You can wait for her there."

They walked down to the room and Alex was wheeled in shortly after they arrived. Alex's eyes were closed and she appeared to be resting.

"Why don't I stay with Alex while you get something to eat?" Jennifer offered.

188

"No, I can get something later. I'm not hungry anyway."

Alex opened her eyes and whispered, "You need to take care of yourself and get something to eat, so I don't have to worry about you."

Jesse smiled, leaned over and kissed Alex. "If it will make you rest, I'll eat something."

While Jesse was gone, Jennifer tried to delicately bring up the topic of Alex's baby. She explained, "I know how sad you must feel right now. When Hope died, I was in so much grief, just getting up every day was a challenge at first. I didn't want Hope's death to go unnoticed, though. That was when God led me to create Hope Academy. It may not be evident right now, but God has a plan for you also. Put your faith in him. He will help you heal and find your path in life."

Alex was silent for a moment as a tear ran down her face. "I didn't even know I was pregnant, so how could I be so sad over something I never knew I had before this morning? I can't imagine how you ever recovered from losing Hope."

"It's normal to grieve the loss of the baby because it was part of you and Jesse. Just don't let the grief consume your life. Let God help you to heal and guide you toward your destiny. Feel free to call me anytime you start to feel overwhelmed and need a sympathetic ear."

She wiped the tear from her face as Jesse walked back in the room.

Jesse could see they were having a serious conversation and tried to lighten the mood. "I think the food in the cafeteria is as bad as the food the patients are served."

"I'm very tired. I am going to try to sleep for a little while," Alex said.

Jennifer took the hint and got up to leave. "Call me, Jesse, if there is anything you need."

"Mom, can you stop by the house and let Max out and give him some food?"

"Sure, I'll also play with him for a while and keep him company, so he doesn't miss you. Take care of Alex. Let me know if there is anything else I can do."

After three days in the hospital, Alex was released with orders to rest at home for at least two weeks. She encouraged Jesse to return to work. She assured him that she would be fine during the day without him. She decided, since she was not able to work, she would go ahead and give her notice at her job. That way when she was well enough she could start working with Jesse at his animal hospital.

During Alex's first week at home alone, Jennifer thought she might need some company, so she stopped by with Abby and Matthew to visit.

"Hey guys, I am so glad you stopped by." Alex held out her arms to Abby and asked, "Can you climb in to my lap?"

Jennifer leaned down and helped Abby onto the sofa beside Alex. Abby started chatting away while Matthew was more interested in playing with Max. Hopefully, spending time with her niece and nephew would cheer her up and not make her think about what she had lost.

"Alex, you seem to be healing quickly. Your skin's not as pale, and it looks like you have put on a few pounds. Do you know how much longer you have to stay home from work?"

"I hoped to be back at work, at least part time, next week. I'm looking forward to starting my new job with Jesse. I am feeling much stronger. I just have to be careful when I move, or the pain comes back. I am going crazy sitting around the house with Max all day long, and just need to get back to a routine."

"I totally understand. I am a horrible patient. I hate it when I can't take care of myself and everyone else," Jennifer laughed. "When I was pregnant with Jesse and ordered to bed until I delivered, I thought I would go nuts. Rest while you can though, so you can get your strength back. You will be back at work in no time and be all too busy again soon."

∗∗∗

Alex's doctor gave her permission to return to work part time at first. She could only work four hours a day and was not allowed to lift anything over ten pounds. She was also instructed to stay off her feet as much as possible.

She was thrilled to get out of the house and start working with Jesse. Due to her restrictions, she was assigned to the front desk from eight o'clock until noon each morning, checking in patients.

One morning was quiet with few appointments scheduled, when a grimy looking little boy came into the veterinary hospital. He looked to be about five years old and was carrying a puppy in his arms. "What do we have here?" Alex asked. She reached over to pat the puppy.

"My puppy is hurt. Can you help him?" the little boy responded.

190

"Where is your puppy hurt?" Alex asked.

"He won't eat and whines every time I pick him up."

Alex squatted down to the boy's level and asked, "What is your name?"

"Chip."

"Chip, what is your puppy's name?"

"Skippy."

"My name is Alex. Can you tell me what happened to Skippy?"

Chip hesitated, and then said, "Someone kicked Skippy in the side."

Skippy looked to be only around twelve weeks old and weighed about ten pounds. Alex held out her arms and asked Chip, "Can I hold Skippy for a minute to see if he is okay?"

Chip handed Alex the puppy and the puppy started to whine. Alex feared the puppy might have some broken ribs.

"You were right to bring Skippy to us. Why don't we walk back to the examination room? I will get the doctor to take care of Skippy."

Alex saw Jesse in the hall and motioned for him to follow her into the exam room. When Jesse walked in Alex explained, "This is Chip and Skippy. Skippy may have some broken ribs where he was kicked."

Jesse looked at Alex to let her know he understood what she was trying to relay about possible animal abuse. "Well, let me take a look." Jesse gently lifted the puppy onto the exam table. The puppy was dirty and covered in fleas. Jesse could feel some swelling around the puppy's abdomen that concerned him.

"I need to take an x-ray to determine the extent of Skippy's injuries. Alex, can you take Chip to my office while I take care of Skippy?"

"Can I stay with Skippy?" Chip asked.

Alex took Chip by the hand, "Jesse is very good with animals and will take good care of Skippy. As soon as he is finished examining Skippy he will come and get us."

Jesse left with the puppy in his arms. Alex led Chip down the hall.

"Let's go to the sink to wash our hands. Then, I will find something for us to eat. Jesse always keeps a stash of food and drinks in his office."

Alex helped Chip scrub his dirty hands and then led him to Jesse's office. "Why don't you sit here while I see what Jesse has hidden in his desk to eat?"

The boy was very skinny, with dirty clothes and hair. Alex feared he may also be abused.

"Would you like some chocolate chip cookies?"

Chip nervously looked at the floor, not responding. Alex wondered what Chip had gone through to make him so withdrawn. "Chocolate chip cookies are my favorite," Alex said, trying to get Chip to feel comfortable around her. She handed him some cookies and a bottle of milk.

Chip shyly ate the cookies and slowly drank all the milk. He acted like he was going to be punished for doing so.

Alex knew Chip must be scared. She came up with an idea to reassure him she was not going to hurt him. She hoped he would open up and talk to her. "Jesse and I have a dog named Max. Would you like to see a picture?"

Chip nodded his head yes.

Alex picked up the framed picture of her and Max on Jesse's desk. She held it out for Chip to see. "Jesse rescued Max and saved him after he nearly died."

Chip asked, "What happened?"

"Max was mistreated and half-starved before someone found him. He was brought into the animal hospital. Jesse nursed Max back to health. He now lives with us and is a very happy dog."

Alex asked, "How old are you?"

He held up five fingers.

"Have you started school yet?"

Chip looked at the ground and shook his head no.

"Do you live close by with your parents?"

Chip paused and said, "I live in a foster home."

Alex felt horrible for Chip. He obviously was not being properly cared for. "How about we go sit at the front desk? You can help me check in the other patients being examined today."

Chip nodded his head yes. Alex reached for Chip's small hand and walked with him back to the lobby. Alex pulled up a chair next to hers for Chip to sit on. "Would you like to color?"

Chip sat quietly with his head down, not saying a word. Alex handed him a coloring book along with some crayons.

Chip turned the pages of the coloring book and found a picture of a dog. He started coloring quietly while Alex worked. She wondered if she should contact family services. She didn't want to get Chip in trouble and lose his trust.

After about an hour, Jesse walked out. "Skippy will be fine. He just had some fluid around his lungs that needed to be removed. Would it be all right if you left him here with me overnight? I will take very good care of him," Jesse assured Chip.

Chip nodded his head up and down, still looking at the floor.

"Chip, you stay right here while I talk to Jesse for a minute," Alex instructed.

Alex reached for Jesse's arm and pulled him down the hall, so Chip couldn't hear their conversation.

"We need to do something. We can't let Chip go back to his foster home. Something bad may happen to him. It's obvious he is not being taken care of."

"Maybe you are overreacting. You know how dirty boys can get. Why don't you offer to drive Chip home, that way you can meet his foster Mom and see what the house looks like?"

Maybe Jesse was right. She was overreacting, Alex thought. "Okay it's time for me to leave for the day anyway. I'll take Chip home and call you with what I find."

When Alex returned to the lobby, Chip was gone. She walked back to the exam rooms to see if he wandered off looking for Skippy, but couldn't find him. She ran outside and saw nothing but a busy street, with cars racing by in front of the veterinary hospital. She grabbed her purse and rushed to her car to see if she could track down Chip walking home. She drove all around the surrounding neighborhoods and side streets in the area, but there was no sign of Chip. With nothing else left for her to do, she drove home.

When Alex arrived home, she called Jesse. "I wasn't able to locate Chip. Do you think I should call someone?"

"Why don't you call my Mom? She has experience dealing with children with problems. She will know what to do."

"Thanks, that's a great idea. I will let you know what she says."

Alex dialed Jennifer at home. "Hi Jennifer, it's Alex. I need to ask your advice on something."

"Is everything all right? How are you feeling?"

"I am fine. It's not about me. I had this little boy named Chip bring a puppy into the office today. He was very withdrawn and didn't look like he was being well taken care of. He told me he lived in a foster home, but he disappeared before I could find out where. I am concerned about his well-being. Is there someone I can call to make sure he is all right?"

"I worked with Family Services on several occasions when I was teaching. I know someone who might be able to help. Let me give her a call, and I will call you right back."

"That would be great." Alex hung up the phone and anxiously waited for Jennifer to call back.

In less than thirty minutes, the phone rang, and Alex jumped to grab it.

"Family Services is all too familiar with the foster home where Chip is living. They have been sited for violations in the past for failure to properly care for their foster children. She had hoped that conditions for the children had improved. They are going to do a wellness visit to make sure Chip is all right."

Alex was relieved to hear someone would check on Chip, but felt sorry for the little boy. "Hopefully he will return to the animal hospital tomorrow to check on Skippy. Then I can talk to him some more. Thanks again for your help."

Jesse walked in the door a few minutes later carrying Skippy in his arms. He had been bathed and smelled much better.

Alex reached to pat the puppy. "How is Skippy doing?"

Max also investigated the new member of their household, nudging Skippy with his nose.

"He will be fine. I removed the fluid from his lungs, and he ate a little food. I will keep an eye on him tonight. What did you find out about Chip?"

Alex filled Jesse in on her conversation with Jennifer. Then she blurted out, "Have you ever thought about becoming a foster parent or adopting a child?"

Jesse knew where this was coming from. Alex feared she wouldn't be able to get pregnant again, and she wanted to have children. "I haven't really considered it, to be honest. Is this something you might like to pursue?"

"After meeting Chip today, I started wondering how many other children are out there that need a good home. Maybe Chip's visit today was God's way of pushing us in that direction."

"If you want to pursue becoming foster parents, I will support you." Jesse leaned over and kissed Alex. "You would make a great mother."

The next day Alex went to the animal hospital with Jesse and Skippy. She anxiously waited for Chip to return to check on Skippy. When he didn't return, Alex started to worry that something must have happened to him. When she arrived home, she called Jennifer. "Chip didn't return to the office today. Do you know if Family Services visited Chip's home yet?"

"Why don't I give them a call and find out if the wellness visit occurred? I'll call you right back."

Alex tried to stay busy around the house while she waited for Jennifer to call back. Finally, the phone rang and Alex grabbed it. "What did you find out?"

"Family Services did visit Chip's home first thing this morning. They removed him after determining he was not being properly cared for. You did the right thing by alerting authorities, so he can now be placed in a more loving home."

"I talked to Jesse last night. We would like to be approved as foster parents. Can you direct us through the proper channels, so we can obtain approval to foster children, and help Chip?"

"I think that is an excellent idea. I will email you the forms to complete, along with the name and number of the person to call. She will be able to expedite the process for you."

Alex felt like this was the path God was directing her to go, after losing her baby. She completed the forms before Jesse arrived home from work. All he had to do was review and sign them, so they could be submitted.

The next day, Alex hand carried the application to Jennifer's friend at the Family Services and set up an appointment for an interview in two days.

The day of the interview Alex was a nervous wreck. "Thank goodness the interview is at eight in the morning, so I don't have to worry about it all day."

As Alex dressed, Jesse told her, "Don't worry. I am sure they will see what wonderful parents we would make and grant us approval."

"I hope you are right."

The interview went well. Jesse and Alex found out that Chip had been placed in another foster home. It was only temporary though, because they already had six children. The Family Service director told them, "Once the application process is complete, there should be no problem moving Chip to your home. An evening class is being offered this week that you will need to take. Then I will plan a home visit to inspect your house."

Jesse and Alex were elated. They attended the evening class and spent the next couple of days cleaning and making their home spotless for the inspection.

A lady from Family Services arrived at their home and looked through the house and asked a few questions. "I see no reason why you shouldn't be approved as foster parents. I can complete the paperwork today and obtain the final approvals. If you like, I can arrange to bring Chip in a couple of days."

Alex could hardly stop from yelling with delight, "That would be wonderful!"

"I will contact you tomorrow to let you know the day and time you can expect Chip to arrive."

"Thank you so much! We can't wait for Chip to be part of our family."

Once the Family Service representative left, Alex couldn't hold back her excitement any longer. She jumped into Jesse's arms and gave him a big kiss.

The day came for Chip to arrive. Jesse cancelled his afternoon appointments, so he could be home with Alex. Skippy had been staying with them and was doing much better. Max seemed to enjoy having another dog around the house to keep him company. Skippy would sleep curled up next to Max at night to stay warm. Max was very gentle with Skippy since he was so much larger. Jesse knew Chip was going to be so happy to see Skippy again.

Alex jumped up to look out the window every time a car drove by to see if it was Chip.

Jesse joked, "I am going to have to replace the carpet if you don't sit down and stop pacing."

"I am just so scared and excited at the same time. What if Chip doesn't like it here?"

"Of course he will like it here. He will have us as parents, who will spoil him rotten. I can teach him how to play ball, ride a bike, and of course, surf."

Then Alex heard a car pull into the driveway, and she rushed outside. She could see Chip in the back seat strapped in a car seat. Alex opened the car door and was greeted by a much different boy. He had been bathed and was wearing clean clothes. He had a smile on his face. The first thing he asked before he got out of the car was, "How is Skippy?"

"You can see for yourself." Jesse approached the car with Skippy in his arms.

Chip yelled, "Skippy!" He reached for his puppy and gave him a hug. "I missed you so much." Skippy seemed just as excited to see Chip again and licked him all over his face, at the delight of Chip.

The Family Service representative laughed, "Chip was so excited when he was told he was going to be living with you. He had his clothes packed and was standing at the front door this morning when I arrived."

"We are so grateful for your help in allowing us to take care of Chip," Alex said.

"Chip looks to be the lucky one. Call if you have any questions." She watched Chip happily playing with Skippy before she left.

Jesse and Alex showed Chip to his room.

His face lit up. "I have the whole room to myself?"

"You will have to share it with Skippy," Jesse replied.

Chip hadn't let go of Skippy since he arrived. He sat on the bedroom floor with Skippy and started to talk to him like he was his best friend. Skippy jumped in Chip's lap and licked him some more as if he understood every word Chip was telling him.

Laughter filled the house from this point forward. Chip was no longer the shy, scared boy Alex originally met. He opened his heart to them and became a permanent part of their family. After six months, they were granted approval to adopt Chip. Jesse and Alex's family slowly grew as they took in three more foster children ages two to eight. Each one arrived withdrawn and untrusting. These children had been let down so many times in their short lives. They had experienced so little love. With time, the love their family had to offer won them over. Jesse and Alex shared their love for animals which really helped the children come out of their shell. Along with two dogs, they now had a turtle named Pete and a rabbit named Bugs. Jesse and Alex's home was now filled with children and animals, just as they had dreamed.

Chapter Twenty-Seven

"Therefore I say unto you, Take no thought for your life, what ye shall eat, or what ye shall drink; nor yet for your body, what ye shall put on. Is not the life more than meat, and the body than raiment?" *(St. Matthew 6:25)*

As the years passed by, the grandchildren grew up and started school. Jennifer was no longer needed to babysit during the day. She still made time for each grandchild during the summer break to do something special. The girls enjoyed shopping, baking, and doing crafts while the boys enjoyed spending time outdoors with Josh surfing and camping.

Now that she had more time on her hands, Jennifer wanted to travel; something she had always loved doing with her parents when she was young, but never had much time or money to do with Josh. Josh agreed to cut back on his hours at the surf shop. He hired a manager to help oversee the day-to-day operations of the business, so he could take some time off.

It was Easter weekend, and the annual Cocoa Beach Easter Surf Competition was taking place. Josh was not competing anymore, but two of their grandsons were surfing. Josh couldn't be prouder that his love for surfing was also enjoyed by his sons and grandsons. Jennifer and Josh sat on the beach under a beach umbrella, cheering on their family that beautiful spring day. It was nice having time for each other again. The day was perfect with good waves, few clouds, and temperatures in the low 80's.

As the sun started to sink below the horizon, Jennifer asked, "Have you had enough sun and surf for one day? Are you ready to go home?"

"I could use a pizza after watching other people surf all day. I am starved," Josh said. "Why don't we stop and pick up one on the way home?"

Jennifer used her cell phone and ordered a pepperoni pizza with extra cheese, their favorite.

As she gathered up their belongings off the beach, Josh reached over and touched the back of her leg. "Do you know you have a mole on the back of your leg behind your knee? Have you had that checked by the dermatologist to make sure it doesn't need to be removed?"

Josh, having lived in the sun most of his life, was very familiar with having moles removed that might be cancerous. He religiously went to the dermatologist every six months to be examined for pre-cancerous cells. Jennifer on the other hand, being from Minnesota, hadn't been so diligent.

"No, I didn't know it was there." She leaned back to look at the area Josh pointed to. "I am sure it's nothing, but will make an appointment to have it checked if it will make you happy." Jennifer leaned over and kissed Josh.

The next day, not really concerned about the mole, but wanting to make Josh happy, she made an appointment with the dermatologist. The first opening was over a month away. With the high retirement population in Florida, dermatologists stayed very busy. She accepted the first available appointment.

Summer was quickly approaching, and Jennifer stayed busy picking up her grandchildren from school. She also helped take them to after school activities when her sons and daughter-in-laws had to work.

Josh and her were looking forward to traveling. They started planning their first summer vacation together. "How about we do a month long tour of Alaska?"

"You, who wears a sweater anytime the temperature drops below eighty degrees, wants to go to Alaska?"

"Yes, from pictures I've seen, it's beautiful. I will bring plenty of warm clothes, so I won't get cold."

"All right, Alaska it is."

Taylor was still running Hope Academy and classes would be ending the last week in May. She would be spending the summer with her children, Abby and Matthew. Alex had cut back her hours at the veterinary hospital, so she could spend more time at home with her four children during the summer. That would leave time for Josh and Jennifer to go on an adventure of a lifetime.

Jennifer's dermatologist appointment was May twenty-first, so she planned to leave for vacation right afterward. Josh and her busied themselves planning all the places they wanted to visit while in Alaska, and prepared for the trip. Since they lived in Florida, they were afraid their thin winter clothes may not be enough to handle the cold nights in Alaska and decided to order some heavier jackets online. They found a used camper top that fit on the back of Josh's truck. The camper would give them someplace dry to stash their supplies for the trip and provide a place to sleep at night.

Jennifer's dermatologist appointment finally arrived, and she was looking forward to getting it out of the way. She never really cared for doctors much and avoided seeing them, if at all possible. The doctor had her answer the normal questionnaire about allergies and previous medical conditions. Then he examined her closely using a magnifying glass for any signs of skin cancer.

"I need to remove the mole behind your knee and some of the surrounding skin, so it can be tested to make sure there are no cancerous cells."

She knew the mole and skin removal was standard procedure. Josh had come home many times with patches of skin removed. He always received a good report afterwards.

The doctor numbed the area and sliced away at the back of her leg. She couldn't feel any pain, but knew once the Novocain wore off, she would be sore for a few days. She went home with a bandage behind her knee and waited for the doctor to call with her test results.

Two days later, she received a phone call from the dermatologist office. "The doctor would like to discuss your test results with you." The receptionist asked, "Can you come in tomorrow at two?"

"Yes, I can be there at that time." She hung up the phone and thought it was peculiar not to just give her the results over the phone. Josh never had to go back to the doctor's office for his test results. She didn't want to worry Josh, so she didn't mention the appointment to him.

The next day she met with the doctor. She immediately asked, "What were the results of my test?"

"Some cancer cells were detected from the sample I took. I need to remove more tissue around the same area to make sure all the cancer has been removed, so it can't spread."

He took another much larger sample of skin from the area behind her knee and applied several stitches to close the wound.

"I should have the test results tomorrow afternoon and will call to let you know the results."

She slowly left the doctor's office walking carefully, trying not to open the stitches in her leg. She was in much more pain this time and took it easy when she arrived home.

When Josh walked in the door, she decided she better come clean and tell him about her doctor's appointment. She nonchalantly said, "The dermatologist called me back into his office today, so he could remove more skin. I should get the test results tomorrow." She tried to make light of it, even though she was worried. "He is just being thorough to make sure all the cancerous tissue has been removed."

"Are you all right? That looks like an awful big area he removed."

"I'm just a little sore, but will be up and running around again in time to do some hiking in Alaska," she tried to reassure Josh.

"I don't like this. He must think it's serious, since he removed more tissue. Let me know as soon as you hear from the doctor."

The next day she waited for the doctor's call. She was sure he would tell her there was nothing to worry about, that he had removed all the cancer. The call finally came late in the day, but the news was not what she had hoped.

"Your second sample also showed evidence of malignant cancer cells. I am going to schedule you an appointment with an oncologist. He will be able to determine the extent in which your cancer has spread."

The words everyone fears to hear, you have cancer. She was in disbelief. She felt fine, and told herself it was nothing. The oncologist would take care of her, and she could resume her life.

She had never been so wrong about something in her life. This was the beginning of many doctor's appointments, surgery to attempt to remove all the cancer, followed by radiation and chemotherapy to try to stop the cancer from spreading. She had to cancel their vacation to Alaska. She prayed to God to give her the strength she needed to battle the cancer, and if it was His will, to help her heal.

Unfortunately, the months of radiation and chemotherapy treatment hadn't worked, and the cancer had spread to her bone. Her last hope was to have a bone marrow transplant. Jonathan and Jesse were both tested to determine if they were a match to her. She received the good news that Jesse was a match, and he could donate his bone marrow in hopes of saving her life. She had the bone marrow transplant just before Christmas and remained in the hospital for several weeks in isolation to give her immune system a chance to strengthen. She missed spending time with her family over the holidays. She felt like she was in prison and relied on her faith, talking to God daily to help her make it through her ordeal.

After several nerve wracking weeks in the hospital, she received the news she had waited so long to hear. "The bone marrow treatment has worked. Your cancer is in remission," the doctor said.

Jennifer cheered with joy and thanked God. She had won the battle, for now.

She had been given another chance at life and didn't want to waste a minute. After getting her strength back over the spring, Josh and her spent four weeks in Alaska. It was magnificent. They watched bear eating salmon along the river's edge, elk grazing in the fields, and whales swimming in the peninsula. They spent time enjoying the splendors in Denali National Park. They were amazed by the beauty of Mount McKinley. God's inspiration was at every turn in this wilderness as shown in its beauty, and amazing animals that survived the harsh environment.

As they neared the end of their adventure, Josh and her savored their time together. One of their last nights, they lay on their backs on the ground at their campsite. Josh wrapped them both in a blanket, and they cuddled together to stay warm. They watched as the aurora borealis entertained them for hours displaying a light show like they had never seen before. God's presence seemed closer than ever before. Jennifer watched in amazement at the display of lights and was so grateful to be alive. She reflected on her life and realized she had been truly blessed by God.

***

As they started the long journey back to Florida, Jennifer started to tire easily and had a headache that no amount of aspirin seemed to help. Josh became concerned, and called the oncologist from the road to schedule an appointment for the next day. He drove all night while Jennifer slept, to make it back to Florida.

Jennifer told Josh, "You are overreacting," she tried to convince him. "I just overdid it on the trip. After I get some rest, I am sure I will be fine."

Josh pulled into the driveway as the sun was rising. He woke Jennifer and helped her into bed. She stayed in bed with her eyes closed, with the lights off, trying to get rid of her headache. Josh brought her some soup, but she was too nauseous to eat.

That afternoon Josh helped her into the car and he drove her to the doctor's office. The doctor admitted her to the hospital for some tests and to administer fluids for dehydration.

They received the news they feared, "The cancer has returned and has spread to your brain." The doctor discussed the treatment options which included surgery, more chemotherapy and radiation. The doctor admitted, "The prognosis is not good and the treatment may only prolong your life for little while."

That night in the hospital, Josh and Jennifer prayed for God's guidance to show them what they should do. The surgery was very risky, and it could possibly leave Jennifer a vegetable if she survived. When the doctor returned to her room the next morning, she told him, "I've decided to try radiation and chemotherapy again."

"I will schedule you for your first treatment right away. I have to warn you though, this will be a very aggressive dosage to attempt to stop the spread of the cancer. You will feel much weaker and sicker than you did during your last treatment."

She grabbed Josh's hand and told the doctor, "I plan to beat the cancer and fight with everything I have."

"I like your positive attitude. I will do everything I can to try to ease your symptoms from the treatment."

She was released from the hospital that day and started the aggressive treatment the next day. She had to spend every day at the hospital for the next week while she received a cocktail of drugs which were fed intravenously into her body. She was allowed a week off treatment to recover, before another dose of chemotherapy started again. This went on for twelve weeks.

Josh was by her side the entire time making sure she was as comfortable as possible. He forced her to drink, so she wouldn't get dehydrated. Josh tried all kinds of weird concoctions to help her get the vitamins and minerals she needed to keep her strong. Each day Josh would bring her a different smoothie to drink. She was too afraid to ask what he put in them. The smoothies came in several different colors from green to brown and most tasted peculiar. She didn't want to let Josh down, and managed to drink at least some of each one.

By the end of the twelve weeks, she started to wish she would just die, she felt so bad. Her body felt like it was being burned from the inside out. She was becoming very weak and thin from the treatment. She started to think if the cancer didn't kill her, the treatment would. She didn't know how much more she could take.

Finally, she received her last dosage and she was finished with the treatments for now. The doctor instructed her to rest for the next several weeks to get her strength back before returning for more testing.

Josh was so patient and caring. She could tell watching her suffer was slowly eating away at him. She worried if she didn't survive, what would happen to Josh. She had accepted her fate for whatever God had planned for her, but it was not so simple for Josh. She needed to discuss the possibility with him that she may not survive, but she didn't know how to bring the subject up.

During the next week, she found her chance. She had just woken up from a nap and gotten up to get something to drink in the kitchen. She saw Josh sitting on the patio with his face in his hands. He looked visibly upset.

She quietly opened the patio door, sat down next to Josh, and grabbed his hand. "I love you very much and know how hard my illness has been on you. You have been so strong for both of us."

"You have brought me so much happiness," Josh said. "I know God will help me find a way to manage without you, but the thought of losing you is more than I can bear right now."

Jennifer sat in Josh's lap and put her arms around his neck to be close to him. "God has blessed us with a life I couldn't have imagined. We have two wonderful boys and six grandchildren. I couldn't have asked for a better life or man to spend it with. I fear though my time is coming to an end, and I need to know that you will be all right." The tears started to flow down her face as she tried to remain strong.

Josh looked into her eyes and wiped the tears from her cheeks. "I can't imagine living my life without you. You have been a part of me for so long I can't bear the thought."

Josh held her as she cried on his shoulder. She lifted her head, all cried out wiping her tears away and told Josh, "God has given us so many happy memories together. He has been there to guide me every step of the way. I know He is with me now and will help to ease my suffering. I don't know how much longer I have, but I want to spend it with my family, remembering the happy times and not being sad. You have to promise me you will stay strong for our sons and grandchildren if I do not beat this. They will need you more than ever. I hope it will bring you some peace to know you brought me happiness when all I knew was despair. You made my heart whole again and helped me see that God was always with me. You must know whatever happens it's in God's hands and you will survive. God will be there with you as He has been there with me so many times when I needed Him."

Chapter Twenty-Eight

"Precious in the sight of the Lord is the death of his
saints." *(Psalm 116:15)*

"And I heard a voice from heaven saying unto me, Write,
Blessed are the dead which die in the Lord from henceforth: Yea,
saith the Spirit, that they may rest from their labours; and their
works do follow them." *(Revelation 14:13)*

A few weeks later, Jennifer received another brain scan to determine if the tumor had been affected by the treatments. She knew the answer before receiving the test results. Her headaches persisted, so she was not surprised when the doctor said, "The chemotherapy and radiation have had little affect on the tumor. The tumor has shrunk, but not to the extent I had hoped."

"What are my options at this point?"

"Because of the location of the tumor, surgery would be very risky. You can go through another round of chemotherapy and radiation, but I don't know if you are strong enough to survive the treatment. I am sorry to say, in the end, it may only delay the inevitable."

"Let Josh and I discuss the options. I will notify you of my decision tomorrow."

Josh and Jennifer walked hand in hand out of the doctor's office. Once inside the quiet of the car, Josh reached for her hand and looked into her eyes. Then, he said the same thing she was thinking, "I don't want you to suffer through another round of treatments if there is no chance it will save your life."

She leaned over and kissed Josh. "I love you and want to spend whatever time I have left with you and our family."

Jennifer spent the last days of her life enjoying every minute she could with her children and grandchildren. Josh never left Jennifer's side, willing her to keep living as long as she could. One of Jennifer's last wishes was to go to the beach, the place where she was always the happiest. Josh carried Jennifer, now too weak to walk, and placed her on a beach towel on the sand just above where the waves broke. Chilled from the ocean breeze, Josh wrapped a towel over her shoulders and cradled her to keep her warm. She watched the surfers and dolphins riding the waves as the sun glistened off the water. Just like the day they first met the surf conditions were perfect. Those memories of watching Josh surf brought a smile to Jennifer's lips.

Soon after, the day Josh dreaded and couldn't stop, came. Jennifer died on the exact day they had met on the beach, just forty-eight years earlier. She was surrounded by her family as she took her last breath. Jennifer discovered her true path to finding happiness was in God's hands all along. All she had to do was follow her heart and trust in the Lord.

"Blessed are they that mourn: for they shall be comforted." *(St. Matthew 5:4)*

"The Lord preserveth the simple: I was brought low, and he helped me." *(Psalm 116:6)*

"Thy shoes shall be iron and brass; and as thy days, so shall thy strength be." *(Deuteronomy 33:25)*

"For wisdom is better than rubies; and all the things that may be desired are not to be compared to it." *(Proverbs 8:11)*

"Let not your heart be troubled: ye believe in God, believe also in me." *(St. John 14:1)*

"Fear not, for I am with you. Do not be dismayed. I am your God. I will strengthen you; I will help you; I will uphold you with my victorious right hand." *(Isaiah 41:10)*

"The sun shall be no more thy light by day; neither for brightness shall the moon give light unto thee: but the Lord shall be unto thee an everlasting light, and thy God thy glory." *(Isaiah 60:19)*

"God is our refuge and strength, a very present help in trouble." *(Psalm 46:1)*

"If ye abide in me, and my words abide in you, ye shall ask what ye will, and it shall be done unto you." *(St. John 15:7)*

"Consider what I say; and the Lord give thee understanding in all things." *(II Timothy 2:7)*

"Forbearing one another, and forgiving one another, if any man have a quarrel against any: even as Christ forgave you, so also do ye." *(Colossians 3:13)*

"I will say of the Lord, He is my refuge and my fortress: my God; in him will I trust." *(Psalm 91:2)*

"Lay not up for yourselves treasures upon earth, where moth and rust doth corrupt, and where thieves break through and steal:
But lay up for yourselves treasures in heaven, where neither moth nor rust doth corrupt and where thieves do not break through nor steal:
For where your treasure is, there will your heart be also."*(St. Matthew 6:19-21)*

"Trust in the Lord, and do good; so shalt thou dwell in the land, and verily thou shalt be fed." *(Psalm 37:3)*

"I will lift up the cup of salvation and call on the name of the Lord." *(Psalm 116:13)*

"The Lord is my light and my salvation; whom shall I fear? The Lord is the strength of my life; of whom shall I be afraid?" *(Psalm 27:1)*

"Then spake Jesus again unto them, saying, I am the light of the world: he that followeth me shall not walk in darkness, but shall have the light of life." *(St. John 8:12)*

"In him was life; and the life was the light of men." *(St. John 1:4)*

"Though I walk in the midst of trouble, thou wilt revive me: thou shalt stretch forth thine hand against the wrath of mine enemies, and thy right hand shall save me." *(Psalm 138:7)*

"When thou passest through the waters, I will be with thee; and through the rivers, they shall not overflow thee: when thou walkest through the fire, thou shalt not be burned; neither shall the flame kindle upon thee." *(Isaiah 43:2)*

"Man's goings are of the Lord; how can a man then understand his own way?" *(Proverbs 20:24)*

"My son, keep thy father's commandment, and forsake not the law of thy mother." *(Proverb, 6:20)*

"But the Lord said unto Samuel, Look not on his countenance, or on the height of his stature; because I have refused him: for the Lord seeth not as man seeth; for man looketh on the outward appearance, but the Lord looketh on the heart." *(1 Samuel 16:7)*

"That thine alms may be in secret; and thy father which seeth in secret himself shall reward thee openly." *(St. Matthew 6:4)*

"Now faith is the substance of things hoped for, the evidence of things not seen." *(Hebrews 11:1)*

"To every thing there is a season, and a time to every purpose under the heaven." *(Ecclesiastes 3:1)*

"Therefore I say unto you, Take no thought for your life, what ye shall eat, or what ye shall drink; nor yet for your body, what ye shall put on. Is not the life more than meat, and the body than raiment?" *(St. Matthew 6:25)*

"Precious in the sight of the Lord is the death of his saints." *(Psalm, 116:15)*

"And I heard a voice from heaven saying unto me, Write, Blessed are the dead which die in the Lord from henceforth: Yea, saith the Spirit, that they may rest from their labours; and their works do follow them."*(Revelation 14:13)*

About the Author

Diane E. Izzard lives in Welaka, Florida near the St. Johns River. The laid back Florida life style provides her the inspiration she needs to write. She has a bachelor degree in Industrial Engineering and master degree in Management. She worked at Kennedy Space Center until 2013 when she started her writing career. She loves dogs, hiking, biking, skiing, and curling up with a good book. Her latest dog, an Alaskan Malamute, provides the personality for the dogs in her stories. Visit her on Facebook at www.facebook.com/Dianee.Izzard